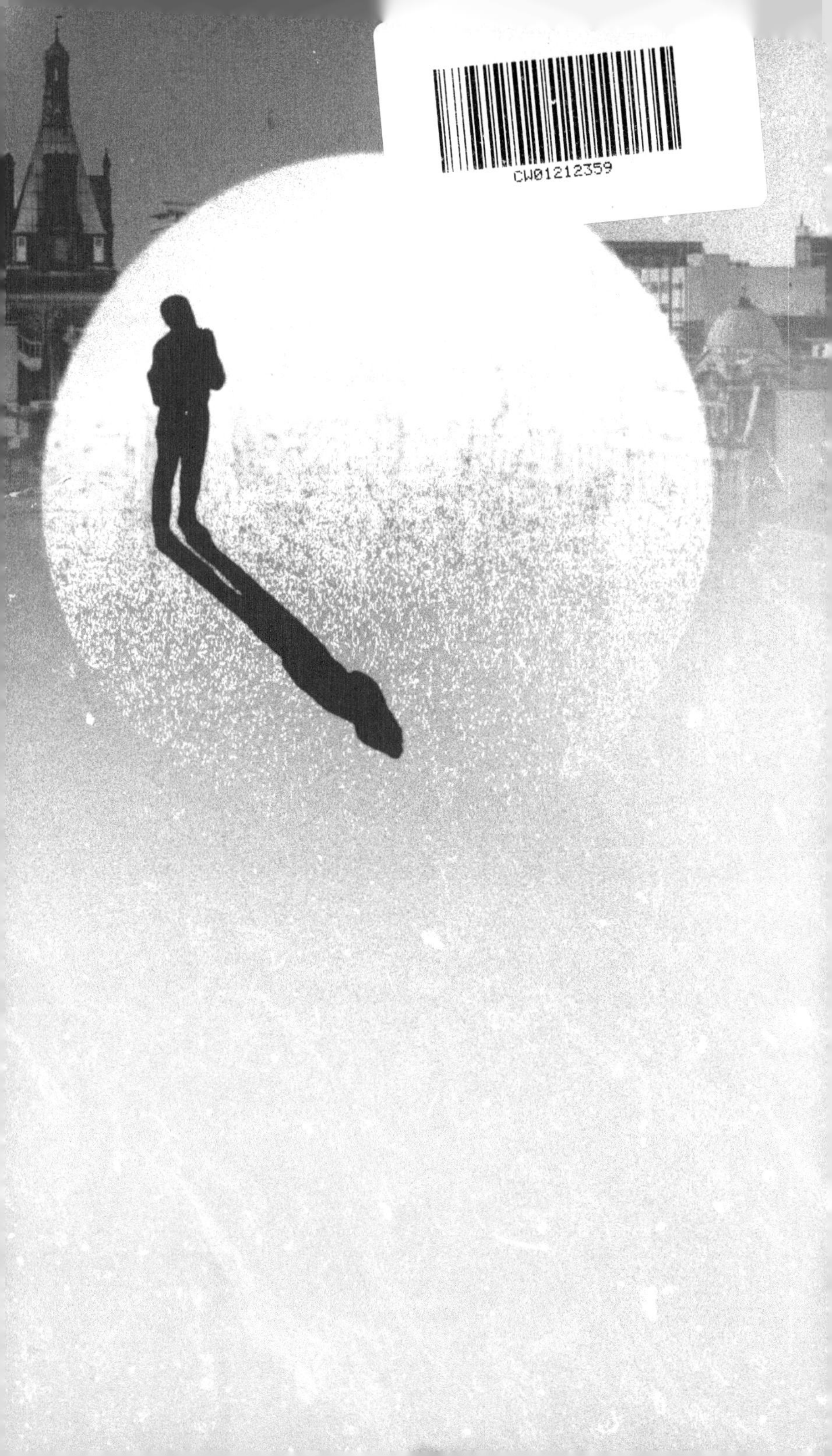

CW01212359

By the same author

The Barra Boy
All We Cannot Leave Behind

The State Trilogy
A Justified State
State of Denial
State of War

FULL SUN

Iain Kelly

The Book Guild Ltd

First published in Great Britain in 2024 by
The Book Guild Ltd
Unit E2 Airfield Business Park,
Harrison Road, Market Harborough,
Leicestershire. LE16 7UL
Tel: 0116 2792299
www.bookguild.co.uk
Email: info@bookguild.co.uk
Twitter: @bookguild

Copyright © 2024 Iain Kelly

The right of Iain Kelly to be identified as the author of this
work has been asserted by them in accordance with the
Copyright, Design and Patents Act 1988.

All rights reserved. No part of this publication may be
reproduced, transmitted, or stored in a retrieval system, in any form or by any means,
without permission in writing from the publisher, nor be otherwise circulated in
any form of binding or cover other than that in which it is published and without
a similar condition being imposed on the subsequent purchaser.

This work is entirely fictitious and bears no resemblance to any persons living or dead.

Typeset in 11pt Minion Pro

Printed on FSC accredited paper
Printed and bound in Great Britain by 4edge Limited

ISBN 978 1835740 989

British Library Cataloguing in Publication Data.
A catalogue record for this book is available from the British Library.

For
Chloe Dawn and Caden Daniel

And
Joanne

PART 1

A MAN AND A WOMAN

1

I am sitting in the back corner of the banquet room, so far back my chair is almost out of the door. That suits me. I am still adjusting to being surrounded by large crowds of people.

At the front of the vast room, at the top table, my newly married sister is sitting next to her husband, flanked by his parents and my mother, Anita Jackson. Our father passed away nine years ago. Just as well. He would not have approved.

I do not want to be here, but she is my little sister and it is her day. Marie asked if I would give her away, in place of our absent father. I declined. She was only asking out of politeness. She doesn't really want me taking any limelight from her on her wedding day. Uncle Liam, Dad's older brother, flew in from Ontario to do the honours. He sits at the top table, next to Mum. But I couldn't say no to the invitation to be here today. Marie is still family.

She looks different with her hair in waves and braids. I am pretty sure those are fake extensions. The veil from the ceremony has gone. The sculpted white corset dress looks expensive, decorated with sparkling gems. Everything in this place looks expensive. It isn't Marie or Mum that is paying for it.

The groom, my new brother-in-law, is Anthony McArthur. He was my best friend growing up. We haven't spoken in a long time.

He wears traditional attire: a kilt and matching waistcoat, coloured in green, yellow and black – the ancient McArthur tartan.

The speeches finish. An army of waiters appear as if by magic and the first of five courses is served to two hundred guests. The starter is *Chicken and Wild Mushroom with Pickled Vegetables, Endive Leaves and Shallot Purée*. At least, that's what it says on the card in front of me. Whatever it is, it's too rich for my blunted taste palate and too small to fill my stomach. I have become conditioned to plain food and meagre rations in the last year. I pick at the small square of meat lost at sea on the large plate. To my left an older lady, who appears, like me, to be unaccompanied, does the same.

'You would think for the cost of all this they would've ordered enough food for everyone to get a whole damn chicken.' She smiles at me. I return her smile, but say nothing in reply.

Roast Pepper Gazpacho Soup follows. I take a mouthful and leave the rest. I think the old lady is about to walk out in protest.

There is an interval before the main course is served. Some guests leave their seats and mingle around other tables. I stay where I am and hope no one will approach me.

'You're a relative of the bride?' the old lady asks, pointing at my place card. 'A Jackson?'

'Her brother.'

'You should be at the front, not back in the cheap seats with me.'

'We're estranged.' I am relieved when she does not ask me to elaborate.

'Nice to meet you, Callum.'

'Cal,' I correct her. 'Always Cal, never Callum.' Unlike Dad, who was always Joseph, never Joe.

'Margaret,' says the old lady, 'usually Maggie, or Mags.' I nod an acknowledgement. 'You don't say much.'

'I like to keep myself to myself.'

'That isn't very sociable.'

'Call it a survival technique.'

'Mysterious. There must be a story there.'

'There is, but I don't say much.'

Maggie smiles at that, the lines around her mouth creasing and causing her lipstick to crack. She concedes and turns her attention to the old couple on the other side of her. I go back to looking around the room.

There are a lot of familiar faces. A lot of faces from school that I haven't seen for years. Marie has stayed loyal, even after we moved away from the village we grew up in. I have tried to leave them behind, especially after the accident. Now she is marrying Tony, I will be pulled back into their world.

I gaze up. Extravagant chandeliers hang from the ceiling, lit by electric candles. Decorative cornicing snakes around the edges. The walls are white panelled wood, highlighted by spotlights and punctuated with bouquets of yellow and white flowers. It is all done in a modern style, belying the old exterior of Erskine House.

I think about escaping. Is after the meal too soon? I resign myself to staying until the first dance has taken place and the evening entertainment has begun. Then I can slip away unnoticed and drive back to Glasgow; I will not have to hang around waiting for a taxi to come all the way out from the city to pick me up. Not drinking has that advantage. Before I go, I should talk to Mum and congratulate Marie and Tony. So far I have only seen them briefly, when I was required to pose for an official photograph with them.

A loud laugh makes me look to the top table. I recognise that laugh. So does everyone in the room. Francis McArthur, Tony's father, demands attention. It is his money that has funded the day. It is Tony and Marie's wedding, but no one on the guest list is here without Francis's approval. Most of the two hundred guests are his friends and acquaintances. This is his day to show off.

I spot a few D-list celebrities: a bit-part actor, a social media influencer, a city councillor, a member of the Scottish government.

Enough famous faces to justify the couple of reporters and press photographers hanging around outside. They were allowed access to the ceremony, and will be allowed in after the meal for the evening dance. Anything they publish will have to be run past Francis McArthur first.

"Local businessman and entrepreneur" would be the tabloid description of Francis McArthur. A vague enough description to be truthful without full disclosure. Marie isn't just marrying his eldest son, she is joining the family, and family means a lot to Francis McArthur.

He is laughing at something he has said. Marie joins in with him, her hand squeezing his arm. Mum manages a half-smile.

The serving staff reappear and guests cut off conversations and return to their seats. I check the menu. *Braised Beef Cheek, Beef Shoulder Bon Bon, Celeriac Mash, Roasted Baby Roots and a Red Wine Jus.* It sounds a lot. It isn't. I eat the meat in two mouthfuls, and the mash in another. I leave the rest. Maggie is picking through her plate with a look of disgust. I make my excuses and go to find the bathroom.

On the way back, I pass open French doors that lead onto a rooftop balcony. Not desperate to discover what the dessert will be, I head out for some fresh air.

It is quite a view beyond the flat lawns of the house grounds. Round to the left is the golf estate attached to the property, which rolls up to the backdrop of the hills and woods of Inverclyde. To the right, beyond a small knot of trees, is the River Clyde, widening as it makes its way out to the Firth. In the distance, I can just make out Dumbarton Rock, with its distinctive double peak. It is a warm late afternoon with only a few wisps of cloud across the cerulean sky. The forecasts say we are in for a heatwave over the next few weeks, something to do with the warm air pushing up from Saharan Africa. I take a deep breath of fresh air. It is one of the simple things I missed while I was in prison.

I lean against the weathered stone balustrade. If I'd had one in my pocket, I would have lit a cigarette, but smoking has gone the same way as alcohol. A simple pleasure I deny myself. The vices that helped me get through long periods of my life have now lost their lustre.

I hear the crunch of footsteps a moment before I hear the voice.

'Callum Jackson.'

Malcolm Thomson. Francis McArthur's bulldog.

'Malky,' I greet him with a forced smile as I turn around. Malky Thomson is not a man you upset, unless you enjoy pain.

'Enjoying the day?'

'Sure.'

'Tell your face. You're not happy for your sister?'

'Delighted.'

'I'll pretend I didn't hear the sarcasm.' He towers over me as he stands next to me. It occurs to me that he could push me over the side of the balcony with a flick of one thick arm and I would plummet to the concrete steps below. 'Thought you'd be pleased to be here. Can't have had many days like this in the last year. How does it feel to be a free man?'

'I'm still getting used to it.'

'Francis was willing to help you out. He was a bit offended when you refused him.'

'I deserved what I got. It was right that I did the time. It's been good for me.'

Malky looks me up and down. 'If you say so.'

Laughter and chatter from the banquet room drift out of the door. Malky looks that way and decides he wants to get back.

'He wants to see you. After the meal. I'll come and find you. Don't disappear.' Malky walks away.

My heart sinks. It is starting already. There is no escaping it. For a split second, I think about doing a runner, jumping in my car and getting away. There is no point. Not unless I am able to get out of Scotland. But the conditions of my parole do not allow that, and even then I would not be safe. Francis McArthur has reach.

I get back to the table to find dessert waiting for me.

'Now, if you're not going to eat that, I'll take it,' says Maggie.

White and Dark Chocolate Dome filled with Glayva Gel, served on a Light Shortbread Biscuit.

It sounds pretty good. It looks pretty good. I push my plate towards Maggie. 'All yours.'

I have lost my appetite.

2

'Ladies and Gentlemen, if you could make your way out to the reception hall, please, while we prepare the main room for the evening entertainment. Thank you.'

The Master of Ceremonies dismisses us. The satiated guests file out of the room and the staff swoop in to clear tables and prepare the dancefloor. Malky finds me hiding in the back corner.

'Follow me.'

He takes me through the east wing of the house to the central entrance hall. The noise and chatter from the wedding recedes behind us. Here, the house is softly quiet. A grand carpeted staircase sweeps upwards. I follow Malky to the second floor and along a corridor. This part of the old house has been converted into accommodation for guests. Dark oak doors face each other on opposite sides of the corridor. Each room has its own name. The Caithness Suite, the Mar Suite, the Galloway Suite. They are all named after Scottish Earldoms. The corridor splits left and right at the end of the hallway. The Sutherland Honeymoon Suite is at the front of the house. Marie and Tony will spend the night there. Malky turns the other way, to the suite that occupies the rear corner. The sign calls it the Erskine Suite, named after the ancestral owner of the house.

Malky raps his large knuckles on the heavy wooden door and waits. A moment later, the handle turns and the soundless door swings inwards. I follow Malky inside. The room is huge. Large bay windows let in the evening sunlight. There is a king-size bed, a sofa, an antique *escritoire*, a huge flat-screen television mounted to the wall, a dining table and chairs. The thick carpet is Erskine tartan, lines of light and dark green. The walls are freshly painted off-white. Paintings of rolling Scottish hills adorn each wall.

At the far side of the room, inset into the round turret of the house, is a large desk. Francis McArthur has just got to his feet behind it. At his shoulder, standing behind the chair, I recognise Murdo Smith. In front of the desk a woman stands up abruptly. Malky places a hand on my chest and moves me aside to let the woman pass us on her way out. She is one of the wedding guests, dressed for the occasion in a teal ruched dress with a flowing sleeve coat, but her face has lost the celebratory spirit somewhere along the way. She gives me a look of thunder as she exits. I vaguely recognise her face. She is a politician of some kind. I have seen her on the television news, minus the wedding get-up. The door closes behind her.

Malky ushers me forward. Francis McArthur comes out from behind the desk and meets me in the middle of the room. He is the same height as me, a shade under six-foot tall. His grey hair has started to thin since I saw him last, but tanned skin and clear green eyes give off an air of energetic good health. He wears the same McArthur tartan as his son, the same kilt and waistcoat. He holds out his hand to greet me.

'Cal, good to see you.' His left hand slaps me on the upper arm while he shakes my right hand with a solid grip.

'Mr McArthur.'

'Francis, please. After all, we're family now.' It is always Francis, never Frank.

'Francis.' He finally stops shaking my hand and lets it go.

'Glad you could make it today. Marie mentioned you were having second thoughts about coming.'

'I'm still adjusting to being back in the real world. There's a lot of faces from the past here.'

Francis smiles. 'Some of whom you would rather not see again, am I right?'

'I wouldn't want to insult any of your guests.'

'You've learned to be diplomatic.' He laughs and the smile grows wider then vanishes, replaced by a look of concern. 'And how are you finding things? Adapting okay?'

'Getting there. Keeping to myself. Taking it slow.' I can feel the sweat starting to gather on my brow. Malky still stands behind me at the door. Murdo Smith remains behind the desk, his sharp eyes never leaving my face.

Francis nods and pats both my upper arms. He steps back and pulls a pocket watch attached to a chain from his waistcoat, clicks it open and checks the time. The pocket watch is an affectation Francis McArthur has had since I first met him twenty years ago. The story goes it was handed down to him by his father, who got it in turn from his father, who had been a horologist, a watchmaker, way back when. I hear Francis's voice telling us young impressionable teenagers why he still kept it and used it instead of getting a wristwatch. *It's to remind me of where I come from. Never forget your roots, lads. It keeps you humble and honest.* I guess honesty is a fluid concept and is kept in the eye of the beholder.

He snaps the brass cover closed and places the watch back in his pocket, the gold chain dangling across the front of his waistcoat. 'I've wasted enough time on business today already, so I'm going to let Murdo take over here.' He looks me in the eyes, fixing his glare on me. 'You're family now, and I take care of my family. Listen to what Murdo has to say and we'll talk some more. Maybe get you round to the house with your sister.'

'Sure.'

He grasps my hand again and gives it another enthusiastic shake. 'Good to see you out, Cal. A fresh start, eh?'

I turn and watch him go. Malky opens the door for him and closes it behind his retreating figure. Without McArthur's large personality, the room goes cold.

'Sit,' Murdo Smith orders me and points at the chair in front of the desk. A fresh veil of sweat breaks out on my back. The air closes in on me.

Murdo perches himself on the corner of the desk as I sit in front of him. He looks down at me. 'Assaulting a police officer. I thought you were smarter than that.'

'Not smart enough, I guess. In my defence, I didn't know he was a police officer until after I'd hit him.'

Murdo's pincer eyes bore into me. He is a small, slight man, bald with the remaining hair around the sides of his head shaved in close to the skin. He is a few years older than his boss, which means he must be over sixty now. As Francis McArthur's right-hand man, he is the power behind the throne, the protector of the family secrets. Around Glasgow he is feared as much as McArthur himself, but Francis McArthur hides his rough edges behind the public image of a clean-cut, personable man of business and civic society. Murdo Smith wears no such mask. He is a simple man who operates on a straightforward basis. For forty years it has served him well.

'We could have made sure you didn't do any jail time, if you'd let us help.'

'I deserved what I got,' I say for the second time today.

'How very honourable.' He shakes his head, dismissing my misplaced faith in the justice system with a glance to the ceiling and a wave of his hand. 'You didn't feel like that on the previous occasion.'

'I was younger then. Maybe I learned my lesson.'

I wait for him to get to the real reason I have been summoned.

'Well,' he looks at me with a smile that could cut glass, 'unfortunately your brush with the law presents us with a bit of a problem now that you're part of the family.'

'It does?'

'Mr McArthur is a man of a certain reputation, a certain standing in society. He runs many businesses. Having a convicted criminal as his son's brother-in-law doesn't reflect well on Mr McArthur, or Anthony, or your sister for that matter.'

'If it makes you feel any better, I tried to talk her out of it.'

That smile again. 'Surprisingly, we agree on something. I advised Mr McArthur against allowing Anthony to go ahead with the marriage. I felt he could do much better.'

He wants the insult to my sister to anger me. I don't let it. 'Mr McArthur didn't take your advice?'

'He agreed with me. Don't let his jovial manner today fool you. He thinks Anthony could do much better. He thinks there's a fair chance his son will soon regret his choice.'

He waits for me to take the bait and defend my little sister. He is enjoying toying with me. I hear Malky shuffling around behind me, but I dare not turn my attention away from Murdo Smith as he holds me in his gaze.

'I'm more than happy to keep as far away from Mr McArthur, his family and his business as possible.'

Murdo gives a sharp laugh and stands up and walks around to the other side of the desk. He looks out of the window. 'Again, we think along the same lines. Perhaps you are not as stupid as I think you are.'

'Sorry to disappoint.'

He turns back to face me. 'Unfortunately, Mr McArthur is a more charitable man than I am. He thinks you deserve a second chance. Call it familial duty.'

I try to think of what my second chance might entail.

'Have you been working since you got out?'

'I haven't been looking.'

'What are you planning to do? Sign on the dole?'

I shrug. 'Maybe.'

Murdo shakes his head and leans towards me, his hands palm down on the wooden desk. 'Mr McArthur will not have a member of his family claiming welfare from the State.'

'I didn't ask to be in his family.'

'And yet here we are,' Murdo snaps, then steps back. 'We'd like to offer you a job within our organisation.'

'A job?'

'You're aware of what a job is?' Again the sharp eyes pin their focus on mine. 'You know we run a number of establishments in the city centre. Mr McArthur thinks you would be ideally suited to help out at one of his clubs.'

I see an easy way out and grasp it with eagerness. 'I'm not sure the conditions of my parole allow me to work in a licensed establishment.'

'You don't have to worry about that. Mr McArthur has an arrangement with the local authorities when it comes to employing people with a past. There have been far worse than you rehabilitated thanks to Mr McArthur's generosity.'

It will have to be the difficult way then. 'You can tell Mr McArthur I appreciate the offer but I will have to decline.'

Murdo pauses and stares at me for an uncomfortable moment. 'Be careful, son. People who go against Mr McArthur tend to regret it.'

'And yet here we are.'

Malky clears his throat behind me. The quiet room chills further. For the first time today, I want to be back in the banquet hall among the other guests.

He gives it one last try. 'You're sure? You need the money, you need the routine. You're drifting without purpose. And offers of employment aren't going to roll in for a convicted violent criminal.'

Marie has obviously provided the McArthurs with the update on my current financial status. I shake my head. 'It's still a no.'

'Okay,' Murdo raises his hands in acceptance of defeat. 'I will let Mr McArthur know your decision.'

'Tell him, if it helps, that I plan to stay as far away from him and his family, including my sister, as I can, within the limits of my parole, which means I have to stay in the country.'

Murdo turns to the desk and starts looking at some paperwork. 'Malcolm, would you show Mr Jackson back to the wedding reception.'

Our meeting is over.

3

I follow Malky's broad shoulders back along the hallway and down the stairs. At the bottom of the staircase, he stops.

'You want to be careful with how you deal with him. You don't want Murdo Smith as an enemy.'

'I don't want anyone as an enemy. I just want to be left alone.'

Malky shrugs. 'Don't say I didn't warn you. See you around, Cal.' With that, he heads back up the stairs.

The main entrance faces me. It is tempting to slip away into the evening and be done with them all. My conscience makes me stay.

The band has started in the banquet room, now transformed into a ballroom, with tables cleared to the side and a sparkling dancefloor revealed. I have missed the first dance. A few women are on their feet, swaying and spinning and moving awkwardly in high heels that will soon be dispensed with. Marie is in the middle of the group, the centre of attention. I recognise the song. It's a cover version of something I have heard on the radio. I can't remember the name of it or the artist. My music taste dates back a few decades. Most of the guests sit around the edge of the dancefloor, huddled in groups and leaning towards each other, shouting to be heard over the loud guitar and lead singer. I see Francis McArthur, sitting at a table with his wife Sheila, Tony and members of his entourage. He is watching the group on the dancefloor. His gaze meets mine and he nods. Murdo Smith has not yet conveyed my rejection. Mum is at the same table as them, in conversation with Sheila, who appears to be trying to get her up to join the action on the dancefloor. Mum politely resists.

I have no desire to sit near McArthur and I never dance when sober, so I leave the main hall and go to the bar in the adjoining side room. The music is quieter here, the din of the guests muted. You can hear yourself think.

'Soda water and lime.'

The girl behind the bar looks about twenty. She pours the drink and uses tongs to add a slice of lime. 'You look like you're having the time of your life.'

'Nowhere else I'd rather be.'

'Maybe you need something stronger?'

'No, thanks.' I hand over a note to her. I'm still waiting for the bank to send me a card for my new account. 'Keep the change.'

'Can't. No tips.' The bartender hands some coins back to me. I forgot this was a classy place.

I take my drink to the end of the bar and have a sip. I don't like the taste, but it's better than non-alcoholic beer. I lean my elbow on the bar and face into the room. The alcove that leads back into the main hall provides cover to keep out of sight. I can lie low here until I get a chance to congratulate Marie and make my exit.

The woman catches my eye as soon as she walks into the room. Maybe it's the dress, a low-cut, tight wrap configuration that hugs her body. Maybe it's the dark black hair or the brown eyes, the full lips or the high cheekbones. She has all the parts that make up a young Sophia Loren, but falls just short. I guess only Sophia Loren can pull off being Sophia Loren. Maybe it's the way she sways across the room, a curious mix of sophisticated swagger tainted by just a little too much consumed alcohol.

'Vodka straight, and fill it up,' she orders the young bartender, who obliges. She turns to me. 'You're the brother?'

'Guilty.'

'So I heard. Hiding in here?' Her words have a slight slur to them. From her choice of drink, she isn't about to stop.

'Not my kind of music.' On cue the guitar next door strikes a new chord. The crowd responds and there's a stampede onto the dancefloor for Van Morrison's *Brown Eyed Girl*.

'I'm hiding from the people,' she tells me.

'I can relate. Although I should tell you off for insulting my recently acquired family and friends. Anyone in particular?'

She declines to answer, only dips her head and flutters her dark eyelashes. We both look towards the dancefloor as a choir of dissonant voices join in with the lead singer for the chorus.

'You don't remember me, do you?'

I find it hard to believe I could have forgotten her, but studying her face rings no bells. 'Remind me.'

'We went to school together. I was a year above you.'

It has been fifteen years. A lot has happened in that time. 'Were we friends?'

'Not really, no.'

'Did you have a name back then?'

'Same one I have now. Elise.'

A rush of teenage memories flash before my eyes. The old school uniform – white shirt, blue and grey striped tie, grey trousers for the boys, grey skirt for the girls. Teeth in braces, acne-covered skin, hairstyles based on US sitcoms and Hollywood stars. Awkward awakenings and dalliances and embarrassed feelings hidden. The cliques and playground groups, the outsiders and the in-crowd. Her name stood out from the crowd more than her face.

'The French teacher's daughter?' Madame Moreau. I did not have fond memories of her class. I was terrible at French. Madame Moreau was known to be stern. She was also the object of desire for hormonal teenage boys blinded by the dark features of a foreign woman from Paris, the city of love.

'*Très bien*. Well remembered.' Now I notice the soft accent. Glaswegian, but with a Gallic twist. Her smile and the look she gives me under her dark eyelashes make me nervous. It feels like she's flirting with me. It's been a long time since that happened, so I can't be sure.

'I knew you, but I don't think we ever spoke.'

'Everyone knew of me, thanks to my mum teaching at the school.'

'How is your mum?'

'Been better.' Her eyes tell me there is a painful story behind the answer, but she changes topic before I can ask more. 'You were mates with Tony.'

'Back then, yes.'

'Not now?'

'I'm here for my sister and mother.'

The song ends and a slower melody fills the air. The band have misjudged their set list. The dancefloor empties. It's too early in the evening for a romantic number. Through the door I see Murdo Smith and Malky. They head towards Francis McArthur's table. Will they deliver my refusal to him just now? They won't want to spoil his evening. Besides, my minor rebuff can't be that important to a man of his stature.

Elise swallows the last of the vodka from her glass. It has disappeared in two mouthfuls. 'Care to buy me another?' She waggles the empty glass at me and the tip of her tongue runs round her red lips.

I don't want to admit that the bar prices are stretching what little funds I have with me. I am starting to enjoy myself for the first time in a long time, but I can't afford to keep this going much longer. The last of the money I left prison with is running out.

'Don't you think you've had enough?'

'I haven't had a drink in two months. Give me a pass for one night.'

The young bartender pours another large measure of vodka into a fresh glass. I use the last note in my wallet to pay for it and pocket the change. 'Has everything doubled in price since I went away?'

Elise picks up her drink. 'Depends where you shop. A place like this has to charge more, even if it's the same stuff you get out of a bottle from the off-licence.'

'So you're friends with Tony, or my sister?' I ask.

Elise starts to answer, then hesitates and takes a gulp of vodka. 'Neither. Yvonne, the bridesmaid.'

'You're with her?'

'Just friends. Sorry to disappoint. We're both between relationships at the moment, so I'm here for moral support.'

Heading towards blind drunkenness standing at the bar doesn't seem like great moral support to me, but I let it pass.

We stand together looking out to the main hall. I take a sip from my glass. I am surprised I don't feel awkward standing next to her. After all, this has been the longest conversation I've had with a woman in over a year, apart from my mother and sister. Maybe it's because she seems as lost as I am amongst the celebratory gathering.

The slow song comes to an end. The singer announces they will be taking a break for half an hour and the evening buffet is now open. Piped music comes through speakers mounted on the walls and the lights are faded up. A surprising number of guests who have just eaten a five-course meal join the buffet queue. Marie leaves the dancefloor and walks over to our mum, who has been left alone at the table. The McArthurs have moved on to mingle with other guests. It seems like the perfect opportunity for me to speak to them both, and after that I will be free to leave.

Elise senses I am about to abandon her and gets in first. 'Never look a free meal in the mouth.' She drains the last of the vodka away and slaps the glass on to the bar top. 'See you around, Cal.'

She sways across the bar, but doesn't head towards the buffet. Instead, she goes the opposite way, out of the door towards the main reception area. I have no reason to expect to see her again. I watch her walk away and think that would be a shame. Not because of the way she looks in that wrap dress, but because she seems to have the same disregard for the people we are surrounded by at this wedding. Just as she reaches the door, she stumbles in her heels. She may have been bumped by the man coming the other way, or it may be that she's rushed one vodka too many. I suspect the latter.

I pick up my soda water and lime, which is still half-full – at these prices, I'm going to make it last – and make my way over to my mother and sister. A few familiar faces mumble greetings as I pass; a few familiar faces bob their heads in my direction. No one wants to approach me beyond brief acknowledgement. That suits me. As I walk across the empty floor, I catch the sharp eyes following my progress. Murdo Smith has perfected the art of staring daggers.

4

I approach the table where Mum and Marie sit together. The smiles they are sharing look genuine. I hate to ruin it for them.

Marie sees me first. 'You're still here?'

'Just about to head off. Didn't want to miss the first dance,' I reply, even though I did miss it. I don't know if Marie is aware that her new father-in-law has pulled me aside for a private meeting, or if she knows about the job offer. 'Thought I'd better say goodbye before I leave.'

'I'm glad you came.' I can't tell if she means it or not.

'When do you leave?'

'Tomorrow afternoon. A week in St Lucia.'

'Enjoy it. Maybe see you when you get back.'

'Maybe.' She stands up and turns to Mum. 'I'll see you on the dancefloor later. Promise?'

Mum smiles and agrees and squeezes Marie's hand.

Marie starts to walk away. I call after her. She stops and turns.

'You look stunning,' I say, and I mean it.

'I know I do.' She smiles and, just for a second, we are brother and sister again, playing and annoying and kidding each other in the house growing up together. Then she is gone. I watch her cross the hall and find Tony. She says something to him and he looks in my direction and raises a hand. I return the gesture and then sit next to Mum.

* * *

Up until ten years ago, Mum led a pretty happy existence. She was married to Joseph, had two children and we were comfortable, if not rich. It all started to fall apart when I was involved in a road accident.

A young teenage girl, a pedestrian, was hit by the car Tony McArthur and I were in. It was Tony's car but I was driving. Tony was in the passenger seat. The girl survived with life-changing injuries. The police were involved, charges were pursued, but in the end I got away with a few hours of community service and a crippling sense of guilt. Tony escaped with a warning. The influence and connections of Tony's father helped to obtain the lenient sentences, and kept us out of prison.

Francis McArthur's help came at a cost though. He insisted that the injured girl and her family be compensated. He was a fair man. He recognised that a wrong had been committed and we had to take responsibility. He paid for the girl's private medical care, he paid for the required renovations to their house to make it accessible, he insisted on paying for a tutor to help her catch up on her missed exams and then supported her through university. Tony paid off the debt he owed his father by working for him without wages. Francis could have shouldered all the costs himself, but he insisted that my family contributed some of the burden for my part in the accident. My dad agreed that a slice of his monthly wage would go to McArthur. The cost was something Mum could budget for. Life would be a little less comfortable, but it was better than seeing me behind bars.

However, there was a bigger cost than the financial penalty. Indebted to McArthur, Dad could now be called upon for a favour.

He had no option but to agree to anything that Francis asked for, or risk my future if he pushed back. Mum never knew the exact nature of what McArthur asked her husband to do. Dad was only a mid-level Planning Officer with the city council. Francis owned a lot of property around the city and did a lot of property development and construction. Mum was smart enough to make the connection.

Whether it was my increasingly wayward behaviour after the car accident, the financial strain, the murky favours he was required to do for Francis McArthur, or just depression, a mid-life crisis or an unhappy marriage, Dad never explained in the note that was found next to him. It was eighteen months after the car accident when he took his own life and left Mum and us. It was Marie who found him lying on the bed. She thought he was asleep.

Dad's death did allow Mum to break free from the influence of Francis McArthur. She continued to work as an office clerk with the Glasgow Housing Association. McArthur no longer requested part of her salary. She wasn't in a position to do him any favours. Gradually, she got back on her feet.

Now in my mid-twenties, I continued to cause her worry. I never recovered from the aftermath of the car accident. I dropped out of college and spent time in menial jobs, holding none of them down for long. I took a mix of painkillers, anti-depressants and alcohol to cope with my guilt. I moved out and saw Mum infrequently. She didn't know where I was living for much of the time. Marie stayed with her and, like Mum, showed more fortitude. Mum's worries about Marie might have been over, until the day she picked up with Tony McArthur. When Marie announced their engagement, Mum's anxiety returned.

Soon after Marie's news, I got into a brawl outside a pub in the city centre. I didn't know the man who tried to restrain me was a police officer. The assault was deemed serious enough that I was sentenced to two years in prison, with the chance of parole after twelve months.

Francis McArthur got in touch with Mum. Due to the impending union of their families, and given their past history, he offered to help get me a reduced sentence. Mum told him it was up to me. I rejected Francis's help this time. Mum sensed the assault was part of a downward spiral brought on by Marie's engagement to Tony. The McArthurs were haunting our family once more.

Now Mum sits at the wedding of her daughter to Tony McArthur. She has no choice but to accept Marie's marriage or face losing her as well as her husband and son.

'Enjoying your day?' I ask.

'That's all you're going to say, is it? After nothing for three weeks? I wasn't even sure you were going to turn up today, for your own sister's wedding.'

'You know it isn't as straightforward as that.'

'I don't need you to remind me of that. You could have made it easier by letting me know you were okay at least.'

'I'm doing okay.'

'You haven't been round to see me.'

'I figured you'd be busy with the wedding and Marie.'

'Where are you staying?'

'I've got a small flat. Housing association. In Mount Florida.'

'And you're coping okay, being out?'

'It was only a year.'

'You weren't coping before prison. I'd be surprised if you are doing any better afterwards.'

'You don't need to worry. I'm doing fine.'

She places her hand on top of mine on the table, patting it softly. 'Of course I worry about you.'

I hold her hand for a moment and then let it go. She tells me this, like she does every time she sees me, but ever since the car accident and everything that followed, I think she cares a little less.

'Quite the show they've put on.' I change the subject, motioning to our surroundings.

'Aye, well. The McArthurs like to be the centre of attention.'

'You're okay with it? With Marie and Tony?'

She shrugs. 'Resigned to it. What can I do? I tried to talk her out of it at the start but… I'm glad your dad will never know about it.'

'And you'll be okay in the house on your own?' Francis has already given Tony and Marie a new townhouse to move into in Bearsden as part of their wedding gift. Mum will be in the family home on her own for the first time.

'I'll have to be.'

She has offered my old bedroom to me. I turned her down. Too many memories. I am thirty-two now. It is time to stand on my own two feet. I think she is about to try to persuade me again, but before she can say anything else, Sheila McArthur comes over to us and interrupts.

'Come and get yourself a plate a food, Anita. It's quite the spread, and you'll need to keep your energy up for the rest of the evening.'

'Mrs McArthur,' I greet her.

'Nice to see you, Cal. I hope you're well.' The look of disgust on her face suggests Sheila McArthur actually hopes I am seriously ill, or preferably don't exist. She drags Mum up from her chair and takes her away to the buffet, where the initial queue has died down.

I sit at the table and have a final sip from the glass of soda water. I have got through the day without causing an argument or ruining it for Marie. So long as McArthur takes my rejection of his job offer well, I've got off pretty lightly. With the exception of Elise Moreau, I've managed to avoid getting trapped in a conversation with any of the familiar faces who know about my past.

The band is starting to reassemble on the stage. Now seems like the perfect time to get out while the going is good. I head out of the main hall and pass the bar. There is no sign of Elise. With any luck she is sleeping it off in a room somewhere in the hotel. The doorwoman holds the door open for me to let me out. I am down the sandstone stairs and crossing the gravel courtyard towards the car park when Tony catches up with me.

'You're not even going to congratulate your old mate on his wedding day?'

I am tempted to carry on walking, but there is no escaping it. Better to have the conversation now, like ripping off a plaster. I stop and turn to face him. 'Isn't there supposed to be some rule about best mates and sisters? Like "never the two shall marry"?'

'Come on. You can't act like we're still teenagers. Besides, you quit being my best mate years ago.'

'You better not hurt her, Tony.'

'Now you're the protective big brother? You haven't taken an interest in her life for a long time. You don't get to ride back in, fresh out of prison, and start handing out advice to everyone.'

He has a point. I don't even know why I am arguing with him. 'Look. Congratulations, Tony. I hope you will both be happy together. And thanks for a great day.' I turn to leave, but he holds my arm.

'Did my dad speak to you?' I look at his hand on my arm until he removes it. 'It was my idea to offer you a job. It can't be easy getting back on your feet.'

'I turned him down.'

He looks hurt. 'You know I can't help who my dad is, right? You can't hold that against me. So we might as well take advantage of it, right? A house for us. A new start for you.'

'You might not have a choice, Tony, but I do.' I start to walk away again. Tony doesn't follow this time, he just calls after me.

'Think it over, at least. It might be the only offer you get.'

5

I sit behind the wheel of my beat-up silver Vauxhall Corsa and decompress. It's almost ten o'clock. The sun has dropped behind the low hills and the world is turning grey. The rumble of bass reaches out from the house and disco lights spin and flash through the tall windows of the banquet hall. The engine starts with an unhealthy splutter at the second attempt.

The single-track road that leads to Erskine House is shouldered on either side by trees, creating a tunnel that blocks out the fading light at the end of the day. The gloom descends further. There are no streetlights until I get close to the bridge, its sweeping arch spanning the wide river. I see no other cars until joining the motorway. The countryside falls away as I drive round the outskirts of Glasgow Airport and merge onto the M8, passing Renfrew and the industrial estate at Hillington.

I feel the pull as the junction for the tunnel approaches. I should keep to the right, carry on across the south side of the city and turn off at Tradeston. I will be home within fifteen minutes. Instead, I drift left, cross the lanes of traffic and exit the motorway on the slip road taking me north. The road dips down into the Clyde Tunnel. The lights on the ceiling dazzle as they flick by until I emerge on the other bank of the river.

I take the first exit onto the expressway to Partick, then turn onto Crow Road and follow it until it joins Clarence Drive. On either side now are the red sandstone tenements, four storeys high, with sloping front gardens and steep stairs leading to communal front doors.

I turn into Airlie Street and park. There is no one around. It's ten forty-five. The grey has turned to black, pierced by white LED streetlights. Stepping out of the car, I hear people further away. Students either returning from an evening at the pub or heading into the west end to go to a nightclub. I retrace my way along the pavement back to Clarence Drive. On the corner is a school. Outside that is a bus stop. It is unoccupied. I take a seat on the uncomfortable metal bench under the shelter. The heat from the day is still in the air.

Across the road, the windows of the tenement buildings are closed and curtains are drawn. Behind a few there is a glimpse of light. I look at the first floor of the end building. The windows to the left of the main door are in complete darkness. The bedroom is at the back of the property. She will be in bed by now, I guess. I know she doesn't go out much. That's my fault. What I did to her changed the path of her life.

Rose Black. I found out her name after the car accident. Multiple bone fractures. A bleed on the brain. They weren't sure she would survive at first. If she had died, I would have been sent to prison. No amount of Francis McArthur's money and influence would have made a difference.

Rose was strong, a fighter, they told me. She pulled through. Came out of the coma. They weren't sure what damage had been done. Wheelchair-bound. Permanent brain damage. Scarring.

We were coming home from a night out in the city centre. Tony was too drunk to drive his car. He let me drive. I hadn't had as much. I was sure I was under the limit. We had both had a few beers, but we had driven on similar nights out many times before.

We were on Great Western Road, heading for Tony's house in Bearsden.

I didn't spot the red light.

She was with a group of friends. She was the unlucky one who stepped onto the road first.

The noise still haunts me. The thudding sound of metal crunching into her fragile body. The smash of the windscreen. The screech of the tyres. The screams of her friends. The stillness when the car came to a stop.

Blue lights. Police cars and ambulances. Tony called his father. Francis McArthur arrived with Murdo Smith and Malky Thomson. Tony and I sat on the kerb, our heads in our hands. Murdo spoke to the officers. Malky was sent to the hospital, following Rose in the ambulance when it sped away. He was to update Francis and approach the girl's family. Whatever they needed, he would see to it.

We were breathalysed, handcuffed and put in the back of separate police cars. McArthur's solicitor, Alan Cox, went with Tony. I was on my own. The officers didn't say anything to me in the car. At the station we were put in separate cells.

The cell stank of urine. The single lightbulb in the ceiling flickered. Every ten minutes the metal slot in the door opened and a duty officer checked on me.

I had no idea how much time passed before they came to get me. They took me to a room. Alan Cox was waiting for me. He waited while they charged me with causing serious injury by dangerous driving and driving while under the influence. Tony was charged too, with aiding and abetting, because we were both over the legal alcohol limit. He could have stopped us both getting in that car.

Cox sat me down and closed the door.

'How is the girl?'

'Alive, the last we heard. For your sake, you better hope she survives. If she dies, there's only so much I can do.'

He took me through what would happen next. He would get us out of the cells on Monday, once the magistrate's office opened. Until then, speak to no one. He told me it was important Tony and I told the same story. Don't waver from the facts. Then he told me what the facts were. They weren't the facts that I remembered. If they ask if the traffic light was red, say I was sure it was green. If they ask about the amount we had drunk, say we thought we were under the limit as we only had one small bottle of beer each.

'You're lucky you were with Tony. Francis will make sure his son doesn't go to prison for this. He can call in favours for Tony's sake, but no one would raise a finger to help you. Tony means you get a free pass. You understand? You'll owe him; you'll owe Mr McArthur.'

On Monday morning, Tony and I got out. Malky picked us up outside the station and drove us home.

Dad couldn't look me in the face. 'I warned you about hanging around with Anthony McArthur. Now look what you have done to that poor girl. Look what you've brought on us.' I didn't know what he meant then. Only later did I learn Francis McArthur and Murdo Smith had already visited my parents. They had explained what would happen. My father would owe them money. My father would be in their debt. Joseph Jackson agreed to their plan to keep me out of prison.

I wish he hadn't.

Eighteen months later, the case came to trial in Glasgow Sheriff Court. I sat next to Tony in the dock. We hadn't seen much of each other since the accident. Rose Black and her family came to the trial. We pled guilty. The deal had been arranged. Community service for me. It should have been at least six months in jail. A caution for Tony. The Black family looked broken. When the sentences were read out by the judge, Rose's mother wept and put her arms around her daughter. Rose didn't move. Her father was motionless as we shook hands with Alan Cox and Murdo Smith.

Francis McArthur had stayed away. By then, the Black family had agreed to let Francis help them. They accepted his offer of money. Francis McArthur fixed it.

That could have been the end of it. It should have been. We could all have put it behind us.

Except I couldn't. I couldn't shake the guilt. I couldn't shake the fact I had got away with ruining a young girl's life. I should have been punished. It was arranged by McArthur and Alan Cox and Murdo Smith for my benefit. Mum and Dad knew what had happened, they knew about the favours and deals done in the judge's chambers and the men's clubs. Marie was never told the full details. If the police or the Crown Office and Procurator Fiscal Service knew, no one said anything. If any of the witnesses saw different from the official crime report read out in court, none of them said anything, but at least one of them must have seen the truth in the aftermath of the accident. The drunken state of the driver stumbling out of the car. I had run the red light. I had driven while under the influence. I had been the one to destroy the Black family and all their dreams and hopes for their daughter. I had been the one to shatter Rose Black.

Francis McArthur may have salvaged my life, but not my soul.

Before the accident Rose Black had been an outgoing, bright young girl, on the cusp of becoming a confident woman, set for further education. She could have been whatever she chose to be. She could have succeeded at anything she set her mind to. Her father said all this at the trial in his witness impact statement.

I couldn't get her out of my mind. She had spent time in a wheelchair, then she'd used crutches while her bones healed and she learned to walk again. When she left the court, she limped. She wore her hair long and brushed across her face. It hid the scars that would never fade.

I wanted to tell her how sorry I was. I wanted to make amends. Alan Cox advised me to stay away from her and her family. I spiralled out of control. I was drinking too much, I wasn't sleeping. The doctor prescribed antidepressants. I abused them. I took other drugs. I dropped out of college. I acted like I was the victim. My father gave up on me. Then he gave up on life. When he died, my mother and sister gave up on me as well. Mum blamed me – me and Francis McArthur.

I drifted. On days when a black cloud descended, I would search for Rose Black.

I never approached her; I never spoke to her. I followed her. I thought of myself as her guardian angel, ready to save her if she needed to be saved. It never occurred to me that she didn't need saving, least of all by me. It never occurred to me that I was doing anything wrong. Through her years at university, when she got her first job, when she moved out from her parent's home, I was there, watching. She didn't need a guardian angel. In truth, I needed her. I needed to see that she was doing well, that she was safe, that I hadn't destroyed an innocent life after all. I wanted to make amends, but I didn't know how. She made new friends, she had a brief relationship with a boy from her course. It didn't last. Was that because of the scars I had caused?

I know there is nothing I can do to make it up to her. I know I shouldn't be here. I know a part of me is broken and can't move on, even when I know Rose has healed and moved on. Now shame mixes with guilt.

I haven't seen her in over a year, since before I went to prison. She might not even live on Clarence Drive anymore. All I can do is wait and hope.

If she sees me, what will she do? She could call the police. I'm a two-time offender now, I've done time, I'm an ex-convict. It's a risk just being here, sitting at the bus stop and watching and waiting.

It is wrong, but I tell myself I'm not doing any harm, so long as she never sees me. That won't stand up in a court of law.

It is after midnight. I have been sitting at the bus stop for over an hour. No one has passed on the empty street apart from the odd car every now and then. One car passes more than once; at least, I think it's the same car. When it passes for a third time, I decide it's best to leave. It's probably no one, but even no one will be suspicious of a man sitting at a bus stop for over an hour, when the buses stopped running two hours ago.

I walk back to the car and drive off into the night. Rose Black's flat remains in darkness.

6

Alongside being able to drive myself home after a late night out, the other benefit of no longer drinking alcohol is the lack of a hangover the next morning. My sleep pattern is still unsettled. I can't adjust to the lack of a set routine. Even though it was after one before I got to bed, I still wake up at six. It doesn't help that I've forgotten to close the curtains – something else you don't have to worry about in a prison cell.

I lie on the bed, letting the sunlight warm my face. There is nothing to do today. With the wedding out of the way, there is nothing scheduled in my future. I can lie here and not get up and nothing will be any different in the world. No one's life will be affected.

Around nine, I start to hear the noise growing outside. It is a Saturday morning. There's no weekday rush hour but the traffic is building. There are voices, loud conversations, some shouts and the odd bit of singing. By half past nine, I have to get up and look out of the window to see what is going on. Groups of people are walking past on the street below my ground-floor window. Mostly men, a few women, a few kids. They are split into two tribes: those that wear blue and those that wear green. An incongruous sound adds to the mix. Horses' hoofs clopping along the concrete road. Mounted police appear.

It is Cup final day. The national stadium, Hampden Park, is only a couple of streets away from Cumming Drive. To make matters worse, it's Celtic against Rangers, the two Glasgow rivals with a mutual hatred for each other. Any chance of a quiet day evaporates. I can see Cathcart Road, the main street that leads to the stadium, is rammed with early crowds. Some spill onto Cumming Drive to find a quieter route, and pass my front window. It is still hours until the kick-off at three in the afternoon, but that hasn't stopped supporters of both sides getting here early. Coaches trundle towards the stadium. One man decides to relieve himself on the patch of grass in front of my flat. It isn't worth the argument to open the window and shout at him.

There are two choices for the residents in the surrounding streets. Get out of town until the match is over and the crowds have dissipated late in the evening, or hole up for the day, barricaded behind locked doors and shut windows. I have nowhere to be and nowhere to go. I go back to bed and put my head under the pillow. My beat-up Corsa, parked in the residents' spaces on the street, will have to take its chances with the football supporters of Glasgow.

I make it until mid-morning before giving up on bed and moving to the sofa in the living room. I put on the television to drown out the noise outside. I flick through cookery shows and political talk shows and sport preview shows. Nothing holds my attention. I turn it off and put the radio on instead. In the small kitchen, I scrape bits of green mould from the last piece of bread and make myself a slice of toast. There is nothing to put on it. I take two dry bites and throw the rest in the bin.

I change out of the t-shirt I slept in and put on fresh underwear, crumpled jeans picked up from the bedroom floor and a clean top. I make a mug of coffee and sit back on the sofa. Twenty minutes later I have taken two sips and the coffee has gone cold. I pour it down the sink.

It is difficult to occupy my mind, cooped up in the small, messy flat with just the damp-stained walls and ceiling to look at. Marie and Tony will be at the airport now, about to jet off on their honeymoon. Mum will be back at the house. Inertia creeps over me. Thoughts of Elise Moreau compete with memories of Rose Black. The Cup final will be on the television. That will pass the afternoon, even if I don't care which team wins.

Then there is a bang on the door. I figure it will be a drunken fan, caught short in the street, wanting to use the bathroom. I ignore it.

They keep knocking. I go to the hallway and stare at the door, willing whoever it is to leave me alone. No one has been to the flat since I moved in. I haven't invited anyone; I haven't given my address to anyone. My parole officer and the housing association are the only ones who know I live here. I haven't spoken to any of the neighbours.

Another insistent rap on the door.

'Who is it?'

'Police, open up.'

A female voice. Some street cop to tell me a worse-for-wear Rangers supporter has puked over my front lawn.

I open the door.

She isn't wearing a uniform, so she isn't your average street cop.

'Hi Callum,' she smiles. It doesn't reassure me. She holds up an open wallet and shows me her identification. Detective Simone Millar. Specialist Crime Division. Definitely not your average cop.

'It's Cal.'

'Can I come in?'

'What's this about?'

'Easier to tell you inside, away from Glasgow's finest,' she points over her shoulder at the hordes in the street, still filtering their way down to the stadium. I open the door for her. She walks past me, ducks her head in each door as she goes down the hallway and turns into the living room. I shut the front door behind her and follow.

She stands in the middle of the room. She has short, sandy hair in a functional cut just above her shoulders. She's thin but wiry in black jeans and t-shirt and a tan leather jacket. She wears black boots with a small heel. She has the look of someone who spends an hour each morning in the gym before starting her shift. Five-ten, an inch shorter than me. She dominates the room; she is used to being in charge.

'Have a seat,' she instructs me, like it is her office instead of my living room. 'I like what you've done with the place.'

'Haven't got round to decorating yet.' I pick up last night's suit, which lies crumpled on the sofa, and throw it in the corner. 'Sorry about the mess.'

'I've seen worse, especially from ex-convicts living on their own.' It doesn't sound like a compliment.

I try to pre-empt her reason for being here. 'I checked in with my parole officer last week.'

'Good. Well done. Make sure you keep that up.' She is still looking at the surroundings. What she is looking for, I'm not sure.

'So what's this about? I have plans for today.'

'Sure you do, Cal.' She gives me a wry look. I sit down on the sofa. Detective Simone Millar continues to stand. 'Late night last night?' The way she asks the question, she already knows the answer. 'But you left the wedding early.'

'You followed me?'

'Let's say we were keeping an eye on comings and goings.'

'I'm not big on social occasions.'

'Your sister's wedding though?'

'We're not close anymore.'

'A spell in the nick will do that to relationships, even family. But it was quite a prestigious occasion. You're part of Glasgow royalty now,' she persists.

'I'd rather be a commoner, given the choice.'

She laughs at that and shakes her head. 'Unfortunately, people like you, Cal, don't get much of a choice in life.'

'People like me?' I'm not enjoying the conversation, either where it is going or Detective Millar's attitude towards me.

'How can I put this without offending your sensitive feelings? You're one of life's losers, Cal. You were always destined to be. Some of it wasn't your fault. You weren't to know, growing up, that your best friend at school was also the son of a Glasgow mobster. Or maybe you did? You must have had some idea. Your dad must have warned you to be careful. No?'

So it is about McArthur. What exactly, I'm not sure I want to find out, but like Millar says, I don't have a choice.

When I don't respond, she shrugs. 'Then the inevitable for you, the car accident. How did you manage to avoid a prison sentence for that? Mowing down an innocent young woman, leaving her in a coma? You came out of it unscathed, but at what cost? In debt to Anthony's dad. Your dad knew you had got caught up in a web of criminality.'

Two mentions of my dad. Two too many. 'If you've come to remind me of my past mistakes, I can live without it.'

'You're right, Cal, I apologise for raking over old ground. Let's talk about the present instead.' As far as I am aware, I have no present, beyond stumbling along in my new-found freedom without purpose. 'You're part of Francis McArthur's family now and it may surprise you to learn that we take an interest in the McArthur family business. Turns out not all of his dealings are strictly above board.'

'How long did it take you lot to work that out?'

'It's been known about for some time, but unlike in the past, there's a will now for something to be done about it.'

What she means is that McArthur has spent years paying people off, bribing officials and police officers to look the other way. I have first-hand experience of it.

'There are new people at the top now, fresh blood with a new outlook. Not so easily blackmailed or compromised.'

'And you'd be one of these people?'

'I wouldn't go so far as to call myself top brass, Cal, but you're right to say I have a bit of power, a bit of sway. I'm running a task force looking into some of McArthur's property deals around the city. You'd be amazed just how much of the city your sister's new father-in-law owns.'

I'm not surprised at all, but I don't say anything.

'I'm telling you this because I know you're not a big fan of Francis McArthur. Can I trust you?'

'I'm an ex-convict and I'm in the McArthur family now. Should you trust me?'

'I think I'm a good judge of character. You'd do anything to stay away from Francis McArthur. You're not going to rush over to his house in Bearsden and tell him about me. Besides, he knows who I am and what I'm doing already. That's part of the problem.'

There is a loud shout from outside. Detective Millar moves to the window and looks outside. 'Hooligans,' she mutters, before turning back to me. 'The sort of day that makes me glad I'm not in uniform anymore.' She comes back around the room and sits in front of me, resting on the coffee table, looking me straight in the eye. 'McArthur has had years of covering his tracks. He knows all the tricks of the game. We know he's dirty, behind his public façade and good deeds and donations to good causes. He's a criminal. We know it, but we need evidence to prove it. Evidence that can be used against him.'

I have a sinking feeling in the pit of my stomach. Her gaze is intense, like she is trying to look into my soul and see if there is any chance a good man resides within.

'I'm not sure how I can help you,' is my meek reply.

'You're in a privileged position now, Cal. You got a job offer last night.' How does she know about that?

'Just to work at one of his nightclubs. Bar work. Nothing that's going to help you. I turned him down. How did you find out about that?'

She ignores my question. 'We're going to need you to take that job, Cal.'

'And do what, exactly?'

'Keep your eyes and ears open for us. Take a wee note of who visits Mr McArthur. Maybe listen in on some conversations. See if you can pick up anything that might help me.'

'You want me to be your informant? A grass?'

'If you want to call it that.'

'What would you call it?'

'That's what I would call it too, but the thing is, Cal,' she pauses, emphasising my name, 'you don't have a choice.'

'Are you threatening me with something?'

She picks up a manila envelope from the coffee table. I didn't even notice her putting it there. She tosses it onto my lap with an apologetic gesture and stands up again, moving behind me, the back of the sofa between us.

I open the envelope and pull out the pieces of paper inside. It is glossy photograph paper. Black and white images. I turn them the right way up. I manage to swallow the urge to vomit.

She leans over the sofa and whispers into my ear. 'Oops.'

The bus stop on Clarence Drive. The bench, one person sitting on it. Me. It is dark, night time. Not last night; I'm not wearing the suit. From another night, maybe a month ago. It was taken with a long telephoto lens.

I muster some resolve. Worth a try to brazen it out. 'I haven't broken any law.'

'Would Rose Black think so? Or would she be tempted to bring some charges against you?' Millar is stalking around the room now. 'Worse, what would she think of you if she knew you had been following her? Especially when she learns how long you've been following her.'

She is behind me again. She leans over and plucks the photographs and the envelope from my hands. She sits in front of me again as she slides the photographs away and tucks the envelope inside her jacket. 'Of course, she never has to find out about you. At least, not from me.'

7

Detective Millar leaves fifteen minutes later. I watch her from the window as she walks down the path to the gate. The black jeans have a confident swagger. She looks back, sees me watching and gives me a smile and a salute. She puts sunglasses on and gets into a familiar silver coupé that is waiting for her. The same silver coupé that drove past the bus stop three times last night outside Rose Black's flat. Another detective is driving. Her partner, I guess.

The street is clear. Everyone has made their way through the turnstiles and into Hampden Stadium. A temporary calm descends while the game is being played. In two hours, the storm will erupt as supporters from both teams spew forth from the stadium again with one tribe celebrating and the other rioting. I turn the television on to the BBC Scotland channel as the teams come out onto the pitch. From outside, I can hear the roar of the crowd. On the television there is a delay of about thirty seconds, giving a weird echo to events.

The game kicks off. I watch, without taking in anything that is happening. My mind is too busy thinking about Detective Simone Millar and Francis McArthur and the situation I've been forced into.

It isn't just the fact I will be working for Francis McArthur. I will be informing on him to the police. I will be a snitch. I know from prison that police informants are considered the lowest of the low. Nobody likes a grass. If I get caught, there will be only one outcome. Millar says they can protect me. If I need out, they will get me out. They can move me away if it comes to it, give me a fresh start and a new identity somewhere else in the country. Millar says this, but we both know there is nowhere they can put me that would be safe from Francis McArthur if he finds out I betrayed him.

'Why McArthur?' I had asked her as she prowled round my living room. 'There's worse out there that the police turn a blind eye to.'

As much as I don't like McArthur, as far as criminal gang lords go, he has some good qualities. It is well known that he takes a zero-tolerance approach to drugs. Drugs aren't allowed in his nightclubs and he will have nothing to do with drug trafficking. He leaves that to others. Unlike the Glasgow gangs of the past, the McArthur family never lets violence spill out onto the streets. There is no history of murder sprees or dead bodies. As the biggest landlord in the city, his reputation is firm but fair. He is civic-minded, sponsoring arts events and concerts. He funds equal-opportunity endeavours and spends money to help those in poverty – which still blights a vast swathe of the Glasgow populace. To many he is a hero. The local boy made good, who is giving back to his roots. Only those that get too close ever see underneath the veneer, and even then, only if they look carefully. If I were the police commissioner for the city, I'd be grateful for what I had, and fearful of what might take McArthur's place. Why upset the apple cart?

Millar dismissed me. A criminal is a criminal. She wants to peel back that veneer and see what lies behind the shiny, squeaky-clean surface. She figures I will understand. I have more reason to want to bring McArthur down than most. She mentions Dad for the third time. How can I live knowing Francis McArthur drove my dad to take his own life?

It wasn't the only reason, I argued.

'Sure it wasn't,' she said.

I'd tried to find another way out. 'My parole conditions mean I can't work after ten in the evening. I can't serve alcohol.'

Millar brushed these complaints aside. She could fix that.

'What about Marie? I can't betray my own sister.'

'You will be doing it for her own good,' said Millar. 'You'll be saving her before she gets sucked in too deep and becomes complicit.'

'I already told Murdo Smith no. I was pretty adamant. They will be suspicious if I turn up at their door asking for a job. They will never believe me when I tell them I had a change of heart.'

'Convince them,' Millar had said. 'Come up with a persuasive reason. Tell them you've slept on it and considered how much your sister means to you. Tell them you'd be honoured to be part of the McArthur family. Tell them whatever they need to hear. Just make sure you get that job. Otherwise…'

Then she pointed at the envelope again and I knew I had no choice.

Millar knows I have no choice too, but not for the reasons she thinks. Prison time doesn't hold much fear for me anymore. I've done time, I can do it again. It wasn't the most pleasant way to spend a year or two, but it wasn't the worst either. Maybe I am conditioned to it as a way of life now, like the long-term inmates who fear being let out into the real world more than anything else.

What I can't live with is the thought of hurting Rose. The anguish and anger it would cause her if she knew. The hatred she would have for me. That's what I can't face. That's why I will do what Detective Millar is asking me to do.

A noise like a jet aeroplane taking off builds outside and erupts into a collective roar. Thirty seconds later, on the television, Celtic score.

Millar told me not to hang about. She is giving me until the middle of the week to approach McArthur and accept his offer.

I think about getting out, but where would I go? I don't have a passport. I do have a criminal record. I can't leave the country. Scotland isn't a big enough country to stay hidden in for long, unless you're willing to lose yourself in the wild Highlands. I don't have the survival skills required for that. There is no hiding place.

She left me with two phone numbers. One is her work phone number. 'Call me after you've made contact. Keep me informed. When it is all set up we'll sort you out you with a burner – a separate mobile phone you can use to get in touch with me that McArthur won't be able to trace.'

The second phone number belongs to Murdo Smith. 'Call him and ask to see him early next week. Tell him Marie gave you his number.'

There is another thunderous roar from outside. I've been staring at the television without paying any attention to it. The camera cuts to the referee as he blows his whistle for full-time. The green half of the stadium erupts in joy.

8

The first mistake I make is parking the Corsa outside the front of Murdo Smith's house in Milingavie.

I couldn't face calling him on the number Detective Millar left me. Instead, by Sunday lunchtime, while Glasgow City Council workers were busy cleaning up the street outside, I worked up the courage to send him a text message.

My situation's changed. Is the job offer still on the table? Cal.

The reply came instantly.

Tomorrow. 10.30. My house.

'House' can be filed under a violation of the Trade Descriptions Act. The modern building looks like it has been transported into the north-west of Glasgow from the south of Spain: clean straight lines, square corners and glass walls surrounded by fresh whitewashed brickwork. I pass through a steel gate in a perimeter wall, announcing myself to a faceless security guard via an intercom. No one speaks; the gates just swing open to allow entry. A gravel driveway winds around a front lawn and opens onto a courtyard in front of a wide front door, flanked on either side by palm trees that I assume are fake.

'Mr Smith will see you in the drawing room,' says Davidson, Murdo's assistant, like it is the most natural thing to say to an ex-convict living in a housing association one-bedroom flat. Davidson has been around since I was a teenager, always at his master's side. Rumours about the exact nature of their relationship have been around just as long. Murdo Smith has never been married, has never had a partner, female or male. He lives in this huge six-bedroom pile on his own. Davidson is part of the house staff, including a cook, cleaner and chauffeur who tend to him every day, but are not permitted to live under the same roof as him. Anyone who speculates about Murdo Smith's sexuality isn't going to do it to his face, unless they have a death wish. The only thing Murdo Smith has ever devoted himself to is the protection and wellbeing of Francis McArthur.

Dressed in suit trousers and shirt despite the early morning heat, Davidson leads me across the foyer, up the stairs and along a hallway to a room that overlooks the front of the property. He chaps the door and opens it without waiting for a response.

'Callum Jackson to see you.' He announces me like the butler in an Agatha Christie novel.

Murdo is at the window, looking out over the front courtyard. Unlike his assistant, he wears a casual t-shirt and shorts. His legs, arms and bald head are tanned more than is naturally possible in Glasgow. 'Give your car keys to Davidson.' He turns and faces us. I hand my car keys over. 'Move Mr Jackson's car round to the back gate.'

'Yes, sir.' Davidson pockets my keys and closes the door behind him as he backs out of the room.

'As admirable as it is that your car still manages to start at all, it ruins the aesthetic of the view from here.' I can't argue with that. I join him at the window and admire the view. The clear blue sky, the palm trees, the white walls. Beyond, the hilltops of the Campsie Fells shimmer through the rising heat haze. It could be the south of Spain.

The front door opens below us and Davidson strides out to my car. We watch him get in. It takes him three attempts before the engine catches. He revs it hard before crunching it into gear and driving away. A plume of dirty grey smoke trails from the exhaust. Murdo takes a last satisfied look at the restored impeccable view and turns away.

'Too nice to be sat inside on a morning like this. Let's go to the garden to talk.'

'Sure.'

Instead of descending by the stairs inside the house, he leads me to a balcony at the rear that has an external staircase down to the grounds. There are more palm trees at the back, but they are dwarfed by tall pines that border the property on the other side of the white perimeter wall. The grass is lush and green and artificial. There is a swimming pool in the middle of the lawn, blue tiles and clear water shimmering in the May sun, further giving the impression that the designs for this house have been imported from the Mediterranean. I wonder how often anyone ever uses the pool, even in the short weeks that constitute the Scottish summer. Maybe he is future-proofing for climate change.

A tiled roof comes out from the back wall of the house and rests on white pillars, creating a covered terrace, adding to the feel of a Spanish hacienda. A table and chairs sit in the shade. Murdo beckons me to take one of them and sits next to me, looking out to the garden. From an unseen doorway, Davidson appears and delivers an iced tea in a clear glass.

'Anything?' Murdo asks me. I shake my head and he dismisses Davidson with a wave of his hand. 'How long since you were here?' he asks.

'I don't remember there being a pool.'

'I had that put in about ten years ago.'

'Sounds about right.'

'A shame you chose to stay away.'

'It was difficult, after the accident.'

'I thought you and Tony would have been friends for life.' He waits for me to say something. I have nothing to add. 'And now he's your brother-in-law.'

'That was nothing to do with me.'

'But where does that leave you? That's why you want to talk about the job, isn't it?'

'I'm not interested in being mates with Tony.'

'But you do want a job? You realise you'll see Tony? And Francis.'

'Need rather than want.' After mulling it over all day on Sunday, this was the best I could come up with to explain my change of heart. It helps that it is partially true. I need an income and I need a job. Bartender for Francis McArthur isn't at the top of my list, but criminals can't be choosers. Reacquainting myself with Tony and his dad is exactly what Detective Millar wants me to do, but I will be doing it through gritted teeth.

A pair of magpies land in one of the tall trees bordering the garden. They squawk at each other, their harsh chattering breaking the peaceful quiet. 'Bloody things have made a nest up there. They're lucky I don't chop the tree down.' He sips his iced tea. Condensation from the glass drips onto the front of his t-shirt. 'You seemed pretty adamant that you didn't want to work for Mr McArthur under any circumstances when we last spoke.'

'Under normal circumstances I wouldn't.'

'But?'

'But my circumstances aren't normal. I wasn't thinking clearly at the wedding. I had a lot of emotions being there, a lot of history stirred up.'

'On cooler reflection though, you think it would be a good thing?'

Sweat runs down my back again. It isn't just the heat that is causing it. Murdo Smith has this effect on people, even when he's being civilised. 'I think I can't change the fact that Marie is married to Tony. I might as well take from it what I can.' His piercing stare concentrates itself on my face. I manage to hold his gaze for a second before I turn away and look at the garden. I am sure he can see right through me. I try to deflect. 'You use that swimming pool much?'

'Every morning. It's heated. Nothing more invigorating in the winter, or cooling in the summer.' Murdo Smith is the sort of man who always appears to keep an even temper. He doesn't need a swimming pool to help him. 'I'll tell Mr McArthur you've reconsidered.'

'Thanks.' I would like to get up and leave it at that, but you don't walk away from Murdo Smith until you have been dismissed. So I sit there, looking at the water rippling on the surface of the pool.

Murdo sips his iced tea again and places the glass on the table. He leans towards me. 'Look at me, son.' I don't want to, but it is a command that is not to be ignored. 'I still think it's a mistake to bring you in. You've walked away from Mr McArthur's help before. I don't like ungrateful people, especially when they owe him. So I'll be watching you, you understand?' I nod. 'Closely.'

He sits back in his chair and picks up his glass again. He makes a contented sigh. I think I must have imagined the threat that has just been delivered. It's like it never happened, but it has, because I can feel my pulse hammering around my body. It is impossible to fool Murdo Smith. Harder men than me, career criminals and connected gang lords haven't managed to outfox him yet. Who do I think I am to try?

'I appreciate your help. You won't have to worry about me. I just want a quiet life.' I am lying to him already.

'You and me both, son,' he says. The magpies kick off another squabble of grating calls. He points at the tree. 'But sometimes life won't let it be that way. You know the Plein Soleil on Argyle Street?' His clipped Glaswegian accent mangles the French pronunciation.

'That used to be the Cain and Abel?'

'You have been away for a long time. Aye, that's the one. Be there on Thursday night, six p.m.'

Now I have permission to go. I stand up without saying anything else.

'You can get your car at the back gate and leave that way.' He doesn't want to risk anyone seeing my Corsa leave the front of his house. On cue, Davidson appears and guides me through the garden to a small gate in the wall, hidden behind one of the palm trees. Up close, it turns out the trees are real. I wonder where Murdo has got them shipped in from.

My car is parked just outside, like a leper cast into the shadows.

I get in and turn the key that Davidson has returned to me. The engine kicks in first time. I drive off and leave a puff of dirty smoke behind me, clouding the pristine white perimeter wall.

PART 2

DAY FOR NIGHT

9

Thursday evening outside Plein Soleil. Full Sun. An ironic name given the club only opens when the sun has set and the building has no windows, black walls and the main dancefloor is in the basement.

McArthur names all of his nightclubs, bars and restaurants after French films from the seventies and earlier, usually but not always starring the actor Alain Delon. Soleil Rouge is the name of the strip club McArthur owns in the city centre. His Japanese restaurant in the West End is called Le Samouraï. The Red Circle is a casino down by the river. He owns two student nightclubs at the top end of Sauchiehall Street – Breathless and Rififi. His latest venture is a cabaret club that is due to open in the Merchant City to cash in on the current craze for drag shows and burlesque. It is to be called La Grande Illusion. Perhaps McArthur thinks the names lend his venues a sense of sophistication, like Delon in his iconic fedora and trench coat; a reminder of a more refined place and time and style. As far as I can tell, it hasn't rubbed off on the good people of Glasgow so far. Maybe he just likes French cinema.

Plein Soleil caters for the slightly older nightclub clientele, those in their mid- to late-twenties and beyond, with disposable incomes and well-paid graduate jobs. It is the most upmarket of

Francis McArthur's properties, and as such has become the centre of his entertainment empire. The upper floor contains work offices, the ground floor a bar, and the dancefloor is below in the basement. Big names in the music industry hire it out as a venue for intimate gigs and record launches. Celebrities, influencers and footballers often put in appearances. Glasgow's recent resurgence as a location for American films and dramas has seen a few Hollywood names stop by for an evening. There is a strict dress code of formal attire – no jeans or trainers. Dresses and heels, suit trousers and shoes. For my first night there, I turn up in the same suit and shoes I bought cheap for Marie and Tony's wedding.

I park on one of the streets off Byres Road, surrounded by the old sandstone administration buildings of the university. The temperature has risen further over the week. The forecast is for it to top 35°C by the middle of next week. There isn't a breath of fresh air. Walking down the street in my suit causes me to break out into a warm sweat. Glasgow isn't built to cope with heat, and 35°C counts as extreme for the west of Scotland.

The sign over the door is written in yellow letters on a black background, the same typeface used on the original movie poster, with a red sun behind. The front entrance is locked. Doors won't open until ten. I walk round the side and find a door with a "Staff Entrance" sign nailed to it. That is locked too. I consider turning around and leaving, but I have already come too far for that to be an option. A CCTV camera is mounted on the wall. My presence will already have been noted. I press the buzzer by the door.

'Who is it?' A voice comes out of the speaker next to the buzzer.
'Cal Jackson.'

Nothing happens for two minutes. Then the door opens and Malky Thomson is there to greet me, his huge shoulders and chest packed into a plain black t-shirt and black trousers, the official uniform of a nightclub bouncer. He is more than that though. Malky runs the security for all of McArthur's clubs and bars.

He beams his expensive veneered teeth at me. 'Glad you took my advice, Cal.' I let him think it was his warning that has changed my mind. 'Come on in.'

Malky leads me through a narrow corridor, pointing out rooms as we pass. 'Staff room, staff toilet, staff kitchen. Through there is the basement bar and main dancefloor. Stairs up to the main bar. Cleaning cupboard. Cellar where all the food and drink supplies are stored.' The place smells of chlorine solution mixed with musty staleness. There are people in some of these rooms, but Malky doesn't stop to introduce me to anyone.

Up one flight of stairs, we enter the main bar. Through another set of double doors, the black walls are left behind, replaced by white. 'Up there is the manager's office,' Malky points up to the top of the staircase. 'Mr McArthur uses it when he's here. You don't go up there unless you're invited. Off limits to staff.'

'Understood.' He doubles back across the bar and down again towards the staff rooms. 'You work here?' I ask his back as I trail behind him.

'Not every night. I travel between all our places, make sure my security staff are behaving. Murdo asked me to meet you here and show you around. I've got to head off to the Rififi. Someone called in sick. The goddamn students are the worst to deal with.'

'You know what I'm going to be doing?'

'Not up to me. The club manager will sort you out. You know Mr McArthur's rules?'

'Rules?'

He stops and turns to face me, checking off the rules on his fingers as he says them. 'No drugs, period. No alcohol while on shift. Be on time. Treat all customers equally and with courtesy. No skimming from the till. No favours for friends without Mr McArthur's express permission. Follow the rules and you'll be fine.'

'Great, got it.'

'You do good here and there could be a bright future for you with the organisation.'

I'm sure he doesn't mean it to sound sinister, but I get the feeling that if I don't do good, the alternative is a very bleak future.

We are back at the staff room. 'I'll leave you here. Remember the rules.' Malky taps my shoulder and heads back along the corridor. I watch him exit out of the staff entrance and then I push open the door to the staff room.

Grey lockers line one side of a square space. The walls are grey brick, the floor grey concrete. No one has felt the need to decorate this space. A small table sits in the corner with three chairs around it. A fridge is in the corner with a microwave resting on top of it. I pull out a chair and sit down to wait. I feel a long way from being able to help Detective Millar.

Five minutes later the door opens and the young bartender from the wedding walks in. She had been in a blouse and trousers at the weekend, now she is in a black t-shirt. Despite the heat, she looks fresh. She wears her short bleach-blonde hair in the same style, spiked and swept up in a quiff, shaved in around the neck and sides. Her youthful face is adorned with a nose stud and each ear hosts a collection of rings and studs that had been removed when I saw her behind the bar at Erskine House. If she is surprised to see me sitting there, she doesn't show it.

'So you're Cal Jackson?'

'Guilty.'

'Malky told me he showed you around.'

'A whistle stop tour. I thought you worked at Erskine House?'

'I work for Mr McArthur. He wanted his own staff to work the wedding. I'm Carmen.'

'Interesting name.'

'My father was a big opera fan. Carmen Carmichael.' She holds out a hand. I shake it, painfully aware of her dry skin in my moist grasp. 'You got much experience?'

'Never worked in a club before.'

Carmen rolls her eyes. 'Great, another newbie.'

'A what?'

'Newbie. Mr McArthur likes to send his social outreach cases to us. No offence.'

'None taken.'

'Well, we'll get you trained up over the next few days. Plenty of staff tonight, so you can stay behind the scenes and away from the customers for your first night.' She goes to one of the lockers, opens it and pulls out a fresh t-shirt. 'You mind giving me a moment?'

I stand outside the room while she changes her top. She comes out in a loose black t-shirt with the logo of the club across the front and back – "Plein Soleil" written in the same style as the sign over the entrance.

The staff entrance opens and lets in the last of the natural light and a waft of hot air. Four people walk in, two male, two female. Carmen does the introductions as they file into the staff room. 'Guys, this is Cal. This is Andy, Marc, Georgia and Lauryn.'

'Nice to meet you,' says Andy.

'Alright,' from Georgia.

Nods only from the other two.

'Follow me.' Carmen walks back down the corridor. She is petite, maybe only five-three, and slim. She pushes open the door to the cleaning cupboard. 'Okay, grab yourself a cloth and bucket.'

I stare at her. 'I'm on cleaning duty?'

'We all have to start somewhere. Think of it as a rite of passage.'

'I'm not sure this is what Mr McArthur meant when he offered me a job. Maybe I should speak to the club manager first.'

'Sorry to tell you, Cal,' Carmen smiles, 'you already are. And whatever Mr McArthur promised you, I get to run my club and my staff however I choose.'

* * *

I don't see Carmen again until the end of the night. After I've wiped down the basement bar and the main bar, I am shown to the cellar. My job is to cart bottles of beer, wine and spirits to restock the bars as they are needed. Andy shows me how to change a keg of beer and whenever a bartender calls down on the internal line, I have to lug one of the metal barrels over, switch it for the empty one on the pump and stack the empty ones out the back.

I can hear the chatter and laughter as the club fills. At ten the music in the basement dancefloor starts and the thumping bass doesn't relent for the next five hours. It isn't hard work, but it is dull. Fortunately, I am used to passing long periods of time on my own with nothing to do. I've had good practice for the last year.

At one point a huge guy dressed in black shirt and tie bursts through the door that leads up to the main bar and storms along the corridor, smacking the wall as he goes, swearing loudly. He goes into the toilet, where I hear more walls being beaten and running tap water. He comes back out five minutes later, calm and composed, and sees me looking at him.

'What are you looking at? Goddamn drunks.'

Off he goes. I guess he is one of the bouncers and there has been some sort of incident, but nothing else happens. It isn't worth reporting to Detective Millar. A similar scene will play out several times in every club and pub across the city this weekend.

The music finally stops at one minute before three in the morning. The last of the customers leave and cleaning staff arrive. I help collect the used plastic containers, wipe down the bar tops again and tidy up the storage cellar.

I leave at the same time as the other bar staff. There is an easy rapport between them. Lauryn is bitching about a male customer who has spent the night perched at the bar trying to chat her up. They are all younger than me. I figure they are students or recent graduates, working in the club to earn some spending money, waiting for their break into graduate work. They don't remark on my age or ask why a thirty-two-year-old has started working with them. Maybe they are used to older ex-cons passing through thanks to McArthur's social outreach project.

Georgia starts vaping as soon as she steps out of the door into the Glasgow night. They all say, 'See you tomorrow.' Marc and Andy walk off together. Georgia and Lauryn jump into a private taxi that is waiting for them. They are kids. They have probably never even met Francis McArthur or Murdo Smith. They aren't going to be able to tell me anything.

'Enjoy your first shift?' Carmen is locking up the staff entrance.

'Sure, great,' I reply, hoping she will catch the sarcasm.

'Hey, you don't want to be here, you don't have to be here.'

'It's not really a choice for me.'

'You think any of those guys choose to do this?' She points at her departing bar staff.

'I didn't mean it that way.'

'I get it. You're here because Francis made you an offer.' I am surprised she refers to him by his first name. 'Look, I don't want to know about whatever is going on with you and your sister's new father-in-law. Keep your family life away from here. All I care about is that my club runs smoothly and my life is hassle-free. You think you can promise me you won't upset that?'

'I guess I can try.'

'Come back early tomorrow, at six. I'll teach you to pull a pint and we'll take it from there. You driving?'

'My car's parked over there.'

'I walk this way,' she points in the opposite direction. 'We got a deal, Cal Jackson?'

'Deal,' I say.

She smiles and turns and walks away. I watch her go and then head to my car.

* * *

It is after four before I get back to the flat in Mount Florida. A package on the hall floor jams the front door as I push it open. It is a padded envelope. I open it up and pull out a mobile phone. A basic model, scratched and used. Some sort of refurb. I turn it on. There is one number in the address book, listed as 'S. M.' I take it to my bedroom. I get out of my suit trousers and shirt and lie on top of my duvet in my boxer shorts. The night is warm and muggy.

I type out a text message and send it to 'S. M.': *I'm in.*

10

Murdo Smith is right. I hate to admit it. The routine of having a job helps. It provides a purpose. Maybe I am conditioned to routine after a year in prison.

Carmen gave me an advance on my first wage and told me to buy new work clothes and get a decent haircut. Only then will she think about putting me front of house. My shifts are Thursday to Sunday, seven until closing. I haven't been sleeping through the nights since I got out anyway, so the night work suits me and leaves my days free. For the first fortnight, Carmen has me in at five and trains me up on bar service – mixing drinks, pouring measures, pulling pints. The other staff don't say much to me, but gradually they seem to accept me. Lauryn even gives me a compliment. 'You're not the worst of the convicted felons we've had to deal with.' Backhanded, sure, but it is still a thaw in relations.

May turns to June. The heatwave doesn't break. It just adds thunderstorms and torrential downpours. Each one holds the promise of clearing the air, but the temperature doesn't drop and the atmosphere is still sticky and close.

Nothing of note happens in the club in those first two weeks. I don't see Francis McArthur or Murdo Smith. Malky doesn't return. Or if they did appear, no one told me and they don't venture down to the staff area or cellar where I am pulling my shifts. Detective Millar may have wanted me to snoop around and ask questions, but I lack the inclination. I start to think this isn't so bad. I am working for McArthur, but if I don't ever have to see him, I can cope. And if I never have anything worthwhile to tell Detective Millar, maybe she will back off, forget about me and find someone else to do the dirty work for her. I check the burner mobile every night. I keep it hidden in a gap behind a loose skirting board in my bedroom. She hasn't messaged or called.

'You ready to work behind the bar this evening?' Carmen asks on a Friday evening after she's watched me with a critical eye pour a decent pint of Guinness with just the right amount of head.

'If you think I'm ready.'

'I wouldn't ask if I didn't think you were ready.'

Carmen Carmichael is a tough kid. It is easy to see why McArthur has put her in charge of his prize venue even though she is only twenty-five and looks younger. She is street-smart and no-nonsense and makes it look effortless. Men twice her size and twice her age are cowed before her. It could be because she carries Francis McArthur's authority with her, but I reckon she would be able to handle herself just fine without any help. The bouncers look to her for a decision when dealing with any rowdy clientele. Like a Roman emperor in the colosseum, Carmen Carmichael holds the fate of the populace of the Plein Soleil in her hand.

My first shift behind the main bar passes without anything untoward happening, save for a couple of poorly poured pints that I have to ditch and redo. There are the usual drunken arguments and lovers' tiffs, but by Glasgow nightclub standards it is all pretty mild. The bouncers are well drilled and step in before anything is allowed to escalate, which means I don't have to get involved. Georgia and Marc are behind the bar with me. They point me in the right direction when I can't find the right spirit among the optics, or I mess up the price I am meant to charge. Lauryn waits on the tables. She can carry two trays laden with drinks across the crowded room and doesn't spill a drop all night.

'You did well,' Carmen says as she locks up. 'You can work the main bar from now on. The customers like to see an older face there instead of just the students.'

'No more training?'

'You can learn on the job from now on. The kids will keep you right.'

I'm starting to enjoy the one-on-one conversations with Carmen. 'Maybe we could grab a drink some time?' I don't mean for it to sound like I am asking her out on a date, but it comes out like that.

'You're not my type, Cal.'

'I didn't mean— An ex-con?'

She shakes her head and laughs, enjoying my discomfort. 'A man. Plus, I can't be mixing with the staff, not even as friends. One day I'll probably have to fire you, and I wouldn't want to do that to a friend.'

'I just meant for a chat, some company. I didn't mean—'

'Please stop. I've got a partner and a two-year-old waiting for me at home who give me all the company I need. You'll need to find a drinking buddy somewhere else.'

When I get in at four, I check the burner phone. The screen tells me I have a message from Millar. I open it up and read it. *Congratulations on your promotion. Now remember, keep your eyes and ears open.* It crosses my mind again that she is incredibly well informed, even without my help.

* * *

Sunday evening. I am serving behind the main bar with Marc and Georgia again. Lauryn has called in sick so we're short-handed, but it's quiet. The heat is keeping people indoors and out of the city.

The music thumps below our feet, but the dancefloor down there is empty. There's a relaxed atmosphere in the bar too. No crowd demands service. Georgia takes the opportunity to show me some basic cocktail mixing. I'm happy to leave it to her.

At eleven, the curtain that separates the bar from the front entrance moves aside and in she walks.

Like the night of the wedding, heads turn to follow her across the room. It's the way she carries herself. She has an aura, a glow about her. It's not attractiveness, although she has that too. It's something else, like she demands you notice her. She heads straight towards me, although it's the bar that she's aiming for rather than me in particular. Her dark hair is styled the same as it was the last time I saw her, but now she's wearing trousers and a strap top that's cut a millimetre lower than it needs to be. The sway this time has lost the drunken lilt it had before. This time, Elise Moreau is in complete control.

When she reaches the bar and sees me behind it, her eyes flicker and the corners of her red lips curl upwards.

'Well, well, well. Not who I expected to find here.' Any hope that she turned up just to see me vanishes before it has barely flickered into life.

'I just started.'

'Didn't you tell me you didn't want to be around your new family?'

'That's right.'

'And yet here I find you working behind the bar of one of his clubs.'

'Didn't you tell me something similar?'

A shrug is all I get. 'I'm looking for Francis. Is he in?'

'I haven't seen him.'

Elise turns and looks around the room, as if expecting to see McArthur sitting at one of the tables.

'Are the honeymooners back?'

'They were due back last Sunday.' I know this because Mum gave me a rare phone call while Marie was away on her honeymoon. She must have been desperate for someone to talk to.

The curtain moves aside again and a group of four people enter, dressed in business suits. One woman, three men. The woman leads, the men are subordinates. She looks around the bar, squinting into the dim light, searching for someone. She doesn't find them. She sends one of her assistants towards the bar, while the rest of the group sit in an empty booth along the far wall.

Elise watches them. 'I'm not the only one looking for Francis.'

'You know her?'

'Andrea Fulton. Leader of Glasgow City Council. She must have a meeting.'

'On a Sunday night?'

'That's the kind of pull Francis McArthur has.'

'Two halves of Tennent's and a soda water.' Marc has taken the order from the councillor's assistant and is asking me to help with the straightforward drinks while he starts a cocktail mix.

'You want anything while I'm at it?' I ask Elise.

'I'll take a soda water as well.' She answers my raised eyebrow, 'I'm back on the wagon.'

'She was at the wedding.' I motion towards Andrea Fulton. 'She had a private meeting with McArthur then as well.' I didn't recognise her at first, dressed in her office clothes with her hair down and straightened, unlike the gown and make-up ensemble she wore at Erskine House. 'She stormed out, didn't look happy.'

'I imagine meetings with Francis often end that way for the other party involved.'

The background music mixes from one anonymous chilled dance track to the next. Conversations carry on uninterrupted. I wipe the bar and clean some of the empty wine and cocktail glasses Georgia has collected. Elise sips her drink and looks bored. I try to think of something to say and fall back on the one thing I know about her.

'So how is Madame Moreau?' She always insisted on being called Madame by her pupils, never Miss or Mrs.

'Not great,' Elise answers, but she doesn't expand on her mother's troubles.

'You mentioned at the wedding she's been better.'

A painful smile. 'Dementia. Early onset Alzheimer's.'

'Sorry to hear that.'

'She has good days and bad days. The worst is when she doesn't recognise me anymore.'

'It's an awful thing.'

She changes the subject. 'When did you lose your dad?'

'How do you know I have?'

'He wasn't at his daughter's wedding, so I assumed.'

'Almost ten years ago now. Your dad still about to help look after your mum?'

Elise laughs and then notices my look of confusion. 'I never had a dad. It's always just been Mum and me.'

'I had no idea.' There's something else, something she's not telling me, but before I can ask anything else, Malky Thomson comes through the curtain at the front door and holds it open. Francis McArthur strides into his club, followed by Murdo Smith and a couple of other serious-looking bodyguards.

Elise puts her glass on the bar and slides off the stool she's been perched on. She moves across the bar floor in the direction of McArthur. He doesn't seem to notice her, but Murdo Smith does and signals to Malky. Malky hustles around a couple of tables and intercepts Elise before she's halfway across the room in McArthur's direction. Dante, one of the regular bouncers at the club, sees his boss in action and swoops in to assist. They form a barrier Elise can't get around. She protests but they guide her away, managing to do so without resorting to physical intervention until Elise becomes aware they are guiding her right out the door. Too late, she tries to double back, but Malky takes her arm, deftly folds it behind her back and escorts her through the curtain and out into the night.

It all happens so fast, I don't have time to react; not that there's much I could have done to help her. I see Malky point out the door as he says something to Dante, who acknowledges he understands the instruction. I'm sure it's something along the lines of "don't let that woman back in here".

While all this has been going on, McArthur, like a swan on the water, has glided over to Councillor Andrea Fulton's booth and greeted her and her team. Warm handshakes all round. They all stand and follow McArthur to the double doors that lead to the office upstairs. Murdo and Malky follow them. Carmen appears. She's been downstairs but someone has told her the boss has arrived. She comes to the bar and gives Georgia a drinks order. Once Georgia has made up the drinks, including a bottle of expensive champagne in a bucket, Carmen takes the tray and heads up to the office with it. I haven't seen her serve drinks to any customer in the previous fortnight.

The club doesn't get any busier. An hour after they disappeared upstairs for their meeting, Councillor Fulton and her entourage emerge and head straight out the door. She looks a lot happier this time than she did after the meeting at the wedding. McArthur and Murdo Smith leave five minutes later, without a word to anyone.

Malky makes a point of coming to see me before he follows them. 'You know that girl?'

'Which girl?'

'The one who was here earlier. You were talking to her.'

'Used to go to school with her. Her mum was my French teacher.'

'What was she saying to you?'

'Nothing much. Just catching up on old times. Haven't seen her since school.'

'You're not friends?'

'Like I say, it's been fifteen years since I saw her.'

'Best keep it that way. She's not welcome back here. Understand?'

'Sure, no skin off my nose.'

With that, Malky follows the others out the door and the rest of the night passes away without incident. I contemplate asking Carmen what the story is with Elise. What has she done to get barred from the club? *Shame*, I think, same as when she walked away from me at the wedding. Elise seems like someone I could get along with, and there aren't many people like that these days. I don't get the chance to ask Carmen anything. With the club quiet, she heads off early and leaves Dante and Marc in charge of locking up.

* * *

I lie in bed surrounded by the dark, just the bright screen of the burner phone shining in a halo around my face. I read back what I've typed: *Andrea Fulton at the club. Had meeting with McArthur and Murdo Smith. No idea what they spoke about.*

It's not much, but it's the first bit of intelligence that might be remotely interesting for Detective Millar to learn. It helps that I'm being honest. I have no idea what they spoke about and they weren't hiding the fact they were meeting. So far, I haven't betrayed anyone – and Rose Black is none the wiser about my behaviour.

11

Marie looks disgustingly healthy after a week in the Caribbean sun. Her skin has a bronze shine and freckles dapple her nose and cheeks and the top of her shoulders. Her hair is freshly cut, changed from her wedding day into a light wave that falls around her face and tumbles down her back. Her clothes, a white strap top and high-waisted pleated trousers manage to look plain, simple and expensive all at the same time. Accessories sparkle around her neck, from her ears and on her fingers. She still looks like the perfect bride three weeks after the event. The only thing that looks out of place are her surroundings. She is standing on my doorstep in front of weathered council flats, looking like she should be in Milan or Paris for Fashion Week.

'Are you going to invite me in?' She steps past me without waiting for an answer. 'Christ, Cal. You live like a pig.'

'It's the cleaner's week off.' She scoops a pile of clothes from the sofa and takes a seat. 'Tea? Coffee?'

'I'll take a coffee.'

'I only have regular.' I call over my shoulder as I go to the kitchen. She doesn't follow me. I find a clean mug in the cupboard and blow the dust off it, then fill the kettle and leave it to boil. 'How was it then?' I ask from the living room door.

'Like a dream. Another world.'

'Do much sightseeing or just lounge by the pool?'

'We spent most of the time on the beach. Took a couple of day trips and walked to the local market every other day. Wonderful people. Just a different way of life.'

'If climate change keeps on going like the last few weeks, we'll all soon be moving to Prestwick and Ayr and having villas by the sea.'

'Somehow I don't think the Ayrshire coast will hold the same allure.'

The kettle clicks and I retreat back to the kitchen. 'Just milk?' I shout through.

'Oat milk if you've got it.'

I don't, so I tip in semi-skimmed and guess the strength.

I place her coffee on the table and sit on the other end of the sofa, on top of the pile of clothes.

It is Wednesday morning. The advantage of working in the club at night is having the day to myself. The disadvantage is having nothing to fill them with. Mount Florida and the Southside are good places to walk around. After being cooped up for a year behind bars, I am enjoying being out. There are plenty of spaces to escape to nearby. Queen's Park and King's Park become overcrowded in the sunshine, but a little further on, Pollok Park is vast enough to find space to be alone in amongst the paths and woods. The heat has made everyone lazy and I'm not immune. June has already set a new record high temperature for Scotland; somewhere in the Borders hit 36°C. A stroll round the local park is less pleasant when you break into a heat sweat three steps after leaving your front door. After Sunday evening at work, the furthest I've ventured this week was to the shops on Cathcart Road. A lot of the shop owners have closed up and gone to the coast for the cooler air and an ice cream.

I've avoided Clarence Drive and Rose Black ever since Millar paid me a visit. I want to see Rose again to find out how she is. How her life is now. What she looks like after another year. Have her scars faded further? Has the limp disappeared at last?

'Tony tells me you took a job at the club.'

'How does he feel about that? Hope it didn't ruin the honeymoon romance.'

'Francis told him when we got back.' I should have known my employment status didn't warrant a newsflash in St Lucia. 'How are you finding it?'

'Good. Uneventful.'

'I'm glad you took Francis up on the offer.'

'It wasn't like I had a lot of options.' A half-truth. I wait for the reason I have been graced with my sister's presence.

'You've spoken to Mum?' Marie asks.

'She called. I think she is lonely. Missing you being around for a chat.'

'I met her yesterday, at the house. She's thinking of selling now I've moved out. It's a big house for her on her own.'

I fear Marie is about to suggest I move back in with Mum, but even she knows that isn't going to happen. She shifts on the sofa, trying to disguise her discomfort in my penurious accommodation. She adjusts her top and flicks her hair away from her face.

'You need to get some air conditioning in here.'

'I'll ask the housing association to prioritise it.'

She rolls her eyes at my sarcasm. 'Tony and I would love to have you over to the new house sometime.'

That's what we've been building up to. The olive branch is being offered. A chance for reconciliation with my sister and my new brother-in-law.

Instinct tells me to flat out reject it. Detective Millar will want me to accept. She's replied to my text message on Sunday night about Andrea Fulton's appearance at the club: *I need more than that.*

I hedge my bets by not committing. 'I took the job because I had to. I'm not sure I'm ready to become friends with the McArthurs again just yet.'

'It's been ten years since Dad died, Cal.'

'That doesn't make it right.'

'After everything that Tony did for you? He helped keep you out of prison.'

'Tony did what his dad told him to do, nothing more.'

'He could have been honest. He could have told the police the truth.'

'He wouldn't have said anything unless Francis told him to say it.'

'You never think they might have done it because they liked you? Because they wanted to help you?'

'Maybe they did,' I shrug, 'but they used it as an opportunity to get a hold over Dad, to get their claws into him. To take advantage of him and push him until he couldn't take it anymore.'

'For God's sake, Cal.' Her voice rises for the first time. 'Don't you ever take responsibility? Don't you ever think it was you who killed Dad? It all came from you.'

I don't respond. I don't want another fight. I learned to avoid confrontation in prison. It has made me a calmer person.

'I'll think about it.' I concede some ground on the invite to placate her.

Marie takes it as acceptance. 'I'll let you know a day and time.'

'You could always stop by the club one night,' I suggest. At least that way I will be at work. Other people would be around.

'Maybe.' She stands up to leave. 'You should really tidy this place up, Cal.'

'You're right, I should.' I follow her to the door to see her out. 'I'm glad you're happy,' I say. That is true. She deserves that much at least, a little happiness.

'I'll be in touch,' she replies.

She steps out into the sunlight.

'You remember Elise Moreau?'

Marie stops on the doorstep and turns back. Her face looks like thunder. 'What about her?'

'She got thrown out of Plein Soleil at the weekend. No idea why. Your father-in-law had her removed.'

'Good. It's all she deserves.'

'That's a bit much. She was good enough to be at your wedding three weeks ago.'

'What? I didn't invite her to my wedding.'

'I spoke to her at the bar in the evening. She said she was there with Yvonne.'

We both look at one another. It's hard to tell who is the most confused.

'Yvonne was with Fraser. She's been with him for over a year now.'

'Why would Elise be there if she wasn't invited?'

'Because she's insane. She's been after Tony for months now. Always pestering him. Never leaving him alone. All because they went out together for about two days, years ago.'

Elise didn't strike me as insane in the moments I spoke with her. I don't say that to Marie. I'm pretty sure that isn't what she wants to hear. Something tells me there is more to it than jealousy and unrequited love.

'Forget I mentioned it,' I say.

'I wish I could.' She goes this time, walking down the path and getting into her brand-new electric BMW, which is parked next to my wreck.

Something does not sit right about Elise. She didn't say anything about Tony McArthur to me. She didn't mention they had ever had a thing together. She lied at the wedding. She must have sneaked in somehow. And it was Francis McArthur that she had been waiting to see at the club, not Tony.

I grab a bag of ice from the freezer and lie on the sofa with it on my forehead to cool me down. Typical Marie. One five-minute visit and I have a headache. I have an evening with Tony McArthur to look forward to and Rose Black and Elise Moreau circle around my head. I figure this must be what having heat stroke feels like.

12

Pollok Park. The Cricket Clubhouse. 10 a.m.

Friday morning. I leave the house at nine to get there in plenty of time. After an uneventful shift behind the bar, I got home at four a.m. and managed two hours sleep. The text alert on the burner phone pinged at seven thirty, while I was lying awake on top of the duvet.

There are a few joggers and walkers managing to stumble along the single-track road, struggling in the heat. Cars crawl through, towards The Burrell Collection museum and the car park. I sit on a white bench in the shade, under the eaves of the old clubhouse. It isn't a cricket clubhouse anymore. They moved out and a football academy has taken it over – a sign of Scottish sporting priorities. The clubhouse is locked. A sign in the window says activities will start at six p.m. Daytime classes have been suspended until the temperatures drop to safe levels. The oval of grass is still well kept but is now scored with rectangular white lines marking out several junior football pitches. Beyond a fence at the back, the famous herd of Pollok Highland cattle loll, content to chew on the grass and shuffle around in the sunshine. A few seek shelter from the burning sun under the trees that run around the edge of their field.

A minute after ten o'clock, a plain grey sedan pulls into the car park.

Simone Millar gets out and walks over, wearing light cotton trousers, a white t-shirt and sunglasses, and carrying two polystyrene cups of coffee in a cardboard holder. As she approaches she takes a look around at the surroundings. 'Let's take a walk,' she says.

'Do we have to?'

'We'll go through the trees, keep in the shade.'

I follow her back out of the car park and across the road. Instead of heading towards the main hub of the museum and car park, we turn the other way and follow the road to the quieter, secluded north side of the park.

'You couldn't just come to my house?'

'Can't have the neighbours seeing a police detective turning up to see you on more than one occasion. People talk, especially if Francis McArthur and Murdo Smith are asking the questions.'

She offers one of the coffee cups. A hot drink is the last thing I need in the heat. I take it from her anyway. She takes the plastic lid off her cup, takes a sip and replaces the lid. The coffee would stay warmer with the lid off in this heat.

'How are things going at the club?'

'Fine.'

'Good. Anything more to tell?'

'Not really. I just serve drinks behind the bar. I'm not sure what you're expecting me to look for.'

'Eyes and ears, that's all. These things take time. If you have an opportunity to work yourself into McArthur's good graces, that's a bonus.'

The road turns gradually to the left and slopes upwards. Millar strides ahead, lithe and agile. There isn't a bead of sweat on her forehead. I amble along beside her, drowning in perspiration. A dog appears and sniffs around us before dashing off into the woods that line the route. A minute later the owner follows and nods a greeting as she passes.

'We're interested in the councillor,' Millar continues.

'I told you everything I know already. She came to the club. Had some sort of late-night meeting with McArthur and Murdo.'

'A meeting off the public record books late at night is suspicious in itself.' Another sip of coffee. 'Andrea Fulton chairs the City Development Plan for the council. Francis McArthur owns a lot of land that the council want to regenerate. McArthur also owns the biggest construction business in the west of Scotland.'

'Doesn't that mean it's perfectly normal for them to be talking to each other?'

'Sure. It could all be perfectly above board. That's what we want to find out. It's also true that in the last five years, over seventy-five percent of city council building contracts have been given to McArthur's firms. Over half of the council's new infrastructure initiatives have benefitted McArthur, whether through demolition contracts, buying his land, building on it, or building on someone else's land.'

'Look, I'm not an expert on city development, but isn't that just how business is done?'

Millar dismisses my naïve reasoning. 'Let me worry about that. If McArthur's not doing anything wrong, then he's got nothing to worry about.'

'But you think differently?'

'We *know* differently. We just need proof to build a case. You've heard of the term racketeering?'

I say I have.

'That's what this is – a racket. Legitimate businesses on the surface, but behind them, McArthur and his empire controlling it all.'

'How? Blackmail?'

'More subtle than that. Coercion, embezzlement, slush funds, conflicts of interest, abuse of power, bungs. All of the above.'

It all sounds vague to me. I'm not going to pretend I am an expert in fraud and financial law.

A group of cyclists zoom past, middle-aged men in Lycra. Some suit it more than others.

'We know Fulton is going to be at the club again tonight.' Millar is well-informed. It strikes me again that I can't be the only person she has on the inside of McArthur's operation. 'If you get the chance to get in the room with them, it could be useful.'

'I hate to break it to you, but I don't see any way that will happen.'

'Keep your eyes open for an opportunity is all I'm saying.' She is very big on me keeping my eyes and ears open to things, while I want to keep them tightly shut. 'Are you going to drink any of that?' She points at the coffee in my hand, then takes it from me and gives me her empty cup. She takes a sip from the second cup.

We walk on, down the other side of the slope that comes out at Pollok House, the Georgian stately home that now houses an art collection and a café. More people are around here, a mix of tourists and locals.

'Hang around here for ten minutes, then walk back along the river path. I'll be in touch.' She turns to head back along the main central road that will take her back to the cricket clubhouse.

'There is one other thing,' I call after her. Millar stops and steps back to me. 'The same night that Andrea Fulton was at the club, there was another woman. McArthur had her thrown out when she tried to talk to him.'

'I'm not interested in drunken customers getting thrown out of his club.'

'She wasn't drunk. As far as I could see she didn't do anything. Maybe you could look into it as a favour for me.'

Millar stares at me. 'You're not really in a position to bargain.'

'Elise Moreau. She used to go to school with us – Tony and me and my sister. I didn't know her well. She was at the wedding too, uninvited, it turns out.'

'You think something has happened to her?'

'No idea, but there's something going on, and McArthur didn't want her around. Maybe she knows something.'

'Alright. I'll look into it.'

I feel an unexpected relief. Maybe I am more concerned about Elise than I realised. Maybe I have a gut feeling that something has happened to her. People who upset McArthur and come away unscathed are few and far between.

Millar walks away along the path. She stops once more and turns back to me. 'She doesn't live there anymore. Rose Black. You know that, right?'

I don't have an answer. She keeps going along the straight road. I stand there. I want to follow her and ask her where Rose has gone. Is she safe? Where does she live now? There is no point. Millar isn't going to tell me that. It's probably better that I don't know – for Rose and for myself.

I wander down to the house. There is an entrance fee to get inside. I walk around to the side and find a neat parterre garden with a maze of hedges. I go down some stairs and come out at the front of the house, which faces onto the White Cart Water that flows under the old stone Polloktoun Bridge. In the morning sun, under the blue sky, it looks like something from a Jane Austen novel, or one of the many identical period dramas on television. It's far from the dirty industrial landscape most people associate with Glasgow. There isn't a cloud on the horizon.

I follow the path through walled gardens and beyond to a dirt track that follows the White Cart all the way round the fields of Highland cattle and the ex-cricket grounds and back to the clubhouse. Millar's car is gone by the time I get back. I keep walking out of the park and back to the main road, through Shawlands and on towards home.

13

Later that same day, I am at my usual place behind the main bar at the Plein Soleil. It is busier than the last few nights thanks to the addition of a large party on a work night out. They are noisy, but not causing any trouble. Lauryn is behind the bar with me and Georgia is working the floor. Dante is on the door with another fearsome-looking member of Malky's team who doesn't introduce herself. Carmen, Marc and Andy are downstairs. Another group enter, younger than the normal clientele of this place, but there's no reason to object to them. They're smartly dressed and polite when they order their drinks, and none of them seems to have drunk too much so far.

There are enough customers that I'm kept busy, serving up round after round without much of a break. Lauryn takes care of the cocktails. Despite Georgia's best efforts, I still haven't mastered the finer points of mixology.

Eleven o'clock and right on time, the curtain is held open for Councillor Andrea Fulton to make her appearance. Whoever is giving Millar her information is a reliable source. Same deal as before. She's accompanied by the same three assistants. They're wearing the same clothes as before, or at least not different enough that you would notice a change. They take a seat at a different booth against the back wall, keeping to the shadows. The same gofer is sent over to order the drinks. I see him coming and start pouring the half pints before he's even asked.

Carmen appears from downstairs and greets the councillor in passing, doing her bit as hostess. As much as I rack my brains, I can't think of any way I can get closer to the action once McArthur arrives. Maybe I can get talking to the guy who comes to the bar to order the drinks, if he comes over again. But making sociable small talk isn't my forte. How do you ask someone what their boss is up to at a private meeting without it seeming obvious that you're prying?

A cool jazz piece backed by a subtle trip hop beat starts up and, in perfect synchronisation, Francis McArthur and Murdo Smith walk through the door as though it's their entrance music. It couldn't have worked better if it had been staged for a movie. Malky follows, after a brief catch-up with his door staff. Carmen greets them and takes them to Andrea Fulton's table. Greetings all round. Andrea rises and her minions follow, and they all follow McArthur through the double doors and up the stairs.

Life has taught me I'm not a lucky guy by nature, but for once, Lady Luck decides to shine a light on me – although in the future, I'd rather she sticks to making my lottery numbers come up or the roulette wheel roll in my favour.

She takes the unlikely form of a West End hipster from the young group that came in half an hour ago, all slim tweed coat with elbow patches, well-groomed beard and circular spectacles. I don't see what happens in the lead up, but there's a spilled drink, half on the floor and half on an elegant lady from the work party. She's not happy about it and her loud exclamation and subsequent shouts draw the attention of a couple of alpha males in her group, who want a word with our hipster friend. In true Glasgow fashion, things go quickly from a word to raised threats, and before Dante can make up the distance across the bar, a fist holding a glass is thrown and connects with the hipster's head. Now members of both groups are on their feet and it all threatens to turn ugly. Dante sets to work and throws a couple of fully grown men out the way, knocking over a couple of stools and upsetting a table full of glassware.

Carmen appears from upstairs and sees the drama unfolding. Hipster has blood pouring from a wound on the side of his head, seeping through his well-groomed beard and down onto his designer tweed. The bouncers cow the warring tribes and seats are retaken. The two aggressive males who assaulted Hipster are bundled through the front door and onto the street. Dante follows. Carmen speaks to those who remain and reassures surrounding patrons. She comes over to me.

'I need to stay down here and sort this out. The police and an ambulance are on their way. Georgia and Lauryn can handle the bar. You know Francis and Murdo; you can handle upstairs. A bottle of Louis Roederer in a bucket, two club sodas and one Tanqueray and lime, and a bottle of Leffe Blonde. Ask Murdo if you are needed to stay or not.'

'Sure thing.'

The way into the upper echelons of the club has fallen into my lap. Carmen goes over to Hipster and, with the help of one of his group, gets him to his feet and onto a chair. The woman wearing half of his drink down her front stares daggers at him, but the incident has de-escalated.

* * *

The upstairs of the Plein Soleil is like a different building altogether: white walls around the sides, glass interior walls, glass panel doors, an open-plan area and light and airy luxury office spaces. Francis McArthur's office is at the front of the building, overlooking the entrance to the club. The yellow light from the sign outside shines up from below the front-facing window.

Francis sits behind a large modern desk. Councillor Fulton sits opposite, flanked on either side by her assistants. Malky stands at the office door, which seems to be the position he takes up in any room, like he's afraid to venture in any further. Murdo Smith is seated on a sofa at the back of the office, cross-legged and relaxed.

Malky, seeing I have my hands full with a tray of drinks and an ice bucket, opens the door for me.

'On the table,' Murdo says, gesturing to the low coffee table in front of him.

My entrance pauses whatever was being discussed before I came in. I put the tray and the ice bucket down. 'You want me to open the champagne?'

Francis says he does. I untwist the metal muselet and take care to catch the cork in my hand. Some fizz spills out into the ice bucket. I start to pour the glasses. As I do, their attention returns to their discussion. *Eyes and ears,* I hear Millar telling me.

Francis McArthur: 'I'm glad you've come round to our way of thinking.'

Andrea Fulton: 'You left us little choice.'

McArthur: 'This way, everybody gets what they want. You're sure your counterparts in South Lanarkshire are on board?'

Fulton: 'They need the investment even more than we do.'

McArthur smiles and nods and leans forward, elbows on his desk, fingers intertwined.

McArthur: 'You trust them?'

Fulton: 'I do.'

McArthur: 'Can I trust them? I'm taking your word for it, so if anything untoward happens, it's you I'll come to.'

This gives the councillor a moment of pause. I pause too, waiting for the next word, champagne bottle tilted over flute glass.

Fulton: 'You have my word.'

McArthur: 'Good. And our friend in Holyrood?'

Fulton: 'They're happy to proceed and won't interfere.'

McArthur leans back and smiles like a Cheshire cat. 'Then I think the champagne has arrived just at the right time.'

One of the councillor's assistants plucks up the courage to speak and clears his throat. 'And the favour we need done?'

The smile drops for a moment from McArthur's face. 'I thought it was understood that is included in the arrangement. You don't need to mention that again to anybody. Consider it taken care of.' He turns to me, the first time he's spoken to me since the day of his son's wedding to my sister. 'Cal, hand out the glasses.'

I take the tray of glasses around the room and each person picks a glass, except Malky, who is on duty. That means there is one glass left over. McArthur spots it remaining on the tray. 'Why don't you join us for a toast, Cal? Can't let this champagne go to waste.'

I'm not sure if I should accept the offer or not. I look to Murdo Smith. He nods assent, although he looks far from happy about my invitation. I put the tray back on the table, pick up the glass and stand back from the group now on their feet, gathered around the desk.

'To new ventures, new opportunities and new partnerships,' says McArthur, raising his glass flute. Everyone takes a sip, but no one seems as enthusiastic as Francis McArthur. Andrea Fulton places her still three-quarters full glass on the desk and makes it clear that she's going. Her associates follow her lead.

'Malky, Cal, be so kind as to escort the councillor out,' instructs McArthur. Malky holds the door for them, and he and I follow them out and down the stairs. As I look back through the glass door, I see Murdo standing over the desk, saying something to McArthur, who waves his hand like he's swatting a fly, dismissing whatever concern Murdo is raising.

Back down in the bar, everything has returned to equilibrium. There's no sign of injured Hipster, his blood stains, or his assailants. The remaining members of each group have returned to their own tables and are carrying on their evening as though nothing ever happened. Georgia is circulating, collecting empty glasses and plastic cups, and Lauryn is behind the bar. Malky walks the councillor to the door. I take up my position behind the bar.

Carmen appears beside me. 'Everything go okay?'

'Fine. I even got a taste of the expensive champagne.'

'Drinking behind the bar? I could dock that from your wages.'

She's joking, I think.

14

The ring from the mobile phone pierces the night. I'm not unused to hearing a ringtone in the dead of night. Being caught with a personal mobile phone in prison is punishable by a further two years being added to your sentence. That's what the law states. In practice, inmates who did not care what the law said had phones and prison officers looked the other way. Every few months a crackdown would be announced. Cells would be searched. Nothing was ever found. The following night the electronic ringtones would sound again.

This time the phone call is for me and I have to answer it to stop the ringing. I manage to cut my finger removing the skirting board. There's a skelf of wood embedded in my finger; initial sharp pain gives way to throbbing discomfort.

I sit on the edge of my bed, slide my shoes off using my feet and lie back, still dressed in work uniform. I loosen my black tie and look up at the ceiling, I swipe the green icon and answer the call.

'How did it go?' Millar asks.

'Eventful.'

'We know she went into the club.' So they had surveillance, either outside or inside the place. 'You saw her?'

'I saw her.' I rub my forehead with my injured hand, circling the skin around my temples.

'You weren't mixed up in the little incident of assault that my colleagues responded to?'

'Nothing to do with me. A misunderstanding over a spilled drink.'

'Isn't it always?'

'You're working?' I ask. I hear rustling on the other end of the line and realise Millar, like me, is lying in bed, awake and unable to sleep. She's on her own too, with no one to share her bed with and unable to sleep through the night. Unless she's got a partner who can sleep through anything.

'Can't sleep.' She doesn't expand on the reasons why. 'Anything you can tell me?'

'The little incident was a stroke of luck for you. If I were the paranoid type, I'd even say you staged the whole thing to get me in the room with McArthur, but you're not that good.'

'No comment.'

I can't tell if that's an admission or not. The smashed glass and the blood looked real enough to me.

'What happened?'

'McArthur and Murdo took her upstairs to the office. Then the fight broke out. I was sent up to the office with the drinks order. Champagne.'

'They were celebrating something?'

'Something about new ventures together. They'd struck some sort of agreement. They mentioned South Lanarkshire. Included in the deal was some sort of favour McArthur was going to do for them.'

Through the electrical signals passing from one handset to the other across the night sky, I sense the change in her attitude. I imagine her sitting up in her bed, eyes now wide awake, mind fully engaged. I am feeding her good dope; she is the dope fiend.

'You are sure it was South Lanarkshire?'

'That's what they said. McArthur wanted to know if he could trust them.'

'Makes sense. As far as we know he doesn't have any business in South Lanarkshire. Maybe he's branching out. No idea what this favour is?'

'Sorry. He clammed up when it was mentioned. Said to consider it done and not to talk about it again.'

'Sounds perfectly above board.' Her sarcasm drips through the phone.

'He asked about a friend in Holyrood. Fulton said they wouldn't interfere. An MSP?'

'Could be a Member of Parliament. Or a civil servant, or a committee, or a government official.'

'That makes it a big deal if you're looking for a conspiracy, right. That's a good thing for your case?'

'Let me worry about that. Anything else?'

'That's it. They shared a toast of the champagne and Fulton left. I left with them. Murdo and McArthur stayed in the office for another half hour. I could have sworn Murdo wasn't happy about something when I left, but no idea what.'

The tension over, she relaxes. I see her leaning back in her bed, knowing there's nothing she can do with this information until the morning. 'You did good, Cal.' It's the first time she's ever given me a compliment. 'Maybe there's hope for you yet.'

'Thanks.' I expect her to end the call but she doesn't hang up. Maybe she's waiting for me to end it. For some reason I stay on the line as well, like we both need some sort of human connection as we lie awake and alone in the dark.

'Your friend you asked about, Elise Moreau.'

'Yeah?'

'She hasn't turned up for work all week. Far as we can tell, no one's seen her.'

'She's missing?'

'No one's reported her missing, so not officially, no.'

'Where does she work?'

'Sky Park, in the city. Some sort of software design company.'

Has something happened to her? Is McArthur involved? No one has seen her since he had her thrown out of his club over a week ago.

'You want my advice?' Millar is going to offer it whether I want it or not. 'Stay out of it. Let her go. If something has happened to her, we'll find out soon enough. She probably just went away for a few days.'

'And didn't tell her work? She cares for her sick mother.'

'It's up to you.'

Another silence.

'Thanks for looking into it for me, Millar.'

'Just don't do anything stupid. You have a habit of doing stupid things.'

'I prefer to think I've been unlucky.'

I take a deep breath and ask the question I know I shouldn't. 'Where did she move to?' She knows me well enough to know I'm not talking about Elise anymore. I'm asking about Rose.

'You know I'm never going to answer that question.'

'I figured. Is she safe? Is she doing well?'

'If I tell you she is, will you stop asking and let her go and get on with her life?' I can't guarantee anything like that. 'Thought not. Goodnight, Cal.'

This time she hangs up and the burner phone goes dead. I toss it onto the bed next to me and lie in the dark. The occasional car goes past along Cathcart Road, taxis delivering the night time stragglers home. Other than that, there's hardly a sound. It will be like this for an hour or so and then the new day will begin.

In the dying embers of the night, I lie on my uncomfortable bed. My hand still throbs. I think about Rose, Elise, Detective Millar, Marie, Mum. All these women connected to me to a greater or lesser extent. It occurs to me that women should steer clear of me. Even without any intent on my part, being around me has had a detrimental effect on their lives. I make a decision. Millar won't like it, she advised against it, but I'll be damned if I'm going to let another one down. Why do I care about her? I've met her twice. I didn't recognise her from school the first time, when she sauntered over to me at the wedding bar. Is it because she flirted with me? Is it because she took the time to talk to me when no one else would? Is it just guilt about Rose Black, spilling over into a new infatuation? Whatever the reason, she left an impression and I know, deep down, that she's in trouble. I'm going to find out what has happened to Elise.

15

The village of Stepps, situated five miles north-east of Glasgow, hasn't changed much since I grew up there. Taking the M8 motorway from the city centre, I turn off at junction 12 and pass Hogganfield Loch on my right, where I learned to ride a bike as a kid, and the playing fields where I had kicked a ball around with the local football team. I pass Millerston and Steppshill, crowded with memories of childhood friends and family events. It makes me think of Marie and summer holidays spent running and cycling around the streets. Days that always seem to be filled with bright sunshine in my memories. Today is the same – 33°C according to the forecast. It feels warmer in my car, the cool air from the weak fans fighting a lost cause.

Much of the surrounding area has been built up. South of the railway tracks, the old coal mine at Cardowan has been redeveloped into a huge housing estate. Across the main road, my old primary school has been demolished and replaced with houses, although the street is still called School Road. A new school has been built on the football pitches I once played on. The local bank on the corner has shut, the newsagents is now a laundry service. But the road through the old part of the village is the same, crossed by the iron-grey bridge I walked over twice a day to and from school. The large park in the middle of the village has survived, with the white war memorial cross at its entrance. I turn at the traffic lights onto Lenzie Road, then left again just before the dentist's, onto Church Street. The old church where I was baptised is at the top of the street, red-orange brick and black slate roof. The lane along the side had been the perfect place for kicking a football around. At the church I turn right onto Whitehill Avenue and carry on until it intersects with Whitehill Farm Road. On the corner where these two roads meet is my destination.

No. 64 Whitehill Avenue is an end-terrace house, built of sandstone over two storeys. By modern build standards it is huge. I park opposite and sit looking out the car window. Beyond the houses lie green fields that stretch on to the horizon and the Campsie Fells to the north. The M80 bypass, built in the 1990s, cuts across the landscape. It took much of the through traffic away from the village when it opened. Overgrown trees and hedges obscure the front of the house from the street. I double-check the piece of paper I scrawled the address on, the address Millar sent to the burner phone after our conversation on Friday night. This is the place, the same place she lived at when I was a kid.

The rest of the weekend at the club passed without further incident. McArthur and Murdo did not come back. I had not been back up to the office. I only slept for two hours when I got in last night.

Now it is Monday morning. Elise Moreau is still missing. It's over a week since she was seen at the club. This is the house she grew up in. Marie and I grew up two streets away. We were never part of the same group of friends, but we would see Elise around the village. She was two years older than me, which meant a lifetime in teenage years. She was always older and cooler and out of reach. Tony McArthur grew up here too. He used to live in the large farm house around the corner. I spent a lot of time playing in his courtyard, garden, the large house and the fields beyond.

When Millar sent the address, I remembered the house on the corner. The way the streets meet at a sharp angle means the house has a strange triangular garden that comes to a sharp point. The French teacher never moved out. After you leave school, you don't think about the life that goes on there beyond your existence. Madame Moreau must have worked at the local high school until she retired. She will be in her mid-sixties now, I guess. Young to be suffering from the onset of dementia.

That is what brings me here. Elise would not abandon her mother. If I am going to find Elise, this is the place to start looking.

The gate is rusty and paint flecks crumble from it as I open it and walk up the path. Weeds are gradually reclaiming the concrete and gravel path that leads to two big concrete steps and a set of storm doors, which lie one side open, one side closed. Beyond them, there is a wooden front door with a glass panel in the centre. There is no doorbell. I knock on the glass pane and wait. The street is still and quiet. Children are in school, adults are at work, the elderly are sheltering inside, out of the heat. I knock again.

No answer. No sign of life.

I back out of the vestibule and step over the weeds to a window. Inside is a living room. A three-piece suite, a television, a mantelpiece. On one chair a woman sits in repose. Not asleep; her eyes are open, but vacant. She seems lifeless. She could be dead. I try chapping the window. There's a twitch, an involuntary movement, but she settles back into the vacant stare.

'Madame Moreau?' I call. It's her. Older, her hair grey and thin, her skin sagging, but I recognise her. 'Are you okay, Madame Moreau?' No response. I can't just leave her there. I go back to the front door and try the handle. It opens an inch or two, then catches on a door chain. 'Madame Moreau, are you able to come and open the door?'

Nothing. I check back at the window. She hasn't moved. Madame Moreau looks like she will sit in that chair until she stops breathing. Breaking and entering is a risk I will have to take. I can call on Millar if I need to explain myself to the police.

Back to the door. It catches on the chain again. I can smell the stale, musty air inside the house. I step back and put my shoulder to the wooden edge of the door. It bangs against the chain and holds firm. I try again. Once, twice. On the third attempt I feel it give a little. I push against it and with a sudden snap the chain gives way, pulling away from the wall. I stumble into the hallway, clattering into a side table and landing on my hands and knees.

'Who the fuck are you?' Madame Moreau is standing over me. 'I'll call the police.'

I brush my t-shirt and arms clean of dust as I stand up. 'Madame Moreau, let me explain.'

'Elise! Elise!' she starts shouting up the staircase. 'There's a burglar breaking in to our house.'

I'm confused. Is she here? We both wait for an answer but no one responds to her calls. 'Is Elise here, Madame Moreau?'

She looks back at me with anger in her face. I remember that look from school when she gave an errant pupil into trouble. 'What do you mean is Elise here? Of course she's here. She's my daughter. She lives here.'

No one comes running down the stairs. No one answers. She doesn't live here. She hasn't for years.

'Madame Moreau, I don't know if you remember me. I went to school with Elise. I was in your French class. Callum Jackson.'

The old woman's haggard face drops, the aggression drains away. The eyes focus and change and her face draws into a smile of recognition. 'Cal Jackson. How lovely to see you. How have you been?' The change throws me. One minute she was confused and angry, now she seems to have forgotten that I've just burst through her front door.

'I'm well, Madame Moreau.'

'How nice of you to visit. I don't see many of my ex-pupils anymore. Will you stay for a coffee?'

I'm tempted to accept her offer. She needs company. She's thin and frail and if Elise hasn't been here for a week I wonder if Madame Moreau has eaten anything or spoken to anyone in that time. 'I don't want to trouble you.'

'No trouble at all.'

'I'm looking for Elise. Has she been to visit you recently?'

'Oh yes, Elise comes every day to check on me. I tell her she doesn't need to. I'm perfectly capable of looking after myself.'

'Has she been here today? Or yesterday?'

Something happens, somewhere inside her brain, where the signals are misfiring and failing to connect. The smile fades and is replaced by the blank stare I saw through the window when she was sitting in the chair.

'Who was here yesterday?' she asks.

'Elise, your daughter.'

'Oh yes,' she brightens again, 'I know Elise is my daughter. Don't be so silly. She should be here any moment. She comes every day to check on me.'

She seems to have forgotten about the offer of a coffee. We are still standing in the hallway, facing each other, the vacant smile on her face as she looks at me. Something in her eyes tells me she has forgotten who I am.

'Coffee!' she starts suddenly and walks towards the back of the house and into the kitchen.

I follow her. There is no sign that suggests Elise has been here in the last week. The kitchen is strewn with dirty plates and cutlery filling the sink and covering the surfaces. An open carton of milk lies out on a worktop, the fridge lies wide open.

'Does anyone else come to look after you, Madame Moreau? Apart from Elise?'

'That lovely young woman next door keeps an eye on me. I forget her name. I forget so much these days. I have her name written down somewhere. She left me her phone number in case of emergencies.' She starts looking around, lifting pieces of paper and discarded food wrappers and newspapers from the worktop and dining table. I notice the bowl of fruit in the middle of the table is filled with shrivelled apples and black bananas.

I give it one more try, although I know it's fruitless. 'So Elise hasn't been round to see you recently?'

She snaps, a dark cloud descends. 'Fucking Elise. Why do you keep fucking asking about Elise? That little tramp. She's ruined her own life. I warned her. I fucking warned her.'

Somewhere in the back of my mind there is a piece of information that I read or someone said to me once, that people with dementia often have uncharacteristic outbursts and use foul language. Partly it's frustration at not remembering things, partly it's anger that their mind is leaving them and there is nothing they can do about it. I have got no desire to distress Madame Moreau any further.

She has started hunting for something again; whether it's the neighbour's note or a clean cup or the coffee jar, I'm not sure.

'I'm going to go now, Madame Moreau.' I start to back out of the kitchen.

'Right you are. Have you brought the fresh milk for me?'

It's hard to keep up. I point to the open milk left on the worktop. 'Milk's just there.'

She looks and smiles and looks back to me, then her face darkens.

'Who are you? Why are you in my kitchen?' She grabs a dirty kitchen knife and backs herself into a corner, the knife pointing at me.

I put my hands up in surrender and back out of the room, down the hallway. She doesn't follow me. Elise underplayed how serious her mum's condition is. Or she has deteriorated a lot in the last week because she has been abandoned and alone.

I step into the living room where Madame Moreau had been sitting. There is no sign that anyone else has been here either. A thick layer of dust covers every surface, along the sideboard, round the mantelpiece, across the television unit in the corner. I scan the room in case there is anything that could tell me where Elise might be. Random pieces of notepaper are strewn around, scribbled reminders to do simple tasks, a vain attempt to restore order to a failing mind. Framed photographs on the sideboard catch my eye. There is Madame Moreau as I remember her – younger, about the age she would have been when she taught me. Elise back then too, as a teenager, but with the same angular features and dark hair; the French heritage is in her face and demeanour. Then a picture of a baby being held. I assume it's Elise too, not long after she was born. The photograph is faded. She is wrapped in a white blanket and she has an unruly mop of dark hair. She is being cradled by someone. Their head is cropped off the top of the picture; it only shows the torso and arms of a man. He's wearing a smart grey suit jacket. I remember Elise telling me she never had a dad, that her mother raised her on her own. I wonder if the hands in the photo belong to him.

There is a noise from the kitchen. Time to go before the confused mother discovers me in her house and we repeat our earlier altercation. I back out of the room and down the hallway before Madame Moreau appears. I pull the front door closed behind me.

I get back to the car but stop before getting in and look back at the house. I can't leave her in there like that. I cross the road and go up the path of the house next door, No. 62. A small Asian woman with kind eyes answers the door. She knows Madame Moreau; she checks on her every so often. I tell her what has happened. I tell her Elise hasn't been visiting. She says she noticed yesterday that the daughter had stopped coming round. She had mentioned it to her husband. She agrees to call Delphine Moreau's doctor, who is also their own family doctor. Up until this point I didn't know Madame Moreau's given name. She assures me she will make sure Delphine is taken care of until her daughter returns.

There is not much else I can do. I thank her and leave. As I walk back down the path I glance over to No. 64. Madame Moreau is back in her chair in the living room. She stares out of the window, her eyes unmoving, her mind wasting away one small memory at a time.

It's a cruel end to a life in a pitiless world.

16

The following Wednesday, my car coughs its way to the north of the city again, this time through the tunnel and on to Bearsden. I think about detouring to Clarence Drive, even though Millar has told me Rose is no longer there. It wouldn't hurt to check but I'm already running late. Marie has made good on her threat and insisted on having me over to her new house for dinner with her new husband. There's no way to avoid it, especially as Mum is expected too. I will admit it to no one, but I am also curious to see where Marie lives now. I know Francis McArthur has bought his son and daughter-in-law a new house on Roman Road and I can't help but want to see where my sister has landed.

Roman Road is a wide avenue, with pavements bordered by low walls, hedges and large trees that shade the exclusive houses hidden behind them. There is no uniform terraced housing here, or modern-day housing estate kit-builds. Each large house is unique, whether old and built from solid sandstone or a modern design of brick and metal and glass. Some press against the road, others are set back beyond gravel driveways and front lawns. They are not quite of the same stature as Murdo Smith's mansion and there isn't space for sprawling grounds, but it's a long way from the bungalow Marie and I grew up in.

Some houses are so far away from the road that I can't see the door numbers. I rely on Marie's directions to locate her house. I pass the junction with Grange Road and it should be on my right. I look out for the gates Marie has described – dark brown faux wood – and a low, modern, cream-coloured wall. I spot the gate and turn in. I buzz an intercom button on the wall and the gate opens. There must be a camera somewhere looking at the entrance. Inside the perimeter wall, tall trees give privacy. There is a short driveway and then an area for car parking. I park the fifteen-year-old Vauxhall Corsa between Marie's brand-new electric BMW i7 and a Porsche Panamera.

It might not be listed as a mansion, but No. 24 Roman Road can't be far off it. It's a new build but looks like an old build, with big sandstone blocks instead of bricks and a black-tiled roof. From the outside, it's anyone's guess how many rooms are inside. There is a decorative porch over the front door, complete with security camera and surveillance doorbell. I expect a servant to answer, but the new Mrs McArthur isn't at that level yet. Marie has to answer the door herself. She opens it and looks me up and down. For a second I think I am about to be denied entry, but she settles for a sarcastic comment instead.

'Glad you made an effort.'

I look down at my trainers, jeans and t-shirt. I would say smart-casual, but maybe that's not enough for the Roman Road set. The back of my t-shirt is sweat-soaked from the car journey; I can feel the clammy moisture clinging to me. Marie has dressed up more than is required for a dinner in the house. She's in a deep blue blouse and matching pencil skirt, with make-up applied and hair styled in waved layers.

'I can go home and change,' I offer.

My little sister smiles and stands aside, holding the door open and granting me entrance. As I step past her, Tony appears, sticking his head out of a door off the reception hall. He's in suit trousers and shirt, but thankfully not jacket and tie.

'You found us okay, then,' he says, stating the obvious. 'Come on through.' He ducks back into the room and I follow him.

Mum is already holding a glass of champagne, sitting on a sofa that's so big it threatens to envelop her.

'I picked Anita up and brought her over,' says Tony. 'You enjoyed the trip in the Porsche, didn't you?' He pronounces it "paw-shuh".

'Why anyone needs a car that big or that goes that fast is beyond me.'

'There's no substitute for the finer things in life, Anita. Why not enjoy them?' Tony takes an empty glass and the open bottle from the coffee table and pours me a drink. 'You can have one, can't you, Cal? Won't put you over the limit.' The night I ran over Rose Black jumps out at me. I am back in that world. Is Tony deliberately reminding me, has he really forgotten or is he just careless?

I take the glass and sit next to Mum on the sofa. It is cooler in here than it is outside. There is the discreet whirring of an air-conditioning unit somewhere in the room.

When Marie joins us in the room, Tony raises his glass and makes a toast. 'To old friends and new family.' I take a sip of the sweet, fizzy liquid and sit the glass on the table. I won't touch another drop. There is an awkward moment of silence. 'I'll just go and see how dinner's coming along,' Tony says, and exits. By this, I take it to mean he's checking how the chef is getting on, and not that he is preparing the food himself.

While we wait, Marie sits next to Mum and shows her photographs on her smartphone from the honeymoon. I look away after the twentieth one of Marie in a bikini on a sun lounger or standing on pure white sand next to the ocean. Along with the pictures, Marie gives a running commentary. Mum gasps and tells her how lucky she is. Tony pops in and out and adds his observations, joking about Marie's desire to spend too much time lying in the sun rather than seeing the local sights, and the temperature being just as warm in Glasgow as it had been in St

Lucia. Pictures of the lavish private bridal villa they stayed in draw the biggest reaction from Mum. It makes even their new home look downmarket by comparison. I let mother and daughter talk. They are closer now than I have ever known them to be. Any objection Mum had to the wedding seems to have evaporated.

It's another forty-five minutes before dinner is ready and we move into a large dining room. The chef serves the food. Tony tells us he has hired him especially to be our private cook tonight. His name sounds French, but his accent doesn't. He comes with a Michelin star.

We take our seats and the first course arrives. The chef announces it with a fancy name. It looks fancy, too – a delicate construction of prawns and other seafood on a bed of salad. It tastes like a prawn cocktail to me.

Wedding and honeymoon conversation continues to dominate. No one seems to mind that I don't contribute and show little interest. Eventually there's a lull and I realise Marie has asked me a direct question. I look round to see them waiting for my reply.

'Sorry?'

'I asked how the job was going. At the club.'

'Fine, yeah.'

'How are you getting on with Carmen?' asks Tony. 'She doesn't suffer fools.'

Is he implying that I am a fool? 'She's been great. I can see why she's in charge.'

'Everyone told Dad he was being stupid promoting her so quickly. She only worked behind the bar for six months before he put her in charge. But he sees potential in people and doesn't believe age is an indicator of ability.'

'Everyone's been great. Although the younger staff keep their distance.'

'That's because you're a thirty-two-year-old ex-con.' I think Tony means this to be a light-hearted joke.

The chef clears the starter plates away. Mum insists on giving a helping hand. After a pointless spoonful of sorbet to cleanse the palette, the main dish is served: a traditional roast with all the trimmings. The conversation becomes sporadic between mouthfuls of succulent beef. Before dessert, Marie insists on giving Mum a tour of the rest of the house. I'm left at the table with Tony. I try to think of the last time we have sat together, alone, like this. It must be at least ten years ago.

'Carmen says you're getting on well, picking up the job quick. I told her you were smart, despite everything.'

'You were checking up on me?'

Tony shrugs. 'Why wouldn't I? It was my idea to bring you in, give you a chance. Forget about what's happened between us. It's all water under the bridge. This is a fresh start for all of us. There's no reason we can't be friends again. In fact, there's more reasons why we *should* be friends. For Marie's sake, for one.' He waits for me to agree. 'Working at the club is just the start. A test. There's plenty of other work you could help us out with. Better opportunities. You can't be a barman for the rest of your life.'

'What if I'm quite happy where I am? I just want to keep my head down and have a quiet life.'

'Nonsense. You'll be bored in a few weeks. I could use someone I can trust. Dad puts a lot of stock in family and friendships.'

I can hear Millar urging me to make the most of this unexpected advance. 'What sort of other work do you have in mind?'

'Let's not talk about that now. I'll be in touch at the right time. Just stick in at the club just now.'

The ladies return and dessert is served – Eton mess and cream. Cheese and biscuits are to follow in the lounge. I assume this is the room we were in earlier, but that turns out to be only a reception room. The lounge is at the back of the house and is twice the size. Sliding glass doors are open and lead out onto a patio and a good-sized garden area.

'Maybe global warming isn't such a bad thing for Scotland,' laughs Tony. 'I could get used to more evenings like this.' He opens a box sitting on the side unit and pulls out a cigar. He offers one to me. I refuse. He pours himself a scotch. 'The wife insists I only smoke these outside.' He steps out into his garden. The only other person I know who smokes cigars in their garden like this is Francis McArthur. Tony is determined to follow in his father's footsteps.

I've agreed to run Mum home, which means I have to stay until she is ready to leave. It's eleven before I suggest I need to make a move. 'I've got work tomorrow night,' I use as an excuse, although I know I will sleep less than a couple of hours in any case.

Tony fetches Mum's coat and they see us to the door. They promise to have us over again soon. Mum thanks them for a wonderful evening.

'You've changed your tune,' I tell her as I drive back along Roman Road in the dusky remains of another scorching day.

'It's happened now,' Mum shrugs. 'Might as well make the most of it. At least I don't have to worry about your sister anymore. Her future's looking pretty secure.'

'A few nice dinners in it for you too.'

'Doesn't hurt. I won't feel guilty about taking from the McArthurs. Might even see if I can get a wee holiday out of it. St Lucia looks tempting.' I have to laugh. 'And you're okay? You didn't say much.'

'You don't have to worry about me. I told Tony tonight, I just want to keep my head down and live a quiet life.'

Mum looks across at me, her eyes drowsy from too much fine wine and fine dining. 'That's what your dad used to say too.'

By the time we are in the tunnel, crossing beneath the River Clyde, she has drifted off to sleep.

PART 3

THE RULES OF THE GAME

17

June rolls into July. The heat intensifies. Every couple of days there is another thunderstorm, rain lashing down for half an hour, soaking everything. The downpours offer little relief. Nothing seems to be able to clear the hot air. I turn up for my shifts at the club. There's no sign of Elise. I check with Millar. She's never returned to her work or the club. There is nowhere else I know to look for her.

Tony collects me from my flat. I wait for the black SUV to pull up and go out to meet him. It's the second time he's asked me to join him, making good on his promise of better opportunities. Millar has encouraged me to take advantage of the situation. Nothing more has happened at the club. McArthur and Murdo have not appeared again. Millar needs me to get deeper into the family, into the organisation. She needs more than vague mentions of politicians and South Lanarkshire.

* * *

The first time Tony insisted I come along with him, I tried to tell him I was happy working at the club. He wouldn't take no for an answer. We went to a construction site in the east end of the city. Social housing is being built by one of McArthur's companies, on land McArthur owns, subsidised by the city council, to be run by McArthur's private housing association on completion. I followed Tony as he spoke to the site manager and the construction boss. They pointed at plans and showed us around. It meant little to me. A banksman guided a huge articulated lorry into the site, loaded with more building material.

'It'll be finished this time next year,' Tony told me as we were leaving. 'It will be a decent earner for us, and the best part is it's social housing for those on benefits. Most of the rent will be covered by the council, so no defaulting and debt collection needed. Guaranteed income.'

'What was here before?' I asked.

'Old warehouses, industrial space, brownfield. All part of the regeneration of the city. Central government money invested by the city council.'

'How did Francis end up owning the land?'

'Got it cheap when businesses went bust in the financial collapse in 2008.'

'Wasn't there a listed building there once? An old fish market?'

'Fire took care of that.' He said it as though there was nothing suspicious about a fire clearing the way for a new development. Glasgow has a long history of fires breaking out in buildings that would be more valuable if they went up in smoke. Convenient accident or deliberate arson? I didn't ask. I am sure Millar will already know all about it.

From there we went to the casino, The Red Circle, in the city centre on the banks of the river. Open twenty-four seven, there were only a few tired-looking older men and women at the tables on a Thursday lunchtime. On the second floor, Francis McArthur was in his office. He was happy to see me with his son.

'Two old friends,' he beamed at us. He asked Tony about progress at the building site. Tony updated him. Then he turned to me. 'Tony's going to be taking over more and more of the day-today running of some of my companies. Time to pass on the baton and think about slowing down in my old age.' He said this in a way that made me think he had no intention of slowing down or handing over control to his son. 'He's going to need help, people he can trust, loyal friends.' The inference was that I would fit the bill. I bit back the urge to tell him there was nothing I would like less than to become wrapped up in his family business.

Tony dropped me back home that evening. 'We need to get you a better place,' he said, looking at my flat.

'It's cheap,' I offered in defence.

'Exactly.'

* * *

It's the same driver today, introduced only as Patrick, a mundane name that doesn't encompass his threatening presence and large frame. Next to him in the front of the car sits Dante, the bouncer from the Plein Soleil. They both wear black sunglasses and black t-shirts and somehow aren't perspiring in the heat.

I get in and we pull away. The interior of the car is air-conditioned and cool. The windows are blacked out. Patrick drives south, away from the city.

'You'll like this,' Tony says to me, while looking out of the tinted window. 'A trip out of the city into the countryside. Blow away the last of those prison cobwebs.'

'Where are we going?' I ask.

'Checking out a potential opportunity in East Kilbride.'

I don't know much about East Kilbride. I haven't been there more than a handful of times. It's one of the biggest towns in Scotland. The shopping centre in the town centre used to be one of the biggest in the country, until the retail landscape went online and shops disappeared. It's got a cinema and an ice rink. That's about all I can remember. But I know it's situated in South Lanarkshire.

Once we pass through Castlemilk, the road heads uphill and buildings give way to farmland and fields. Tony's right; I should have made an effort to get out of the city. The space seems vast and empty. My mind compares it to the six-by-four cell I spent the last year in. It reminds me that, for a small country, Scotland is a place of big landscapes. I need to escape into it more. At the top of the hill, perched above the Clyde Valley and with Glasgow below, we reach East Kilbride. Wide roads and a series of roundabouts connect housing estates, all with their own uniform houses, all managing to appear the same despite the subtle differences in build. Radial roads converge on the town centre, a modernist concrete block with later additions of glass and steel. An ugly clash of styles and sensibilities.

'The owners went into administration last year. Fallout from the pandemic,' explains Tony as we drive up a ramp into a multi-storey car park, which is empty. Patrick parks the car and the four of us get out. Through an automatic door we enter the bright shopping centre. A large department store takes up one end, closed and shuttered after the parent company went out of business two years ago. A series of empty units line either side of the mall, hidden behind garish advertising boards. As we walk further along, shops and cafés are open, but empty. Staff hang around looking bored. The only customers seem to be pensioners out for a walk with the hope of social contact.

Through another set of doors, we climb stairs and arrive at the shopping centre offices. A man greets us and leads us into a meeting room. Patrick stands at the door. Tony sits next to the man at the head of the table. Dante and I take our seats a little further away. The man introduces himself as Bill. He is the lead on the council task force seeking to resolve the town centre problems, both to find a new owner and to redevelop the space to make it suitable for the modern community. High street retail is dead, Bill tells us. It's time for town centres to change their property portfolio and East Kilbride could be a leader in doing so.

Tony listens to all this with admirable patience, then gets down to business. I feel sorry for Bill. He seems completely unaware of the world he is about to be thrust into. He doesn't realise that simply taking this meeting has sealed the future of East Kilbride town centre. He doesn't understand that when Francis McArthur sets his mind to something, he gets it.

'The McArthur family agree wholeheartedly with you, Bill,' begins Tony.

Bill beams in naïve innocence. 'That's great to hear.'

'So here's what will happen.' Tony leans forward; his tone changes. Bill's eyes suddenly look unsure, but he maintains a plastered grin as he glances at Dante and me. He gets no support from either of us. 'Our architects have drawn up our plans for the space.' Dante takes a sheaf of paper from a briefcase and slides it over the table to Bill. 'Housing, retail, social and community space. A nice mix, just like you suggest. You can look over them, take them to your people. We can adjust them; we're open to discussion on the final layout.'

'Great, but aren't we getting a bit ahead of ourselves?' stutters Bill. 'There are a number of bidders for the land—'

Tony silences him with a wave of his hand. I recognise the behaviour and the demeanour. Tony has been learning from his father. 'We'll buy the land at a fair price. One of our companies will handle the demolition and the construction. Our property management company will then run the development for the council. We will obviously work closely with the council throughout. This is a partnership that will benefit us both for years to come. And the best part is, Bill, you don't have to worry about a thing. We'll take care of everything.'

'Now, just hang on a moment.' Bill is so out of his depth, it's a hard watch. 'We're talking to a number of different developers. There will be a public consultation and a transparent tender process for the work at all stages.'

Tony sighs and gives Bill a smile, like a patient parent explaining how the world works to a toddler. 'Bill,' he taps the plans in front of the hapless councillor, 'this is what will happen. It's the best deal for everyone. We were led to believe, in discussions with my father, that South Lanarkshire Council were on board, that things had been agreed. I wouldn't want to report back that we have been wasting our time. Besides, once your other interested parties hear that the McArthurs are involved, you'll find that their interest in bidding will drain away.'

There's one last try from Bill to reclaim some authority. 'I'm aware that the McArthur portfolio in Glasgow is huge, but this isn't the way we do business here.'

Tony stands up. Dante and I follow his lead. Patrick opens the door. 'It is now, Bill, whether you want it to be or not. Better you get with the programme without too much fuss. To use a tired cliché, there's the hard way to do this, or the easy way. Either way, this is what's going to happen. Think it over and get in touch.'

With that, the meeting is over and we leave Bill to contemplate his limited choices.

We walk back through the centre. The whole place feels drowsy and tired in the heat. I can't help thinking the McArthurs can only improve the lives of the locals here. It's a racket for sure, it's definitely not legal, but at least it gets things done. If the alternative is years of bidding and delays and council consultations, the McArthur plan seems like a good option for all involved.

It's nearly midday by the time we get back to the car. For the drive back to Glasgow, I take my suit jacket off and open the car boot to put it in. In the boot are six empty plastic petrol cans. They look brand new, unused. I lay my suit jacket on top of them and don't mention it when I climb into the back seat next to Tony. He seems happy the meeting went well. I'm not sure Bill the councillor would agree.

'That's how we get things done.' Tony is ecstatic. As Patrick pulls out of the multi-storey, Tony's phone pings as a message arrives. He reads it and then tells Dante to put the radio on and find a news bulletin. After a bit of searching, Dante lands on Radio Clyde as a jingle announces the lunchtime headlines. Tony asks him to turn the volume up.

The newsreader speaks in a serious tone. 'Terence McAvoy, the leader of the main opposition party in the Scottish Parliament, is to stand down with immediate effect. Mr McAvoy, a trade union leader for the last thirty years, has become embroiled in scandal in the last few days after allegations of an extra-marital affair and drug abuse. This morning, fresh allegations about gambling debts emerged, forcing him to announce his immediate resignation. In a statement to the press outside his family home, Mr McAvoy again denied any of the allegations made against him and asked for privacy for his family at this time. He said he was standing down in order to prioritise clearing his name and to spend time with his wife and two daughters. As well as being leader of the opposition in parliament, Mr McAvoy was also the head of the parliamentary committee on transport and infrastructure and in recent months has publicly and vocally opposed the government's proposed policies on housing and road expansion, claiming the plans would have catastrophic environmental consequences. His resignation will trigger a by-election in his constituency of Cowdenbeath in Fife, which could take place as early as next month.'

Dante clicks the radio off as the newsreader moves onto other stories.

'That's how we get things done,' repeats Tony, sitting back with a look of satisfaction on his face.

Now I know the outcome of the favour Andrea Fulton's assistant asked about in the office of the Plein Soleil. Now I understand the power that McArthur holds. An elected official, who may be completely innocent, if such a politician can exist, has been brought down. His mistake was to try to stand in the way of

Francis McArthur and his associates, and now his life lies in tatters. This is how McArthur operates, this is how he holds power, this is how he gets things done.

18

Half an hour later we have left the countryside behind and reach the outskirts of the south of the city again. Patrick takes us west, bringing us back a different way through the affluent suburbs of Newton Mearns and Giffnock.

'One more stop before we drop you home,' Tony tells me. He knows I have got to work at the club tonight. There is a private function on, an awards dinner for advertising companies. 'You're starting to see how the McArthurs do business? We cut through the red tape and get things done.' I agree with him, tell him I'm impressed. 'This is what we want you to be part of, Marie and me, and my dad. We look out for you, give you a future, and you look out for us. We keep it all in the family, with people we can trust.' I bite my tongue from suggesting he has been watching too many gangster films.

Kilmarnock Road brings us into Shawlands, with its rows of sandstone tenements, cafés and restaurants. Every street is lined with cars parked by the pavement, the nineteenth-century grid layout completely inadequate for the modern world of private car ownership. Opposite the main shopping arcade, we turn right onto Walton Street. There is nowhere for Patrick to park the large SUV, so he simply stops and blocks the road. We get out. I assume we are visiting another McArthur property. I am starting to appreciate the sheer number of properties McArthur owns and controls across the city.

'You don't need to come in,' Tony tells me. 'This is personal business. Stay with the car and drive it round the block if someone needs to get past.'

'Sure.'

Patrick and Dante follow him up a short path to a communal entrance, No. 49. Tony pushes the intercom buzzer three times. I'm not sure what flat number, but when I look up, I notice a net curtain flick aside on the second floor and a face appears, looking down. Tony looks up and waves. The main entrance door clicks open and they go inside.

I stand against the side of the car. No traffic comes along the road. It's even warmer here, the hot air trapped between the four-storey buildings on either side with no way to circulate. A woman covered in a full black niqab pushes a pram along the pavement. In this heat, that seems like the worst possible garment to have to wear. She eyes the car blocking the road and carries on her way. I look back up at the window. There is movement behind the semi-transparent net curtain; people walking backwards and forwards, like they are circling each other. Then the net curtain is pushed up against the glass. Someone is being held against the window. I can't make out any detail, but I can make out the shape of a woman and her long dark hair.

A loud blast from a car horn makes me jump. An Audi has driven up Walton Street and found the SUV blocking the way. I move to the front of the car and wave an apology as I get into the driver's seat and pull away.

The one-way system on the grid of streets takes me along Tantallan Road and brings me out next to Queen's Park. I loop back round and get stuck at the traffic lights. By the time I get back to Walton Street, Tony, Patrick and Dante are coming out of the door of the tenement. I pull up and get out. They are standing in a group. Next to them is Malky Thomson. Conversation over, Malky goes back inside and slams the door. Tony doesn't look happy. Whatever they were talking about has upset him. Dante puts a guiding arm around him and leads him down the path towards the car. I give the car fob back to Patrick. The happiness Tony was feeling after our meeting in East Kilbride has evaporated and he says very little for the rest of the journey to my flat.

It's four p.m. by the time I am back home. Just enough time to freshen up, pick up my car and get to the club for my usual shift behind the bar.

All the time, I can't stop thinking about the woman in the tenement flat in Shawlands. It was so fleeting – a momentary, shrouded glance of the back of a head – and yet I am sure I recognised her.

* * *

The evening passes without incident in the club. The award ceremony is hosted by a television celebrity I last saw at Marie and Tony's wedding. I don't recognise any of the people winning awards, or any of the advertising that they are responsible for, but everyone seems to be having a good time and the complimentary bottles of wine soon disappear. After that, the constant flow of orders at the bar keeps me occupied until the awards are all dished out and the party moves downstairs, where a local celebrity DJ provides the entertainment. The self-congratulatory nature of the event seems to keep everyone in a happy mood. After midnight, my shift gets quieter, serving just those few who emerge from the basement for respite from the pounding bass, or the occasional drunken couple looking for a quiet corner. I replenish some stock behind the bar, wipe the surfaces down and collect the empty wine glasses.

Carmen is supervising the catering company, who are busy removing the tablecloths and furniture that have been rented for the evening. At one a.m., she comes over to the bar. 'You can take off now. I'll keep an eye on the bar here and Marc and Georgia will be around for closing.'

'You're sure?'

'Yeah, you can do closing tomorrow.'

'Fair enough.' I thank her, head down to the staff area and collect my coat, then head out of the staff entrance into the warm night.

The smell of burning hangs in the air. I look round instinctively, as all people do when they sense something is happening, curious to catch a glimpse of a drama unfolding. The orange glow can be seen above the buildings of the west end, on the other side of Kelvingrove Park, lighting up the darkness. A pluming cloud of dark grey smoke stretches into the night sky. My senses attune as I walk away from the club, and now I hear the sirens of fire engines running through the city. They will be streaming to the fire from stations all around Glasgow, charging along the motorway to Charing Cross.

I know I won't sleep if I go straight home. One o'clock is an early night for me and I am still thinking about the woman in the window. I get to the car and decide to investigate the fire for myself.

* * *

Woodlands Road is closed at The Old Schoolhouse pub. Police have sealed off the area to vehicles. I park up and get out.

'What's happening?' I ask the officer guarding the junction.

'Big fire,' he states the obvious. Over his shoulder, blue lights flash against the side of the buildings along the street. The billowing smoke is thick and the air acrid. I can hear the flames crackling and see them licking the night sky. Firemen flit around; shouts and commands punctuate.

'What's on fire?'

'Convenience store and empty tenements above it.'

'Anyone hurt?'

The officer shrugs. 'Don't think so. No one lived in the block anymore. It was scheduled for redevelopment. Neighbours have had to be evacuated though.' He points towards a church on the other side of Woodlands Road. The tall glass windows on the front of the broad building reflect orange flickering fire and blue emergency lights. In front of them gather local residents and curious night owls. I walk over to join them, moving in amongst them. No one is upset. There's an excited buzz in the crowd.

An elderly woman is on the edge of the crowd. 'Anyone heard what happened?' I ask her.

'Started in the convenience store,' she tells me. 'They never did pay much attention to health and safety. Sold all sorts of cheap Chinese tat; not a surprise it's so flammable.'

'No one was inside though? In the flats above?'

'They've been empty for a couple of years. The new owner came in and kicked everyone out. Had plans to redevelop the whole place into luxury apartments or some such thing. The Yousafs were the last business holding out.'

'They wouldn't sell up?'

'Why should they? Been there thirty years. Guess this is the price they pay.'

'You think it was deliberate?'

'Son, when you get to my age, it's difficult to believe in accidents. Especially when the circumstantial evidence tells you otherwise.'

'Who are the new owners?'

'Beats me, but I guess they're used to getting their own way. Good luck to them. The place needed doing up anyway.'

I stay for another hour, watching the fire service going about their work. Hoses shower the building from the ground and from platforms in the sky, raised on ladders from the trucks.

Fire service personnel rotate in and out of duty, resting on the pavement near us in between shifts manning the hoses and pumps. Police circulate. The spectators come and go. Some drift away to find a place to stay for the night. Locals from a few streets away bring hot food, tea, coffee and blankets, and offer to put friends and strangers up for the night. It takes a disaster such as this to bring out the local spirit. Once the fire is brought under control and the building made safe, those who live next to it will be allowed home. The fire chief tells the crowd he expects that will be some time tomorrow at the earliest. He suggests everyone finds somewhere to bed down for the night; there's nothing more to see here.

Every so often, there's the unmistakable sound of collapsing timber and brick. The front of the building is still standing, but behind it the roof and floors are falling.

Those that haven't got anywhere else to go gradually make their way inside the church.

I make my way back to the car. The same police officer is still on duty at the top of the road.

* * *

I have a shower when I get home at four. I don't normally, but the stench of the smoke is on my skin and in my hair. I feel the need to wash the dirt away.

On the internet you can search the Land Registry of Scotland and discover who owns any property or land in the country. I don't have a computer; I don't yet have internet service in my flat. I could use my phone to search for the name of the owner of the block on Woodlands Road, but I would rather save the data usage. I am almost sure the Land Registry will tell me that it is one of Francis McArthur's companies that owns the property.

Tony would not have filled up the petrol cans in the back of his

SUV himself and he will not have delivered them to Woodlands Road himself, but he will know who they were delivered to in order for the job to be done tonight.

19

Kelvingrove Museum. Van Gogh's Windmill. 1.30 p.m.

Millar knows fine well that I will have to ask what Van Gogh's Windmill is.

'You mean *The Blute-Fin Windmill, Montmartre* by Van Gogh?'

I guess I do. The lady at the information desk points me towards the French Art room on the second floor of the east wing.

The sound of the giant organ swirls around the vast central hall of the museum. The organist is dwarfed by the thousands of pipes that fill the alcove on the second floor. He segues from a religious hymn that I recognise from school into something from *The Sound of Music*. The observers, sat on chairs on the hall floor below and lining the balconies around the central atrium, acknowledge the change in mood with a murmured sing-along and soft hand-clapping.

I edge out of the crowd, my space taken by a mother holding a small child, who looks terrified of the monstrous sound emanating from the historic instrument. I catch a glimpse of Millar across the hallway, on the west side of the building. She moves between the chandeliers that hang from the ceiling above.

I watch her progress across the hall. She circles round behind the organ. I walk the opposite way, approaching our meeting point from the other side of the balcony. My route takes me past the room set aside for the jewel in the museum's collection, Salvador Dali's huge *Christ of Saint John of the Cross*. I step in for a private moment, just me and the painting. Millar can wait. I'm not religious, nor do I know much about art, but the painting of Jesus nailed to the cross, shown from above and looking down onto a sea below, has a strange power. Softly lit, you can make out the repair required when the canvas was attacked and torn open by a mentally disturbed Glaswegian in the 1960s.

Behind me, the organist bursts into *Highland Cathedral* and a loud Dutch couple enter the room, halting my rare communion with the Lord. I make my way along the balcony corridor, passing rooms of Scottish Art on one side and the surreal *Floating Heads* that hang above the east wing hall: fifty white, bald heads, each face with a different expression, watching the visitors as they make their way around the sides of the museum. Happy, sad, angry, annoyed – all emotions are represented.

At the far end of the wing is the French Art room. Detective Millar sits on a bench in the middle of the room, recyclable coffee cup in hand, legs crossed. I'm not an art expert, but I can recognise the style of Monet in the painting in front of her.

She doesn't acknowledge me if she sees me and for a moment I wonder if we are being watched. Has she seen someone?

I wander around the room and eventually find a painting of a windmill. The card on the wall next to it tells me it's Van Gogh's *The Blute-Fin Windmill, Montmartre*, 1886. The French flag hangs atop the grey structure, itself on a hill above grass fields, picket fences and sheds. Millar appears at my elbow.

'You a fan?'

'Of Van Gogh, French art, or art in general?'

'Take your pick.'

'I once did a family portrait in crayon that my mum put on the fridge in our kitchen.'

'Maybe this will inspire you to learn something.'

The room is quiet. Only a handful of other visitors are circulating around the paintings on the walls. A young woman dressed like the textbook definition of an art student comes alongside us. We move away and let her get close to the windmill. We pass harbours and still-life fruit and women in repose. Through an opening we leave the French behind and enter the Dutch room.

'How's your Dutch art knowledge?' Millar asks.

'Rembrandt, right?'

'Very good. They've got a famous one here. *A Man in Armour*.' Millar points and we walk over to a dark painting, a knight of some kind, in profile, fully clad in armour, looking at his sword. 'See how he captures the light playing on the metal surfaces?'

'I'm learning a lot.'

'What can you teach me then?'

'The fire last night, it was a McArthur property?'

'Know anything about it?'

I tell her about my trip to East Kilbride the previous day. 'That's our South Lanarkshire connection.'

'Makes sense. It's the sort of opportunity McArthur thrives on.'

I tell her about the phone message Tony received, the radio news bulletin and Tony's reaction to Terence McAvoy's resignation. 'The favour they spoke about that night at the club.'

Millar tells me the police are already thinking the same thing. 'It makes sense; he was an obstacle to a lot of development plans the council has put forward. But we'll have a hard time proving that McArthur deliberately set out to smear him. What else?'

'How do you know there's something more?'

'I can read people like art critics read paintings. Give.'

I tell her about the petrol cans in the back of the SUV. There's no going back now. I'm an informant. She asks for the registration plate of the car. I tell her.

'We can check the city-wide CCTV and see where they went

after dropping you off. You were working at the club last night?' I nod. 'Good, you have a strong alibi then.'

'I went to look at the fire after I got off work. They said the building was empty, no one was hurt – just one business in the block that got burnt out.'

'I'm sure that's what the defence will argue. Get the charge brought down to involuntary manslaughter.'

I turn from the young man in armour frozen in painted time to Millar, who takes a sip from her coffee cup and carries on looking at the Rembrandt. 'What do you mean?'

'They pulled a body out this morning. Well, the charred bones that remain. Not been able to identify them yet. Don't even know if it's a male or female. Could just be an unlucky squatter.'

'Or?'

'Or a good way to get rid of someone who might have been causing McArthur problems.'

'You think it was murder?'

'That would make you an accessory.'

'What?'

'Might be a stretch for a conviction, but if it turns out you rode around all day with the perpetrators in a car with eight petrol cans in the boot…'

'They were empty.'

Millar shrugs. 'Like I say, a stretch.'

The oils in front of me are swirling. My mind leaps from one event to another. Petrol cans, a burning building, a dead body.

I knew Francis McArthur was bad. I knew he was involved in dodgy dealings. I knew what he did to my father. I knew about his connections. As threatening as he was, as fearful as people were of Murdo Smith and Malky and the rest of his entourage, I never thought it extended to murder. Yet, for some reason, standing there in front of the Dutch Master's artwork, no surprise registers.

'You're telling me McArthur killed someone?'

'For someone who's lived around him all his life, and who's spent time in prison, you're still quite an innocent boy. You think McArthur has stayed at the top for this long, in this city, without playing nasty?'

'But murder?' We move on again, circling round more Dutch art. I'm not taking in the names on the walls anymore. There's a lot of warships, sails billowing over cresting waves. The turmoil of the sea as storms brew seems appropriate. 'What about your fraud case?'

'I may get superseded. It doesn't matter too much. We can still bring fraud charges if we have the evidence. A murder investigation might open doorways for us, let us in to see the books. You're in the lucky position to be a witness for both investigations.'

'Lucky?'

'You will testify to what you saw yesterday?'

I don't answer her question. An unidentified informant is one thing. Exposing myself in court to send McArthur down is another. He is, after all, my sister's father-in-law, and Tony is her husband.

'Isn't there something about "you can't be compelled to give evidence against family members"?'

'You're thinking of husband and wife.'

'I'd be a dead man walking.'

'You want me to tell you we can offer you protection?'

'Aren't you going to?'

'We could try, but frankly, I wouldn't get your hopes up. There's a lot of corrupt coppers and McArthur has a lot of reach and resources.'

'That's reassuring.'

'You want me to sugarcoat it for you? Maybe you'll be okay. You're family after all. McArthur puts a lot of faith in that.'

'Any scenario where I don't end up testifying in front of him in court?'

'Enough hard evidence that we don't need witnesses?' Millar shrugs, suggesting it's a long shot at best.

'So, who do you think it was? In the fire?'

'Like I say, could just be a homeless person. Could be one of the Yousafs who were refusing to sell up. That would send a message. Could be someone else who pissed McArthur off. I'll bet Francis and Tony weren't directly involved, beyond giving an order; probably Murdo or Malky who was left to organise it.'

'Elise Moreau's still not been seen.'

'Your school friend who got kicked out of the club by McArthur? You think it looked like enough of an argument for Francis to have her killed?'

'No idea.' I won't tell Millar about the visit to the flat in Shawlands or the woman glimpsed in the window. Something in the pit of my stomach makes me panic. Malky Thomson's presence there. The discussion in front of the tenement between Tony and Malky. Tony telling me to stay with the car. *You don't need to come in. This is personal business.* What if it was Elise? What if she is dead, burned alive in an empty flat, and I could have stopped it? I could have saved her if I'd just said something to Millar yesterday.

'How's Rose?' It's a habit now, to ask at the end of every meeting, every phone call, every text message. It is also a distraction to take my mind off the unthinkable horror I am imagining.

'You know I'm never going to tell you about Rose.'

'It won't stop me asking. Where is she?'

'You ever think you might be sick in the head?'

'More often than you think. What now?'

'Keep your ear to the ground. If McArthur's involved, and I'm sure he is, there's bound to be some talk about it. Look out for anything unusual. And the property deals are still what I'm interested in the most, so don't forget about that. I'll be in touch in the usual way. Look on the bright side – this might soon be all over for you.'

With that, Millar is gone, tossing her empty coffee cup into a bin as she leaves the gallery. The organ recital has finished. The museum takes on the usual hushed atmosphere of reverence that art inspires. I find myself in front of the young man in armour again. I focus on the way Rembrandt has caught the light reflecting on his shoulder and helmet. 1655. Light that has been trapped, frozen in a permanent glint for three hundred and fifty years, long after the painter and the model have turned to nothing more than dust.

I get the feeling it will be a long time before this is over for me.

20

The end of another night at the Plein Soleil. Wiping down the bar top, stacking chairs. It hasn't been busy. Carmen has been in the office all night, not needing to help out the staff on the floor.

There's been plenty of thinking time to mull over my conversation with Millar this afternoon and the events of yesterday.

"Hard evidence", Millar said. That's my only way out of this. Enough evidence that I wouldn't need to be involved in any court case. No minor witness required. I could walk away with no one suspecting anything. My sister might still get caught up in the fallout – collateral damage if Tony goes down with his father – but her hate wouldn't be directed towards me. But to get hard evidence there has to be risk.

The other thing on my mind is the flat in Shawlands and the woman at the window. The meeting of Tony and Malky. If not Elise, then another person is being held. Putting all the pieces together, that's what I am certain I saw. Someone being held in a flat against her will. Not enough to go to the police. A beat cop sent round to chap on the door won't find anything to warrant further investigation. They are too careful, too clever, to leave themselves open to a casual inquiry. Hard evidence. The refrain rings around my head. I need to prove to Millar that they need to break into that flat.

While I have been serving drinks and Georgia has again been trying to teach me the finer points of mixology, I've been looking for an opportunity. Hard evidence. It could be in any number of places. I have to rule out places that can never be reached: McArthur's personal computer, a safe in his house; the same for Murdo Smith. There's no way I can get access. They won't share anything on the open internet. Anything that's a public record, Millar will already have looked at.

One obvious place presents itself, right above my head. The office at the Plein Soleil. They host meetings here. I saw papers across the desk when I went up to serve the champagne that night. I have not been allowed back up there since.

I need to create the opportunity. I have let the bar restocking slip over the course of the evening.

The others have done all their duties and are ready to leave. Carmen joins us. The group heads down to the basement and the staff room to collect belongings. I hang back with Carmen.

'I still need to restock a few things behind the bar,' I tell her.

'Okay, make it quick. If it's not a lot it can wait until tomorrow before opening.'

'I'd rather get it out the way tonight, leave everything as it should be. That's what you tell us. I can lock up if you want to get away.'

Carmen pulls a blonde spike of hair away from her face and looks at me, deciding whether she can trust me or not with closing the club. 'You'll need to be here at six sharp tomorrow with the keys to open up.'

'No problem.'

'Okay, just make sure you switch everything off and check the doors.' She hands the bunch of keys to me and heads down the corridor, where she joins the others emerging from the staff room.

'See you all tomorrow,' I call after them in as natural a voice as I can manage. Mumbled farewells and half-waves and they exit. The door settles closed behind them, the catch clicking into place, and I am all alone in the quiet, still club. Opportunity created, easier than I thought it would be.

Don't rush it, act natural. The security cameras are still on, still recording. Do what you told Carmen you would do.

I spend the next fifteen minutes collecting bottles from the stock room and carrying them upstairs to the bar until everything is as it should be for opening tomorrow. Then I hit the light switches and lock the internal doors as I make my way downstairs, leaving the club in darkness.

The last thing to be switched off each night are the internal security cameras and monitors. I flick the switch in the small cupboard room where the monitors live. The screens blink off. I back out into the corridor and look up at the camera mounted over the back door. The red light fades out. The club is in darkness. I grab a torch from the shelf in the cupboard room.

My footsteps echo around the empty bar as I cross the wooden floor. What is lit to seem welcoming and comfortable to clients in the evening, seems sinister and menacing alone in the dark. Maybe that's just my subconscious guilt tainting my perception. Black shadows loom out of corners. It is hard to shake the feeling that someone is watching me, or that someone will discover me, even though my rational mind tells me I'm on my own and I have all the time I need.

I fumble the keys as I find the right one to open the double doors that lead upstairs. At the top of the stairs, another locked door. Trial and error and eventually the lock turns.

There are two main offices up here. The larger one doubles as the meeting room. This is the one McArthur uses, the one I've been in before. Carmen uses the smaller office next to it.

I start with the larger room. Inside, I sweep the torch beam across the desk. It's clear. Behind it, in the corner, are the filing cabinet and cupboard I have seen before. That is where I start.

Office stationery. Pamphlets about alcohol licensing laws and notices about not serving underage drinkers. Various marketing materials from brewers, distillers and drinks' companies, received and discarded. Nothing else.

A small key unlocks the filing cabinet. Top drawer. Staff records, including my own. Nothing untoward.

Middle drawer. Spreadsheets. Incomings and outgoings. Takings and other bills to decorators and workmen and utility companies.

Bottom drawer. It isn't a drawer. It doesn't slide open. It's a door panel disguised as a drawer. Behind the door panel is a built-in safe. On the front of it is an electronic keypad. The only way I can get inside is to enter the right code. Anything that might help me is inside that safe, and there is no way I can get inside it.

I close the door and make sure I've left everything as I found it.

Before admitting defeat, I decide to look in the smaller office. There's nothing to lose now.

It has similar furnishings to the first office, but here there are more signs of occupation. Carmen has a few mementos on her desk – a family photograph in a frame, her wife and their kid and a black and white dog. Her laptop lies open. I turn it on but it's password-protected. Another dead end. I try the drawers on the desk. They are not locked. Paracetamol, ibuprofen, a packet of period pads for emergencies. Make-up. Stationery. Nothing unusual.

In the second drawer down, a notebook. I place it on the desk and sit and flick through the pages with one hand, holding the torch in the other. Lists of things to do each day. Reminders. Names and numbers scrawled here and there. Most of them mean nothing. I see my name and phone number. I get to the back of the pad. It's one of those fancy ones with a pocket on the back cover. Carmen has tucked business cards in there. Her own, a local plumber, the head salesperson of a brewer. I tuck them back where I found them and feel the slip of paper inside, pushed to the bottom.

I prise it out. Numbers have been hastily scrawled across it. I recognise the sequence. It's a phone number. I am sure it's the same. I have seen the string of numbers before in the same order. They light up whenever the burner phone in my flat starts ringing. Carmen has Detective Millar's number in her notebook.

Things fall into place. That feeling I had before: Millar has someone else on the inside feeding her information.

Which means that anything that might incriminate McArthur in the club, Carmen has already seen and has already passed on to Millar. I'm wasting my time.

I put the notebook back in the drawer and leave empty-handed.

Nothing about any fraudulent business deals. No hard evidence. Nothing about the flat in Shawlands or a fire in Woodlands or a deal in East Kilbride.

Nothing about Elise.

I lock the staff door and walk back to my car. The external security cameras film my exit. If anyone bothers to check, they might query why it took me half an hour after the internal cameras switched off to leave the building and what I might have been doing in that time. It's a risk I'll have to live with. I'm not sure I even care anymore.

The car starts first time, the growl slicing through the warm night.

I think over what I've just learned. Carmen has been feeding Millar information. I've been used to corroborate some of it. Does Millar not trust Carmen? Am I just insurance, a back-up? Or is Millar hoping I will get better access to the family now that my sister is married to Tony?

I'm sick of being a pawn in this game, caught between Millar and McArthur. Do I care about his dodgy business dealings? Maybe I should care more, but I can't bring myself to.

No one seems to care about Elise. What happened to her?

The more I think back to that glimpse in the window of the second-floor flat on Walton Street, the more I'm convinced it was

Elise I saw there. Is my mind just playing tricks on me? Now, when I picture that glimpse, it's not the back of a woman's head with dark hair pressed up against the net curtain. It's Elise, facing me, looking down at me, pleading with me to help her.

It's time to throw caution to the wind, it's time to get ahead of my problems. It's time to do something reckless.

21

I park the car a mile away on Queen's Drive, just off Langside Road, and walk through Queen's Park towards Shawlands. I don't want to approach the flat in my car and give myself away with the noise of an approaching engine at three thirty in the morning. It's a fifteen-minute walk, passing the boating pond and the football pitches and exiting onto Langside Avenue.

The park is dark, only the white light from streetlights around the perimeter casting a subtle illumination. Spaces like this at night time, when the world has settled and is calm, have always fascinated me. The forecast says a storm is coming that will finally end the heatwave. Tonight the warm air makes it pleasant to walk around. No one else is about.

The walk gives me time to think. I know the chances are that what I am about to do won't end well.

To take my mind off it, I think back to earlier in the day. Between meeting Millar at the Kelvingrove Museum and my amateur detective work at the club, I had my monthly appointment with my probation officer.

I try to count up how many times I lied to her over the course of our half-hour conversation.

'Have you been seeking employment, Mr Jackson?'

'I've got a job.' True.

'That's great.' She checks some paperwork. 'Oh yes, I see. Bar work at Plein Soleil. I see you were given an exemption to allow you to work there. And how's that been going?'

'Fine.' A half-truth.

She starts working her way down her checklist. 'Have you had any contact with the police?'

'No.' Lie.

'Have you taken any illegal substances?'

'No.' True.

'Have you had excessive alcohol?'

'No.' True.

'Have you been involved in any illegal activity?'

'No.' After what Detective Millar told me, that has to count as a lie, but I'm not about to admit to being an accessory to manslaughter or murder.

'Do you intend to take part in any illegal activity in the future?'

'No.' Lie. I already had a half-idea about what I was planning to do that night after my shift at the club.

'Have you had any contact with suspected or convicted criminals?'

'No.' Stone-cold lie.

'Have you been outside of your registered property beyond the hours of your curfew?' She catches herself. 'We can ignore that one, given your new job ... but aside from that?'

'I stayed out late at my sister's wedding. I told you about that last time.'

She ticks the last box on her sheet and files the piece of paper away in a tray on her desk.

'Thank you, Mr Jackson. Anything else you want to discuss, any concerns? How's your flat working out for you?'

I feel sorry for her. It's a thankless task. I like to think I am one of her good customers; one who doesn't cause her grief or concern, one who doesn't threaten her or fail to keep appointments.

'The flat's great.'

'Family supportive?'

'As much as they were before I went to prison.'

She doesn't press for any more detail. 'Good. See you next month then. Stay out of trouble.'

'I plan to.' Lie. I stand up and leave.

Overall, I think I told more truths than lies. I'm in credit. I wonder if the council social work department have been informed by Millar about my current status within the police investigation. Knowing the hapless state of bureaucracy in local government, it's safe to assume they have no idea.

Rose forces her way into my thoughts, refusing to disappear. Where she might be, what she might be doing. I can be objective enough to realise my search for Elise is a displacement of my guardian angel complex over Rose. I'm helpless to do anything for Rose. I can make up for it by helping another person in trouble. I know my mental state is not healthy with regards to Rose, but I also cannot kick the habit.

I have already thought through the consequences of what I am doing tonight. It could mean the end of my career as a bartender at the Plein Soleil. I'm not too bothered about that. It could mean McArthur and his squad of security scouring the city, hunting me down, ready to kill. That is more concerning.

I have thought it through and decided what the hell. I've been sitting on the sidelines for too long.

Unless you count my misdemeanour at the club an hour ago, breaking and entering is something that I have no previous experience of doing. My plan, such as it is, is going to rely on a lot of good fortune. The sensible thing to do would be some preliminary surveillance to take in the lie of the land. How many people does Tony keep at the flat during the night? My guess is one, or two at the most. No one knows a woman is being held in the flat. Too many burly men in black suits would draw unnecessary attention.

That's not what Tony wants. If I am lucky, it's one guard who is feeling tired having been up all night.

The next hope is that the guard can't identify me. I know it's not Dante, because he was on the door at the club this evening. Malky may have been at the flat yesterday, but he won't take on a night shift. There are plenty of people in the McArthur organisation who I have never met and who don't know me. I just need one of them to be on duty tonight. I think the odds are in my favour.

I follow the curve of Tantallon Drive, lined with parked cars on both sides, and approach the south end of Walton Street. There is no one about. The occasional car passes along Kilmarnock Road at the top of the street, a main artery for the city taxis. I've changed out of my hard-soled work shoes into trainers. I can still hear every footstep like it's a hammer blow on the pavement. All the large tenement bay windows are in darkness; no night owls are awake with lights on in living rooms.

I walk up Walton Street and count the house numbers as I pass. Descending odd numbers on the right. Numbers 55, 53, 51. Number 49. I walk past and glance up at the window on the second floor. Nothing moves. It is pitch black; no dim lamp to signify a night vigil taking place. If there is someone being held there, they will be in a room at the back of the property, away from the street and prying eyes. The only way to get to the back of the building is through the communal entrance. I get to the junction at the end of the road and turn the corner. I count sixty seconds, turn back and walk down Walton Street again in the opposite direction. Numbers 45, 47 … this time I stop outside number 49.

I take a deep breath. I have come this far.

I walk up the short path to the door and give it a push on the off-chance it's been left off the latch. I'm not that lucky.

A metal plate by the door has buzzers for each of the eight properties inside the tenement. Ground, 1, 2 and 3. Second floor. Flat 2/1 is the one on the left, the one with the window I looked up at yesterday and saw the woman pressed against, the woman I am sure is Elise. I go to press the buzzer and see my hand shaking. I force myself to push it.

The electronic buzz rings around the street, echoing against the red sandstone, amplified by the quietness. A minute later, a man's voice crackles through the intercom.

'Who is it?' He sounds wary, unsure about the unexpected caller in the middle of the night and prepared for anything.

'Tony sent me.' I've planned what to say in my head.

'Why?'

'Just to check everything's okay.'

'Everything's fine.'

'I need to come in and see for myself. Boss's orders.' He has reason to be suspicious at this break in protocol.

Silence for thirty seconds. He is deciding what to do. I stay close to the doorway, facing the panel, my back to the window above. I know he will be looking down to see who has been sent in the middle of the night to check on him.

The intercom crackles into life again. 'That you, Dante?'

From above and behind, in the shadow of a darkened doorway, in the middle of the night, I guess I could pass for Dante.

'Sure.' The ancient intercom does the job of disguising my voice for me. Most Glaswegian men sound the same.

'Okay, come on up. I'll put the kettle on.'

22

My experience in breaking and entering may be limited, but I do have a criminal record for assault and battery. I'm not proud of it, but at least I know I can throw a decent punch if required.

I don't recognise the man who appears in the hallway from the kitchen with two mugs of coffee in his hands. He is alert enough to notice that it's not Dante who closes the flat door and turns to face him.

He manages to get a 'Who the fu—' out in the time it takes me to cross the square hallway in two strides and plant a right hook into his face. I follow it with a left hand to his solar plexus as he's falling backwards. Rather than shower me with boiling coffee, he keeps a hold of the mugs. The human instinct to not spill a drop is strong. Unfortunately for him, the momentum of my attack sends the liquid backwards and over his arms and chest and face. It must be fresh, because he cries out in shock as the scalding liquid hits him. I keep moving forward and manage to land another strong right to his chin. My next left misses and collides with the wall behind his head. Fortunately it's cheap plasterboard and not brick. I leave a hole in the wall.

The second right hook is enough to put him down on the ground. The mugs roll away from his loose hands. I haven't managed to draw blood. I remember the spray of red liquid that shot out of the off-duty police officer's nose when I hit him. The fateful blow that landed me in prison.

He's out cold. His breathing is laboured. I drag him into the living room and turn on a side light. I look around for something to secure him with. The only thing I can see that might be useful is the cord for the blinds. I dump him on the sofa and rip the cord from the window surround. I turn him face-down on the sofa, pull his hands behind his back and tie them together in as tight a knot as I can manage. I turn him face-up and pat his sides, around his waist and under his shirt. There's no sign of any weapon, but he must have one somewhere. His smartphone is in his pocket. I take it with me and leave him there, still unconscious, to search the rest of the flat.

In the square hallway there are six doors. One leads to the living room I've just come from; one is the entrance door. I go to the door that looks like it leads to a bathroom, a wooden frame with a frosted glass centre and a blind on the other side. It's a narrow bathroom, the toilet at one end, a bath along one side, a sink on the other. No one's there.

Opposite that, next to the living room at the front of the house, is a small bedroom with a single bed, a standing wardrobe and a small desk, and not much room for anything else. The high ceilings give the impression of spaciousness, but the floor space is cramped. The bed has been used, presumably by the guards to get some rest between shifts, but tonight the room is empty. I look in the living room as I pass. He's still out for the count on the sofa. The next door is the kitchen. It is small and worn and neglected. The light is still on after his trip to put the kettle on; a used teaspoon and a bag of sugar sit on the worktop. His suit jacket is hanging on the back of the solitary chair in the middle of the floor. I pick it up and feel the weight in the pocket. I pull out the black handgun.

I have never held a real gun before. I have got no clue how to use it beyond what I've seen in movies. I know which way to point it and that is about it. It is still pretty rare to come across a gun in Scotland. I don't stop to think how lucky I am that this guy is so sloppy at his job that he let me in while unarmed. I don't want to keep his gun. I don't even want to risk tucking it into my waistband in case it goes off. I leave it on the kitchen counter. There's a weight in the other pocket of his jacket too. I pull out a bunch of keys, several small ones and a couple of larger ones all on one keyring. I take them with me and go back to the hallway.

One door left. It must be the main bedroom at the back of the flat. It's closed and when I turn the handle and try to push it open, it doesn't budge. A crude lock has been fitted. On the floor I can see a small heap of sawdust. The lock has been fitted recently. I take the bunch of keys and try the larger ones in the lock. On the third attempt, the teeth bite and the lock turns. I ease the door open and step inside. It is pitch black, but I can make out a double bed. Whether it's the vague shape on the bed or the scent of human sweat in the air, I sense straight away that there is someone else in the room. My hand feels for a light switch on the wall.

'Hello? I'm not here to hurt you.' I speak into the room. The only reply is a shuffling sound from the bed.

My fingers finally locate the light switch.

'I'm going to put the light on, okay?'

I flick the switch.

Light floods the room from a bare bulb hanging in the middle of the ceiling. I flinch as my eyes adjust. Black paper is taped over the windows. There is no other furniture in the room apart from the metal bedstead and a bare mattress with no sheets. The room is warm, the air fetid. The figure on the bed doesn't react to the light. Her eyes are shut, her head to the side, her mouth hangs open. She's wearing only her underwear, a black bra and white pants. Maybe the lack of clothing is a kindness in the current heatwave. Her arms are spread above her head, her wrists are handcuffed to the frame of the bed.

Elise is gaunt and lifeless, her face drawn and hollow. Her arms and legs are thin and fragile, but her stomach is round. The movement of her chest, rising and falling in short, shallow breaths is the only sign she is alive.

I move over to her and wipe her damp hair away from her face.

'Elise, can you hear me?' Her eyes flicker and open and her pupils, tiny points of black, roll away into her head. She is limp in my arms as I try to raise her head. I softly slap her on the cheek and repeat her name. She stirs and mumbles something and falls away again.

'I'm going to get you out of here, okay? But I need you to help me.' I lay her back down and take out the bunch of keys. I unlock the handcuffs with one of the smaller keys. When they click open, I see the red welts where the metal has chaffed and rubbed away the skin. 'I'll be back in a minute. I'm going to get you some water, okay?' She doesn't respond, but curls up in a ball, her arms tucked around her protruding stomach.

I take the handcuffs to the living room. The man is still out for the count on the sofa. I pull him over to the radiator near the door and lie him on the floor. I put a set of handcuffs on each wrist and lock him to the water pipes that come out of the floor and into the radiator. He stirs while I move him. Once he is secure, I grab his hair and smack his head off the wooden floor, partly to keep him unconscious, partly with anger at what has been done to Elise. I close the living room door.

In the kitchen, I fill two tumblers with cold tap water and take them to the bedroom. Elise hasn't stirred. If I'm going to get her out of here, I need her to wake up. I won't be able to carry her all the way to my car. She needs to be able to walk with my support. I throw water from one glass into her face. She coughs and splutters and her eyes open.

'I need you to sit up, Elise.' I put my arm under her shoulders and lever her up into a sitting position, her body leaning against mine. I put the other glass of water to her lips. 'Drink this, come on.' I tip the glass up. Most of the water dribbles down her chin, but some goes in. Her lips are dry and cracked, her skin dull and grey. She's been drugged with sleeping pills or some other sedative. She needs to shake off the drowsy effects.

My mind races with questions. How long has she been held here? She has lost weight since I saw her at the club. Have they been holding her all this time and not feeding her? Why has she been held here? Why have they drugged and held hostage a pregnant woman? How far along is her pregnancy? It wasn't showing the last time I saw her. All the answers can wait. I just have to get her out of here.

She shows signs of coming round. I shuffle her off the bed and onto the floor, propping her back against the metal frame to keep her upright. 'It's me, Cal. You remember me from the wedding and the club?' I tap her face again. She raises a hand and limply touches my face and mumbles my name and then starts to slide away again. 'No, stay with me. I'm going to get you more water, okay?'

I leave her there and when I return from the kitchen, she's slumped over again. I dump another glass of water over her head and then patiently feed her the other. It's slow work when we need to be moving fast. Her eyes are slits, but they are open and she is able to support herself now.

'I need to find you some clothes.' There is a pair of jeans and a top piled in the corner. They must be hers, discarded when they stripped her and shackled her to the bed. I can't see any shoes. 'Come on, put these on.' I spend five minutes trying to get clothes on Elise as she sways backwards and forwards. In the end I lay her on the bed and roll her and push and pull the clothes onto her. They are loose and baggy, but they'll do. I lift her up and drape her arm over my shoulders, taking her slight weight against mine. She walks in small stumbles and I drag her across the room. I don't look in the living room as we cross the hallway to the front door.

With luck, no one will be coming to relieve him of guard duty until the morning. That gives us a couple of hours head start.

I open the door and peer out onto the landing. All clear. I stand Elise against the doorframe. The man's phone is still in my pocket. I take it out and drop it on the floor and stamp on it twice. The screen shatters. For good measure I pick it up and toss it into the bathroom, where it hits the ceramic sink and falls onto the tiled floor.

Outside, I close the door and lock it. I snap the key in the lock. I carry Elise down the stairs, passing the other flats, and drop the bunch of keys inside a wicker umbrella receptacle on the landing.

The street is still empty and quiet as we exit the building. The odd car still passes along Kilmarnock Road, but nothing comes down Walton Street as we start retracing my steps back to the car.

The fresh air brings Elise further out of her drug-induced slumber. I keep up a constant conversation of reassuring words. The last thing I want her to do is start screaming and shouting and drawing attention to us. When we reach Queen's Park, I walk over the grass on the edge of the path, thinking it will be better for her unprotected feet.

'Almost there,' I encourage her, 'just a bit further, come on.' I'm grateful she's light enough for me to support while still moving at a reasonable pace. The early-rising birds are starting their morning song as we make it to the other side of the park. I check over my shoulder. As far as I can tell in the gloom, no one is pursuing us. I have no idea if the alarm has been raised back at the flat. Reaching Langside Road, I pick Elise up, carrying her in my arms like she's a small child. She lazily wraps her arms around my neck and presses her face into my shoulder. I manage to run across the road and turn into Queen's Drive. I lean Elise against the car while I open the door. I put her in the passenger seat and strap on her seatbelt.

The engine fails to start. After three attempts, I swear at it and slam the steering wheel. Not now, not here. On the fourth attempt it coughs into life with a misfire that is sure to wake those living nearby. I take off and drive through the empty streets. Next to me, Elise falls back to sleep, her head resting against the window.

23

I sit by my bed and watch her. She's been sleeping for four hours since we got back to my flat. I try not to think about how long I've got. Should I have called Millar from the flat? How will I explain it to McArthur when the police turn up at his door?

While Elise sleeps, I get the burner phone from its hiding place and call her now. It's eight in the morning; she will be on her way to work. She answers.

'You remember Elise Moreau?'

'How can I forget? It wasn't her in the fire, if that's what you want to know. The body was a male.'

'I know it wasn't her. I've found her.'

'Good. So you can stop obsessing about her now. I take it she's safe and well after all?'

'I found her chained to a bed in a flat in Shawlands, being held by McArthur's men. If you go to Flat 2/1, 49 Walton Street, you'll find a guard handcuffed to a radiator. It's a McArthur property.'

A moment of silence follows as Millar digests my news.

'Where are you know? Are you there?'

'I'm back home. Elise is with me. She's sleeping. I think they drugged her with something.'

'Stay there,' Millar warns me. 'I'll call you back.'

'Okay.'

'You stupid idiot, Cal.' She hangs up.

I knew she wouldn't like what I have done, but it is too late to change anything. Millar has her fraud case to think about. I have jeopardised my part in that. For her, kidnapping is an unwelcome distraction that she cannot ignore.

How much time do we have? Once they find out Elise is gone, how long before they piece it together? I'm pretty sure the guard didn't get a good look at me, and I didn't recognise him. Will he be able to identify me? Not unless he sees me again. But Tony and Malky and Dante know I was at the flat with them. They know I spoke to Elise at the wedding that she wasn't invited to, and at the club. At the very least they will want to talk to me. They're not stupid; they're bound to put two and two together.

The streets get busier outside and the heat from the sun starts to shine through the thin bedroom curtains. Elise stirs. This time, when her eyes open, she is able to focus. She looks around, bewildered at her new surroundings, and sees me at the end of the bed.

'Cal?'

* * *

I bring her toast and coffee in the living room. She's had a shower. I have given her a t-shirt, socks and underwear. She sticks with the same pair of jeans I found at the flat. I've told her how I found her, about the night time rescue, the guard handcuffed to the radiator and our escape to the car.

'I've called someone I trust in the police and told them about the flat. They're going to call me back and let us know what to do next. Now you.'

'Now me what?' Her voice is weak, diminished from the last time I spoke to her. She takes small bites from the dry toast and struggles to swallow. Her face has changed; her angular cheekbones are pointed and sharp.

'What happened? Why were they holding you prisoner in a flat? Was it something to do with what happened at the club with McArthur?'

Elise puts the half-eaten toast down and picks up the coffee. She takes a long drink from it. Caffeine is the best thing for her at the moment. She doesn't answer my questions, so I try again.

'Is it to do with that?' I indicate her stomach. 'You're pregnant?'

'It's showing then,' she says. She puts a protective hand to her midriff and rubs it. It doesn't show so much now she is dressed in my baggy t-shirt. The wrap dress she was wearing at the wedding would be a stretch now.

'How long?'

'Three months, maybe a little more.'

'We should get you checked out. They gave you drugs that might have harmed the baby.'

More coffee. Then I remember something about how caffeine should be avoided during pregnancy and discreetly move the mug away from her. I let her take her time and she tries a bit more toast. 'Your breakfasts are lousy.'

'Afraid it's all I've got to offer.'

She sighs and puts it down again, pushing the plate away from her.

'It's Tony's,' she says.

'Tony's?'

She nods and picks up the coffee mug again. I'm too stunned to stop her.

My initial reaction is to calculate the timing. Three months ago. I was just out of prison. Marie and Tony had been engaged for a year and their wedding was only a few weeks away. And Tony was sleeping with Elise.

'He was having an affair with you?'

'If you want to call it that. We've slept together a few times, off and on, since school. It was never anything more than that. Never serious. Tony would see other women, I would see other men, relationships, whatever. Every so often we would gravitate back to each other.'

'You knew he was engaged?'

Elise shook her head. 'He told me he was seeing someone, but he didn't tell me he was engaged and about to be married. I never knew it was Marie.'

'Would it have made a difference if he had told you?'

'Probably not. It was just a thing we did.'

'Except this time you ended up pregnant?'

'Tony wasn't happy about it. Blamed me, like all men do. Told me he was about to get married and I was on my own. He offered to pay to help me get rid of it.' Her hands touch her stomach again.

'You didn't want to?'

Elise shakes her head. 'Even if it was going to be just me on my own, I decided I wanted to keep it. Tony accepted that. It was the timing that made him panic, what with him getting married.'

'Then why didn't you do it on your own? Why did you turn up at the wedding and the club?'

'Tony was ready to acknowledge he was the father. He wanted to contribute money even if he couldn't be with us. But Francis stopped him, said Tony would have nothing to do with us and we wouldn't get a penny. Told me to do the right thing for everyone and have an abortion. He could have sorted us out for life with one bank transfer.

'I was stupid, I wasn't thinking straight. It wasn't about me. I wasn't jealous of your sister; I didn't want to steal her husband. I was thinking about my own mum and how she had been abandoned to bring me up on her own. I wanted to make sure I didn't put my child through the same thing. I just wanted Tony to stand up for his child, admit to what he had done and make sure we were okay.

I didn't want him to be involved if he didn't want to be, but he can't just walk away with no responsibility. I was fighting for our future.'

'So you threatened to tell everyone? My sister?'

'Not in so many words. I just let it be known that if we were looked after, then Francis and Tony could trust us to be quiet. If not, then I could make Tony's new marriage difficult for him.'

'When you didn't get the answer you wanted, you decided to confront Francis at the club?'

'That was the plan.'

'What did they do to you?' I hesitate to ask the question.

'They came to my flat a couple of days after they threw me out of the club. Four of them. Malky, Dante, the doorman from the club and two others. They hit me, knocked me out. Next thing, I was tied to the bed in that flat.'

'Did they hurt you?'

She shakes her head. 'They didn't hit me again, but they kept me tied up most of the time. They put sleeping pills or something in the water. They fed me sandwiches and crisps once a day. That was it.'

'What were they planning to do to you?'

'They were going to force me to have an abortion. They kept telling me a doctor would come round and cut the baby out of me.'

'And Tony? Did he threaten you?'

'No, Tony had changed. He wanted me to have the baby. He said he would help me. It was Murdo Smith and Malky who threatened me.'

'Never Francis?'

Elise shakes her head again. 'Never him. I didn't see him the whole time I was in the flat, but I know he was behind it.' We both know Murdo and Malky will only do what Francis McArthur tells them to do.

'McArthur is under investigation for murder, racketeering, fraud. Kidnapping can be added to the list.'

'Murder?'

'I'll explain later.'

'You're not angry about your sister? I mean, I'm sorry it happened.'

'I warned my sister about Tony. She didn't listen.' I should be angry at Marie. She has no idea what she's mixed up in, the people she's dealing with or what they are capable of. Can I blame her though? Until recently, I thought McArthur and Murdo and all his money were just down to some dodgy dealings and minor rule-bending. We were equally naïve.

'She doesn't need to know anything about it. You can trust me not to tell her.'

Before I can answer, the burner phone rings from the bedroom.

'Wait here.'

I go to the bedroom and answer the phone. 'Millar.'

'We're too late, Cal.'

'Why, what's happened?'

'We broke into the flat. It's not a McArthur property. He doesn't own anything in Shawlands.'

'Okay, so he rented it for the occasion.'

'There's no one here, Cal, it's empty. No guard handcuffed to a radiator, no sign of anyone having been held hostage, no furniture. The place is clean.'

'I punched a hole in the wall in the hallway.'

'I'm standing in the hallway now, Cal. There's no hole in the wall. There's nothing.'

'What about his phone? I smashed it and threw it into the bathroom. Or the keys – I threw them into an umbrella stand on the landing.'

'Cal, I've looked. There's nothing. Without Elise making a charge, there's nothing we can do. There's no evidence, nothing to link McArthur or Tony to the property. There's just your accusations. Unless Elise comes forward.'

'You can't bring him in for questioning?'

'There is no evidence of any crime. Until Elise reports a crime, we can't touch him.'

'What about the other investigations?' I can hear the panic in my voice. McArthur is out there and he knows Elise is missing and that someone helped her get free. The only way Elise and I will be safe is if McArthur and his friends are locked up. But Millar is telling me that isn't going to happen.

'They are progressing, but it takes time. If we arrest him and charge him too soon, his lawyer will get him out in no time and we'll be back to square one. We don't want to act until we've got a watertight case against him.'

'What's Elise supposed to do while you take your time?'

'Lie low. Convince her to press charges.'

24

Millar hangs up. Elise watches me pace around the living room, stopping to look out the window. Any moment I expect a black SUV to pull up outside. I check the front door and make sure it's locked and the safety chain is attached. For some reason, I believe a locked door will make a difference to a squad of McArthur's foot soldiers.

'Have you got anywhere you can go? Anywhere they won't look for you?' I ask her. I can take her there while the coast is clear, while we still have time.

'My mum's house.'

I shake my head. 'They'll find you there.'

'I haven't seen her in a month.'

'I saw her a couple of weeks ago.' Elise stares at me. 'I was looking for you,' I explain.

'How was she?'

'Fine,' I lie. 'I checked in with the neighbour and asked her to keep an eye on her. Told her you might not be around for a while.'

'Can I stay here for now?'

'I don't know how safe it is here. Tony took me to the flat. He's bound to suspect something. They saw us together that night at the club. Malky Thomson warned me not to go near you.'

***

She goes back to sleep in my bed. By lunchtime there is still no sign of anyone coming for us. If the guy I knocked out in the flat had been able to identify me, they would have been here by now. Maybe I got lucky.

I rustle us up a lunch from the few things I have left in the kitchen and wake her. We sit opposite each other at the small square table in the corner of the kitchen.

'This is worse than what they fed me in the flat,' she says, picking some mould off a piece of bread.

'I'm not used to having guests.'

Some colour has returned to her face. The effects of the drugs are wearing off. She still needs more rest and proper meals.

'I haven't said thank you yet,' she says. 'For getting me out of there.'

I make like it was nothing. 'I couldn't just leave you there.'

'You're not what I expected.'

'What do you mean?'

'When I saw you at the bar, at the wedding, I'd heard all about you. Just out of prison, done for assaulting a police officer. I was expecting someone more...'

'Violent? Rough?'

'Something like that. You know what I mean. This city's full of them. You were never like that at school. Always one of the quieter ones, more respectful, even if you did hang around with Tony. What happened with the police officer?'

'It was nothing really.'

'You hit him for no reason?'

'No good reason. I was drunk, of course. I'd been down, depressed. I have times like that. Ever since I was involved in a car accident. I hurt a young girl pretty badly, and then my dad passed away. I couldn't find a way to get back on the right track. I drank too much, I started taking drugs, mixing with bad people. Like you said, this city is full of us.

'That night I'd been in a pub, drowning my sorrows again. Nothing exceptional, but I guess I was worse than I realised. Trying to walk home, I was shouting at people in the street, you know, screaming at them. I was out of it.

'This off-duty policeman saw me harassing a group of students. Maybe they said something to me, maybe one of them looked at me the wrong way. I don't know why I did anything. That can be enough.

'The police officer got in my face, told me to beat it. Threatened me. So I lashed out. I hit him once and kept going. Another couple of guys pulled me off him. If they hadn't, I don't know, maybe I would have been up on a murder charge. I guess they saved me in a way.'

'What happened to the police officer?'

'I saw him at the trial and after. He came to visit me in prison. Talked it through. He's a better man than I will ever be. Said he forgave me, hoped I was getting the right sort of help inside. Hoped I would be able to use it as a way to turn my life around.'

'Must be one of the good ones.'

'I've heard they do exist out there.'

We finish eating. The phone doesn't ring; no one comes to the door. Elise goes back to bed, telling me to get some decent food in for dinner or she'll find a different hotel to hole up in.

* * *

Decision time. It's Saturday afternoon and I'm due at the Plein Soleil at six to open up with the keys Carmen gave me last night.

Not showing up will be a sure sign of my guilt.

Showing up is walking into the lion's den.

I try to put myself in McArthur's place, in Tony's place, in Murdo Smith's place. They know the girl is gone. They know she had help. They don't know who from. What will they do? They must have a list of suspects. It might be a short list – it might just have my name on it and no one else.

They don't come barging through my front door to confront me. Why not? Because they're not one hundred percent sure it's me? Because there are other people they don't trust? So they wait and watch. Who acts suspiciously? Who doesn't show up where they're supposed to? Who does something different, something out of the ordinary?

If I don't show up at the club tonight, they'll know straight away. If they're watching, they'll see it, or Dante or Carmen will tell them.

I check the road from my window again. All is quiet. No one is coming.

I think about calling Millar. What would she recommend I do? I already know what she will say. Get Elise to give herself up to the police, make a statement, press charges. They can protect her.

I already know what Elise will say. She's seen what McArthur is capable of first-hand. So have I. He's too well connected; he operates above the law. He's got police officers on his payroll along with politicians, judges and lawyers. There's no way to protect Elise from all of them. If he wants either of us out of the way, that is what he will make happen.

What is the alternative? Going on the run together?

I'm still mulling it over when Elise rises again and comes in from the bedroom.

'I'm starving,' she says, and flops down onto the sofa. 'You really should clean this place up a bit.'

'You're not the first person to tell me that.'

'What's for dinner?'

I pick up my phone from the table. 'Pizza?'

The delivery driver drops off two large pizzas half an hour later. One cheese, one pepperoni. It's not healthy, but it's the sort of junk food packed with carbohydrates and calories that Elise needs. Plus, it's cheap and means I don't have to try to cook whatever is left in the cupboards.

We talk over our situation while a quiz show plays on the TV. Someone wins a grand and acts like it's going to change their life forever.

'You should go,' Elise tells me. 'If you're not back by early morning, I'll get out of here.'

'That's reassuring for me.'

'So don't go,' she shrugs, 'but like you say, if you don't show up for work, then they're coming here anyway, so where does that leave us?'

There are no good options left. I surprise myself by not being in a paralysing state of panic. Breaking into the flat, looking for Elise, hitting that guy, taking her out of there – I must have known it would lead to a moment like this.

'We could run away together.' I don't mean it to sound like I'm suggesting some sort of *Thelma & Louise* road journey, but it comes across that way.

'And where exactly are you thinking of running to? The ex-con and the pregnant woman?'

She's right. The only option is to face up to it. Turn up at the club and scope out the lie of the land. With the fire and a murder charge hanging over him, maybe McArthur has other things on his mind, too busy to worry about his wayward son's other woman. Maybe their business deal in East Kilbride is more important than the trivial people at the bottom of the ladder.

'You promise you'll wait here for me?'

'I'm planning a big night of TV and sleep and maybe ordering more pizza in.'

'You seem pretty calm for someone who's been abducted and held captive.'

'Believe it or not, this place is an upgrade.'

Part of me feels like she wants me out of the way, like she has her own plan to get out of here. She flicks through TV channels and polishes off the last of her pizza while I get myself ready for work.

I leave her at five-thirty. I make sure she locks the door behind me. Before I go, I take the burner phone out and send Millar a message: *I'm going to the club. Elise is at my flat. If you don't hear from me by four in the morning, get her out of there.*

25

Three o'clock. Closing time. The evening has been an anti-climax in a good way. Nothing out of the ordinary has happened. The bar remains quiet. The heat continues to build ahead of the promised storm that will end it all. It keeps people out of the city and out of the club. The days are at their longest. People stay in the parks or their gardens until midnight. No one has need for a nightclub.

Carmen is in. If she has heard about any trouble from the boss, she isn't letting on. Georgia and Lauryn are on the bar with me, Marc and Andy are downstairs looking after the dancefloor. There's no sign of McArthur or Murdo or Malky. No one comes looking for me. Dante isn't on the door, but he wasn't supposed to be. I don't recognise the two men who do stand guard, but that's not unusual and they don't show any interest in me.

The music fades and the last couple in the bar gather their belongings, take an end-of-night selfie for their social media updates and head out. The front door is locked behind them. The main lights come on and end the atmosphere of shadowy intimacy.

I wipe the bar down, tidy away the last remaining glasses and start stacking the chairs on top of the tables, ready for the cleaners to arrive, and mop the black floor. Carmen collects the cash from the tills and takes it to be locked in the safe in the office.

By half past, everyone has finished their duties and we head down to the basement and staff room. The four youngsters head out together. The doormen have already left. I hang back with Carmen as she locks up the office and inner doors. We leave through the staff entrance together.

Carmen steps out first and I notice her hesitate. It's not good news. My gut tells me this is the inevitable conclusion of everything that has happened since I got out of prison, since the wedding day, since I took this job, since I met Elise. In that split second, I link it all the way back to Rose Black hitting the windscreen of Tony's car, with me in the driver's seat.

There is no point in running; there is no escape route back through the club.

A rumble of thunder in the distance signals the coming storm. The humidity clings, the air is damp and warm and uncomfortable.

The gang is all here, except for the McArthurs themselves: Murdo Smith, Malky, Dante and the driver, Patrick. They have come in uniform, dark trousers and black coats, looking the part of a death squad. Their victim is cornered.

Murdo is the spokesperson for the group. He addresses Carmen rather than me.

'Eventful evening?' he asks her.

'Quiet again,' Carmen answers.

'It'll pick up soon enough. A break in the weather and everything will get back to normal. Glasgow's still a night city. And it's still a drinking city.'

'I don't doubt it.'

No one moves. Everyone waits for Murdo to decide what happens next. Another rumble of thunder rattles in the distance.

'We'd like a word with your barman if that's okay.'

'He's all yours,' Carmen replies, unwittingly describing my predicament. 'You don't need my permission.'

She walks away and looks back at me as she goes. I can see the pity in her eyes. Whatever they want to talk to me about, she knows it can't be good news with this turnout in the middle of the night. She gets five paces before Murdo calls her name. She turns to face him.

'If anyone ever asks, you didn't see us here tonight. Understood?'

'I left at half past three and got home at four without seeing a single soul.'

'Good girl.' Murdo dismisses her. Carmen takes in each face that she will deny ever having seen and looks at me last. Pity has turned to sorrow and perhaps goodbye. She doesn't think she will see me again after tonight. For her own safety, there is nothing she can do to help me.

The gathered men watch her depart, then four sets of eyes swivel onto me.

I look at Murdo, flanked by his soldiers. Time to brave it out. 'What can I do for you, Murdo?'

'We'd like a wee word, Cal, if you wouldn't mind.'

He makes it seem like I have options. 'Can it wait until tomorrow?'

'I'm afraid not, but we don't have to stand about like this. Let's go somewhere more comfortable.'

'Carmen has the keys to the club.'

'Not to worry. Why don't we all head back to my house? You can ride in my car. Dante here will follow in your car, if you'd be so kind as to give him the key.'

'You're not going to tell me what this is about?' I want to hear him say it.

'All in good time, Cal, all in good time.' A sinister smile spreads across his face as he puts his arm out and shows me the way. I walk ahead. At the top of the path is Murdo's black Range Rover Velar Dynamic. Dante steps round me and opens the back door. I hand my car key over to him. He walks off to collect my car. Murdo gets in the front passenger seat of the SUV. Patrick gets in the driver's seat. Malky follows me in and sits next to me. It's a spacious car, but he's a big man and I feel trapped in the corner. No one speaks as Patrick pulls away and drives through the empty streets.

We turn onto Bearsden Road and head north. Without any traffic to hold us up, it's not long before we are through Bearsden and on Milngavie Road.

My mind races through possible scenarios. None of them offers me much hope. Have they found Elise? Have they been to my flat while I was working? Is she tied up again, in another anonymous house in the city, chained to a bed? I can't think of any way out of the situation. Making a run for it won't get me far. Admit guilt and plead for forgiveness? Appeal to their conscience and try to make them see that what they were doing is wrong? Paint Elise as an innocent who shouldn't be part of their dark world?

It is four in the morning when we pull through the gates of Murdo Smith's mansion. Through the side window I see my car peel away along the road. Even in the middle of the night, Murdo won't have my beat-up rusting Corsa spoil the pristine edifice of his home. Or maybe he doesn't want anyone to see my car at his house because it will link him to my impending disappearance.

The house is unstaffed during the night. There is no Davidson to open the door for us. Malky does the honours. Lights automatically turn on as we enter. They continue the pretence of civility as Murdo leads me into a sitting room at the back of the house with floor-to-ceiling windows that open up onto the back garden, which is shrouded in darkness. Patrick brings up the rear and closes the door behind us.

'Take a seat,' Murdo tells me rather than offers. I sit on the black leather sofa. Murdo takes a seat opposite me. Malky and Patrick remain standing, adopting their formal doorman work pose, legs slightly apart, hands clasped in front. There are serious looks in my direction all round.

Murdo breaks the ice. 'A serious matter, I'm afraid, Cal. Someone has gone missing.'

I don't say anything. Denial is the only option I have until they present some hard evidence that I can't deny.

Murdo tries again. 'Tony made a mistake the other day when he allowed you to see the flat in Shawlands. He trusts too easily, typical of the younger generation. They haven't learned caution yet.' No doubt Tony has already been reprimanded by Murdo and his father for his indiscretion.

I might as well play my part to the full. 'You're saying someone from the flat is missing?'

Murdo leans forward, his face straight. 'That's right, Cal. A girl is missing. You wouldn't know anything about that, would you? Feels like a bit of a coincidence that she disappeared a day after your visit. I don't believe in coincidence.'

'Am I supposed to know this girl?' I can see my feigned ignorance is annoying them. It's a small consolation.

Murdo cannot contain himself any longer. 'Quit playing around, Cal. We know you helped Elise. Tell us where she is and you might still have a way out of this.'

Cards on the table. An admission of what awaits me if I don't comply.

'I don't know where Elise is, I hardly know her. Why on earth would you be holding her in a flat?'

Murdo doesn't answer, only bows his head in exasperation. He doesn't want to deal with things like this – scandal, infidelity, family affairs. He's a businessman. He's acting on his boss's orders, doing it out of duty and loyalty. Thirty years ago, when he and McArthur were busy building their empire, they didn't have to worry about things like this. The world has changed. Now mistresses are a problem to be covered up, not a bit of fun to be bragged about.

'Enough.' He looks straight at me. 'We all know what's been going on, so let's quit the childhood games. You're a grown-up, start acting like it instead of recreating your school days. There's still a chance you can make it right here, Cal. We just want to know where we can find Elise. If we get her back, we can deal with you with greater leniency. You can still make this right for everyone.'

'Honestly, you've lost me.' One last denial, just for kicks.

Murdo doesn't appreciate it. He gives up and signals to Malky. Malky hits a button on a small remote in his hand. Outside, lights come on and flood the garden. Another click and the swimming pool lights come on. I can see the water shimmering. The wind has picked up, causing ripples to break across the water's surface. In the middle of the pool floats a dark object.

'Let's take in some air.'

Malky opens the door and Murdo leads us outside. I follow his slight frame. Patrick remains inside. Dante, having disposed of my car somewhere at the back of the house, is already there. They gather around me as Murdo stops by the side of the pool.

The object floating in the pool is clearer now. The arms and legs of the body are spread-eagled. He is face down in the water, the waterlogged black suit jacket and trousers not enough to weigh him down. He has no shoes on. I wonder where they went.

'When Malky discovered the flat was empty this morning, that Elise had gone, we had to do some house cleaning. We can't have anything that might link us to such criminal behaviour. Unfortunately, that includes Robert here, the night guard. The one you left unconscious, handcuffed to a radiator.'

Staring at the dead body in the middle of the brightly lit pool is having the effect Murdo desires. A cloud of red-pink surrounds the unfortunate Robert, coming from a wound in his head. I can't tell if it's a gunshot wound, a knife wound or just a blow to the head that sent him into the water. Murdo can see the fear in my eyes.

The first heavy drops of rain start to fall as the wind whips through the garden with gathering force.

'This is the consequence of your action, Callum. This blood is on your hands. This is what happens when someone fails in their duty to Mr McArthur. I would hate to see you end up in the same situation. You are, after all, family.

'Tell us where she is, Callum, and this can all end right here. You can go back to being a barman at the club. We can forget you ever did anything.'

Staring at the floating dead man, I find Murdo's promise hard to believe. There is no way back from this. You only betray Francis McArthur once.

'Silence isn't your friend here, Callum,' Murdo says. 'If you won't offer the information to us willingly, then Dante and Malky will have to force it out of you. They can be very enthusiastic interrogators.'

'I don't know where she is. If someone helped her escape, it wasn't me.' All I can think about is buying Elise some time. By now she should know something has gone wrong. I said I would be back by four and it is half past four already. I thought I would feel worse about the situation, but deep down, I knew this was where it would end up. It was always going to end up like this. When Detective Millar turned up at my place, my fate was sealed. Even before that, from the point I agreed to go to my sister's wedding and be drawn into McArthur's world again, I was on a crash course with disaster.

'I was afraid you would say that.' Murdo shrugs and takes a step back. In his place, Malky and Dante step forward.

'Sorry Cal,' Malky says, as he cracks his knuckles. 'I did warn you not to cross Mr McArthur.'

'I won't take it personally.' One last bit of false bravado to mask my terror. I brace myself for the first blow to land.

The rain starts to pour down. The thunder bellows overhead.

26

It is a measure of the contempt with which they regard me that they don't even bother to tie me up or handcuff me. Instead, Dante steps behind me and grabs my arms, pulling them down behind my back, leaving me exposed to the onslaught about to head my way.

Malky steps forward and sets himself. 'You sure you don't want to change your mind? Just tell us where the girl is and this can be over.'

'I can't tell you what I don't know.'

Malky sighs. 'So be it.' I even believe his reluctance for a second, right up until the moment he raises his shovel-sized fist up to shoulder height and I see the look of joy in his eyes and the growing smile that lights up his face. Moments like this are what Malky Thomson lives for.

While I have had some experience in dishing out blows, from the school playground to the drink-soaked streets of the city, I've also managed to avoid too much punishment in return – just the odd black eye in school, like most boys. I was always much better at avoiding conflict than entering into it. I am not sure how I will react to the pummelling I'm about to endure, but I am sure that to accept it will mean I cross a threshold of pain that I would prefer not to experience.

Malky's fist seems to grow in size, covering the moon that peeks through the thick grey clouds in the night sky above. Then it descends towards me in a screaming arc. I can hear the wind whistle as it rushes forward.

It connects with my cheekbone and nose and I hear the crunch as cartilage is crushed. I'm grateful to Dante for holding me up. Without him, I would have crumpled in a heap, folding like a cheap deck of cards after one blow.

The blood bursts from my nose and I know it's broken. My head recoils forward after the initial jolt backwards and I stumble and stagger.

No one seems to take notice of the rain soaking us. My clothes are sodden already, clinging to my body. The large raindrops wash the blood from my face. I see the trail of red-stained water on the patio at my feet as it drains into the pool.

Dante reaches round, grabs my jaw and props my head up so I can face Malky through the haze of red spray. I think all my teeth remain in place. There is a definite ringing in my ears that wasn't there a moment ago.

'Any chance that was enough to convince you?' Malky asks. I think he's slurring his words, until I realise it's my hearing that's malfunctioning. I shake my head at the blurred outline in front of me, but when I try to speak, I choke on the blood and phlegm pouring from my broken nose.

'I'm not that sorry, to be honest,' continues Malky, warming to his task. 'You always did think you were better than the rest of the boys growing up. I always wanted an excuse to show you how small and insignificant you really are.'

'Now's your chance. Knock yourself out,' I slur.

He doesn't appreciate my humour. Dante straightens me up in preparation. I wonder how many more blows I will be able to take, but I know I will fall unconscious or die before I tell them anything about Elise.

Malky has something in his hand. The metal glints in the moonlight, or maybe it's the shimmering lights of the pool. At first I think it's a knife blade, not an uncommon weapon among Glasgow gangs, even though it's heyday in the city has passed. Then I realise it's a knuckle duster. I can see the drops of rain dripping from the metal. Malky sweeps his sodden hair from his eyes. This is going to hurt.

His left fist this time, showing off his ambidextrous skill. It plunges towards me, landing on the opposite cheekbone. I feel the metal slice through my skin and a fresh torrent of blood spurts into the night air. Dante refuses to let me drop to the ground. He is taking almost all of my weight as my legs disintegrate beneath me. My head lolls to the side and down, and around and through the spinning lights I make out Murdo watching on. It would be nice if he interrupted for old times' sake, but he seems content to watch more.

'Third time's a charm,' says a distant voice that sounds like Malky, but comes through a haze of white noise.

No fist rises this time. Instead he completes his hat-trick with a good old Glasgow Kiss. His slab of a forehead crunches into my already pulped nose and this time I feel at least one front tooth give way. I'm conscious enough to stop myself swallowing it. It rolls around my blood-filled mouth.

Malky hasn't broken sweat yet. There's no witty warning this time; he's getting into a rhythm. His fist slams into my solar plexus and I feel the rush of air escape my body, alongside the sound of a cracking rib. Dante lets me drop this time as I double over and slump to the ground. A fork of lightning arcs across the sky behind Malky as he stands over me.

I lie there. A pair of shining black shoes swim into view. A hand grabs the back of my jacket and rolls me over. I look up into the face of Murdo Smith.

'It's a very simple choice, Callum. Tell us where she is and live.

Don't tell us and the next minute will be the last of your miserable life. This is your last chance.'

My maniacal smile looks up at him. I spit my tooth at his face, covering him in a cloud of my blood as it hits him. I laugh into the night sky.

'The poor bastard is enjoying it,' says Murdo, standing and pulling a handkerchief from his pocket and dabbing his face clean.

Enjoying it might be stretching it, but I feel a strange calm. A catharsis is washing over me, like the torrent of biblical rain that is falling from the sky. I deserve this. Malky's beating is what's owed to me by everyone whose life I've ruined. My father, my mother, Marie. Rose Black. Tony. The police officer I hit. Elise. I have had this coming for a while, and now that it has arrived, I can accept it. Prison wasn't enough. I have got away with it for too long. It is good to finally be found out.

Malky and Murdo are talking.

'Even if he does know, he's not going to tell us. Get rid of him.' Murdo's instruction is directed towards Dante.

'Wait,' urges Malky. Now his face fills my view as he crouches next to me. 'For God's sake, Cal. Just tell us. It's bad enough as it is. What am I going to tell your sister if...'

My smile stops him as he looks into my mangled face. 'Fuck you, Malky,' I say. Or at least, that's what I try to say. How it comes out I can't tell, but he gets the message.

All that's left is to decide how they want to finish the job. I hope they make it quick. Dante pulls me up again.

This time the glint is from a blade. Malky's not messing about. It looks like an army knife of some kind, a military weapon, a thick blade with a serrated edge. A hunter's knife. He holds it up to let me see it.

'I'm going to gut you like a pig and listen to you squeal.'

He never was subtle.

Dante wrestles my limp, wet body into position near the pool. I can see why Murdo had it installed now. How many others have perished in these waters in the last ten years, all to protect the McArthur family? I am to join my floating friend tonight. It seems fitting in a way. I am responsible for his death. It's efficient too. Disembowel me over the pool and tip me in. A change of water and no other cleaning up required to hide any evidence. The rain will take care of the rest.

We are all set. Malky takes a step towards me and raises the fearsome weapon. My soft stomach is exposed, facing him, with nothing between it and the blade that will cut through my skin and intestines like a knife through butter.

And then he pauses. He turns. He hears something. I notice the others hear it too. They look around at each other, into the sky, towards the front of the property.

The sound finally penetrates my faltering eardrums and I hear it too. Over the furious wind and the echoing thunderstorm, a sound I never thought I would be this happy to hear.

Police sirens in the distance, drawing closer and filling the night air of Milingavie. Not the lone siren of a single police car. Five, six, a dozen, more. An army of public defenders coming to my aid.

Patrick rushes out from the French doors. 'Police,' he needlessly informs us. 'Hundreds of them.' He's pointing towards the front of the house.

No one seems certain what their next move should be. Dante dumps me on the ground. He and Malky decide to make a run for it. They sprint to the back wall of the garden. There's a flash of light above the wall and I realise what they are doing. They are throwing their weapons away before they get caught red-handed.

Murdo shows no such urgency. He calmly steps under the shelter of his veranda, takes out a phone from his pocket and dials a number.

As the first shouts of 'Police!' are heard and the first door is kicked in by the invading force, Murdo speaks into the phone.

'Alan, sorry to wake you. We're going to need you tonight. Make some calls, but I should think we will be at Helen Street.'

Helen Street is Govan Police Station, the most secure station in the country. The one that appears on the news when a terrorist suspect has been arrested. Alan is Alan Cox, the McArthur family lawyer who kept me out of prison when I ran over Rose.

A lot of thoughts are running through my damaged head. Did Elise call the police? Or Carmen? Is Detective Millar behind the raid? Are they here to rescue me or have they finally decided to act on their fraud and murder investigation? Will this storm finally break the hellish heat of summer?

I am not thinking clearly. I decide to get up and run. I am certainly in breach of my parole conditions, even if I am the victim here. I don't trust the police. I don't trust the McArthurs. I have to know if Elise is safe. So I run.

In the confusion as officers start to spill into the garden, I scramble across to the side wall and find the door I was shown out of the last time I was here. A flash of lightning guides me.

I notice the gap in the tree line that surrounds the garden. One of the tall trees has gone. I think of the magpies and their nest and the noise they made and Murdo Smith's threat to cut the tree down just to get rid of them. He will stop at nothing to get what he desires. Elise won't be safe until she gets far away from him. I risk a look over my shoulder and see Murdo, his arms being held behind his back, handcuffs being slapped on his wrists.

The gate opens onto the road behind the property. On the other side of the wall, it's strangely serene. There's no police presence; they all came in the front door.

My beat-up Corsa sits parked on the pavement where Dante has abandoned it. The door opens. The keys are in the ignition. Either Dante knew no one in Milingavie would stoop so low as to steal this heap of junk, or they were quite happy for some unsuspecting offender to drive off with it and save them the job of discarding the evidence.

Rain batters the metal roof, a cacophony of drumming that matches the thunder inside my head. I turn the key. It starts first time and I thank the reliable old piece of junk out loud. I wipe the blood from my face with my coat sleeve and drive off into the night, leaving the flashing blue lights behind me. What will the rich folk in their gilded mansions think of their neighbour now? Murdo Smith will be the talk of the neighbourhood.

27

I am in no fit state to be driving. Blood is still coming out of my broken nose. I can feel my face swelling up and bruising and my right eye is starting to close over. Adrenalin and shock are running through my body. My hands tremble as I grip the steering wheel. Every change of gear brings a sharp pain to my ribcage as I reach down for the stick.

It's still too early for rush-hour traffic, so the roads remain clear. The windscreen wipers struggle to shift the deluge bombarding us from the dark clouds above. I run a couple of red lights, too impatient to wait when there is no other vehicle around. Squinting in my rear-view mirror, I see only clear road behind me. No one is following. Either I got away unseen, or the police are more interested in what they found in Murdo Smith's swimming pool.

When I emerge on the other side of the Clyde Tunnel, the morning sun has broken through. The clouds have split and moved off to the east. The rain is reduced to a mere heavy shower. The immediate storm has passed, although more are forecast to roll in from the Atlantic Ocean in the coming hours.

The roads are like rivers, a sheen of water through which I battle. The glare from the sun as it bounces up off the glistening road impairs my already-diminished vision. I drive by instinct, by necessity. My only thought at the moment is to get back to my flat. I am certain they have not been there. They did not know where Elise was. They were not just beating me up for kicks. But what if they had got word to someone else, another of Malky's endless squad of hatchet men?

I retch on the bile gathering in my throat, blood and mucus mixing and coagulating. I cough and spit and wipe my face and set loose another cascade of blood down the front of my shirt, already stained red. I feel faint and the car starts to drift to the other side of the road. I seem to be powerless to stop it. A shrill car horn pierces my fading consciousness and I jolt back upright. Focus, Cal, focus.

The thick blood gathers in my mouth again. I roll down the window and let the warm rain hit me as I spit out of the car to clear my throat.

I have no idea how fast or slow I am going; I just follow the white lines. I drive over the motorway and pass Bellahouston Park and Pollok Park and Queen's Park, not two hundred yards from where they held Elise in the flat that now lies empty. The road rises over the hill and dips down to Battlefield. I veer onto Prospecthill Road and Cathcart Road. I almost miss the turn for my own street as my mind slips away once more. The front wheel bounces over the pavement. I see a hubcap spinning away and realise it's one of mine. My foot hits the brake hard and I crash forward, banging my head against the steering wheel. I pull at my seatbelt and realise I failed to clip it into place when I left Murdo's house.

The car engine is still running. I leave it in the middle of the street, flinging the door open and I half-run, half-collapse out onto the wet road. I scramble around the front of the car and stagger to my front gate and up the path.

No one else is around. It must be six in the morning now.

Someone will be looking out of their window and will see me. If they are sensible, they will stay away.

I reach my door and only then can my eyes focus and see that it lies open. My relentless, staggering momentum comes to a screeching halt for the first time since the police showed up and enabled my escape.

I push the door, widening the opening, and peer inside. My right eye has closed up completely now. Myopically, I look into my hallway. I step forward and have the presence of mind to look at the back of the door. The locks are intact. No one has forced their way in. The only sounds are my hard breathing through my battered nose and the rain outside. Blood makes a strange rasping gurgle in my mouth as I move through to the living room.

No one is here. I turn towards the bedroom. The door is closed. Is Elise on the other side? Have they left her dead on my bed? Or is she sleeping peacefully, oblivious to what has happened?

I open the door. The room is empty. There is no one here.

* * *

My body is telling me to stop and rest and recover. If I do that, if I stop and stay here, I'm a dead man. Francis McArthur has too many friends. He will have known what Murdo was doing tonight. He knows what I have done. By now he will know about the police raid on Murdo's house.

I strip off my blood-soaked shirt and trousers in the bathroom and step into the shower. The cold water stings my cut face and body and the bottom of the bath turns pink. I find cotton wool pads in the cupboard and stick one up each nostril to stem the continuing flow of blood. I wipe the condensation from the mirror and Frankenstein's monster stares back at me. My face is swollen and purple. I pick up my shaving razor. The swelling above and below my right eye needs to be relieved; the pressure needs to be eased. I've seen this a thousand times in the aftermath of prison boxing matches.

I wipe the mirror clear again and hold my eye open with my left hand. With my right, I take the razor blade and draw it across the red raw skin at the top of my cheekbone. I bite down, grimace and swallow the scream of torture that is building. Fresh blood pours down my cheek. One more. I take a deep breath through my mouth and repeat the action, this time above my eye, underneath my eyebrow. The blood pours into my eye and blinds me. I drop the razor and collapse to the bathroom floor. I cannot contain the howl of pain that escapes me.

I sit on the floor and recover. I think back. Did Elise encourage me to go to the club to get me out of the way? Did she plan on leaving as soon as I was out the door? I reach up and use the sink to pull myself back up. A damp handcloth wipes away the blood. I open a jar of Vaseline and smear large gobs of it across the stinging cuts. It manages to quell the tide a little. I take plasters and bandages from the small first aid pack and throw them in a bag.

Fresh clothes on. I can't face eating anything even though I know I should. I manage to swallow a glass of tap water and taste the blood as it goes down. A last look around. There's nothing else worth taking apart from another change of clothes.

Before I leave, I pull the skirting board from the bedroom wall and take out the burner phone. A series of missed calls, all from the only number stored in the contacts. Millar has been trying to get in touch since three o'clock, since the end of my shift at the club. The end of my last shift at the Plein Soleil.

* * *

Warm sunlight has already dried away the storm water that fell less than an hour ago. Only isolated puddles remain. The streets have started to come alive, but only with the occasional car and early morning stroller. Only now do I realise it is Sunday morning, so the weekday rush hour has failed to materialise.

My car is still in the road where I abandoned it half an hour ago, door open, engine running. For the second time in only a matter of hours, the car thieves of Glasgow have rejected their golden opportunity. I try not to take it personally.

I throw my bag of clothes onto the front passenger seat. I have no destination in mind, only to get away from here. McArthur will be looking for me. Millar will be looking for me. I don't want to see either of them.

* * *

I drive cautiously, following the rules of the road, stopping at red lights, signalling at junctions, avoiding any unnecessary attention. There is no one tailing me. I join the motorway that takes me east, skirting across the south side of the city, before slinging me north. I have a notion of where to go, a childhood memory of a safe place where I can be anonymous. A haven where I can recover for a few days and allow the dust to settle. I have one last stop to make before I carry on my journey though. At the spaghetti junction of Bailleston Roundabout, I swing back onto the M8 and circle back towards Stepps.

The village is peaceful. Dog walkers go through the park; the village shops on the main road are only just lifting their shutters as I pass. I turn down Church Avenue and Whitehill Road and pull up at the house on the apex of the farm road.

If Elise got away from my house of her own free will, this is the only place I can think she would come. I sit in the car for five minutes. Nothing stirs. I have to go in.

I walk up the pathway. The bushes and trees have been trimmed back and the path has been weeded. I guess the kind neighbour has been as good as her word. I look in the window to the living room.

Madame Moreau is in her chair. She stares into the empty room as she did before, only this time she looks content, happy even, thinking of some far-off place in the past perhaps. There is no sign of anyone else.

'Hello again,' says the neighbour behind me. She stands at her front door, leaning out. 'She hasn't been back, if that's why you're here again.'

'I thought she may have come by this morning, early.'

She sees my face as I turn to her. 'Is she in trouble?'

'I hope not. Why do you think she might be?'

'Your face for one.' I self-consciously press the plasters and feel the blood that has oozed out from underneath.

'For one?'

'And the other men that have been here looking for her. Are they with you?'

'Big men? Black suits?'

'Exactly. They did not look like nice men. I wouldn't have told them anything, even if I did know something.'

'When did they come?'

'Yesterday afternoon. They let themselves in next door and searched the house. I checked on Delphine after they had left. They hadn't touched anything. Delphine hadn't even noticed they'd been there.'

A wave of relief washes over me. McArthur or Murdo or Tony was looking for her; they sent their goons here yesterday because they couldn't find her. Elise was safe in my flat yesterday afternoon. When they didn't find her, they came for me in the night. Wherever Elise has disappeared to, they don't have her.

'Thanks for looking after her. Her daughter will come back to see her one day soon, I hope.'

'I hope someone will come and look after her properly. Such a shame to see a life end this way.'

'It is,' I agree and start to back away.

'Do you have a phone number I can reach you on if there is any news? I have no contact for anyone who knows Delphine. No family, no friends.'

What harm can it do? I give her my phone number. 'If her daughter does stop by, please call me.'

'Of course.'

'Thank you.' I back away again.

'Do you mind me asking?' She stops me once more.

'What?'

'What happened to your face?'

'A long story.'

'Does it have anything to do with the missing daughter?'

'I hope not.'

This time she lets me depart, though she remains standing at her front door until my car starts and I pull away.

In ten minutes I'm back on the motorway and turning north, leaving the city behind me, but not out-running my troubles.

PART 4

CONTEMPT

28

A week later. Far from there.

Unzipping the front of the tent, I stick my head out into a mild Scottish summer morning. The air feels fresh and clean after the rain during the night. The succession of storms passed after two days and the heatwave has given way to a more traditional Scottish climate – warm without being hot, sunny spells mixing with passing clouds, and temperate rainfall.

My neighbours for the last three days packed up and left early this morning. I can see the square of flattened grass where their tent was pitched. It is peak holiday season, so newcomers will no doubt arrive during the day.

Back inside my small tent, I struggle out of the sleeping bag and into my jeans and a t-shirt. Tent life is not conducive to healing a cracked rib. Sleeping on the hard ground has only exacerbated the pain. I pick up my bag of basic toiletries and head over to the toilet block in the centre of the campsite.

Above the trees that run around the edge of the field, the Cairngorms mountain range towers into a blue sky. Tony was right. The open space is something to behold after a year locked up and a lifetime spent in urban confines.

* * *

A week ago, I drove north-east from Glasgow, turning at Perth and following the A9 to the village of Aviemore. By heading east, I caught up with the storm that had exploded over Murdo Smith's garden as it passed over Perthshire and on to the Cairngorms National Park. Rain poured down my windscreen and I struggled to see beyond the tail lights of the car in front. The road through the mountains became a perilous war of attrition, especially in my weakened state. Confident drivers, those familiar with the road, careered past, overtaking and casting a deluge of spray across my small car. I pulled into rest areas when I feared it would all become too much for me. It took me until late afternoon to arrive in the village of Aviemore.

It had changed a lot in the twenty years since we had come on a summer holiday and stayed in a small lodge. The main street looked the same, but at either end housing estates had been bolted on. I parked outside a new retail park and walked down the main street. Small shops selling tourist souvenirs mixed with outdoor activity shops. The small supermarket in the centre of the village was still there, as was the charming train station. A steam train ran every hour, taking tourists back in time. The traditional Cairngorm Hotel sat across the road, and behind it, in contrast, was the modern, large white tower block hotel that had always been completely out of keeping with the rest of the landscape.

From one of the outdoor shops, I picked the cheapest tent they had in stock, plus a sleeping bag and a roll mat. Five hundred yards north of the village centre, I turned into the campsite.

'You're in luck,' the owner behind the reception desk told me when I said I didn't have a booking. 'We just had a cancellation. Storms have put a few folk off this weekend. Afraid you've missed out on the best of the weather this year.'

£16 a night for a pitch without electricity, but with access to the campsite toilet block, including showers, washing machines and sinks. I could manage to spend a month or so here before all my money ran out, although I would have to limit myself to one meal a day. I paid for a week in advance.

On the first night the storm winds pulled at the guy ropes and I thought my tent would be blown away. Other tents weren't so lucky; the taller, bigger family ones weren't able to withstand the onslaught without sustaining tears and rips in the fabric.

Once the rain stopped, the main problem was the midges, which spawned in their millions and infested every corner of the site, swarming around any human brave enough to emerge and run the gauntlet.

I stayed on the campsite for most of the next few days, only taking the car into the village to purchase basic food, some coffee, cutlery and a small stove. I kept my phone turned off to preserve charge. I slept and recovered.

Now, a week later, I can recognise myself in the mirror once more. The swelling has gone down, the purple colouring has faded to a jaundice yellow. I cover the slits above and below my eye with plasters. My nose seems to have set straight, although I still make an unusual sniffing noise when I breathe through it. Sleeping on the ground hasn't helped my injured ribs, but if I don't make any sudden movements, the pain is bearable.

When I do venture away from my tent, I walk through the local countryside. Hikers dressed in professional gear look at me with disdain as they stride towards the foot of the surrounding hills and mountains. I stick to the paths in and around the surrounding woods in my worn jeans, grimy t-shirt and trainers. Yesterday, I took the car to Rothiemurchus Forest at the other end of the village and walked around Loch Morlich along rough track and paths. It is the perfect space to be alone and to clear my mind.

News on the car radio is my only contact with the world outside of the valley in which Aviemore nestles.

The arrest of local businessman and entrepreneur Francis McArthur, along with his long-term associate Murdo Smith and son Anthony, made the headlines on Monday morning. They were charged with various counts of fraud, business malpractice and arson. There was no mention of murder or manslaughter. There was no mention of Elise. There was nothing about a dead body floating in a swimming pool. The Head of Police Scotland read a statement at a press conference. There was no mention of Detective Simone Millar, only of the arrests being the culmination of a long and detailed investigation over a number of months into alleged malpractice. There was no mention of a further suspect, Callum Jackson, last seen fleeing the scene of Murdo Smith's arrest.

By Wednesday, there is an update. McArthur's lawyer, Alan Cox, reads a statement. His clients deny all charges against them. They are the victims of a sustained and deliberate attack from competitors looking to move in on their business. The news reporter ends her piece by announcing that the three men have been released on bail and are due to appear in court at a later date to face the charges against them.

I feel sick. They are out and free to roam the city looking for me again.

* * *

After a shower and a shave and an inspection of my healing wounds, I walk back to my tent, throw my toiletries inside and close it up.

My week's stay at the campsite ends today. I have to decide what to do. I am tempted to pay for another week's stay. Hiding away seems like a sensible thing to continue doing, but for how much longer?

I am in violation of my parole conditions. I have left my stated residence without informing the probation service. I am due at my next appointment with the probation officer in two weeks. If I don't show up for that, a recall notice could send me back to prison. Maybe I would be safer there.

I try to think what could have happened after I fled Murdo's house. How could they have explained away the body floating in the pool? There was no mention of Malky Thomson, or Dante or Patrick. Maybe they took the fall for the murder rap to save their boss? Arson was mentioned, but nothing about the charred body in the fire on Woodlands Road.

From my car, I take the burner phone that has been switched off for the last week. I use a walk into the village to decide what to do next. I could hand myself in and seek the protection of the police. They would only grant me that if I agreed to be a witness against McArthur.

Following the path that runs parallel to the main road, I turn the burner phone on. There's a rapid flurry of beeps as a week's worth of messages and missed calls filters through. All from the same number, all from Millar. There is no other way forward for me but to call her and find out what is going on. I can't hide forever.

I don't bother reading the messages or listening to the voicemail. I dial the number and hold the phone to my ear as it rings.

She picks up on the third ring.

'Where the hell are you?' Millar screams through the phone.

'Lying low.'

'You're a wanted man.'

'I figured I would be.'

'You need to get back here so I can protect you.'

'I heard they're out on bail. The last thing I want to do is go back to meet them in the street.'

'You need to understand, the police are looking for you too. Why did you run?'

'People with guns make me nervous.'

'Running makes you look guilty.'

'I heard reports on the news – no mention of the dead body in the swimming pool, no mention of the dead body in the burnt-out building, no mention of me. Just fraud and dodgy business dealings. Makes it sound like the worst they did was bad accounting. What's going on?'

'There's not enough to charge them with the body yet. They're claiming the guy in the pool was found like that, an accidental drowning.'

'You believe that? That guy was the one I left in the flat when I got Elise out. They killed him for not doing his job.'

'Of course I don't believe them, but that's not enough to press charges. We're investigating the circumstances. We need time to make it stick, then we can add the charges on to the existing ones.'

'In the meantime, they walk around free?'

'We've got Francis, Murdo and Malky under surveillance twenty-four hours a day. They can't make a move without us seeing it.'

'What about the others? Tony, Dante and the rest?'

'We don't have the resources to follow all of them, all of the time. That's why it's easier if we know where you are.'

'They beat me up pretty good.'

'You should have hung around and pressed charges then, instead of running. CCTV picked up your car leaving the house right after we showed up.'

'Did you tell your colleagues I'm on your side?'

'I'm trying, but you need to prove that to them. Come back and be a witness against McArthur. Make a statement about what you saw at the nightclub, in East Kilbride and at the flat. It all adds up to a stronger case.'

I reach the top of the main street. It's busy with families, elderly couples, tourists and walkers coming in and out of the various shops and cafés. I turn down some steps and take a short path that runs next to a small river, under a tunnel and out the other side. A single-track road continues parallel to the main street. On the other side, fields stretch away to the foot of the Cairngorms mountains. Sheep and cows are in the fields. One cow near the fence stops chewing the grass and watches me approach.

'What about Elise? Have you found her?'

'We're not looking for her. There's no evidence she was ever taken. No one has reported her missing.'

'You're still saying that? I told you I found her tied up in a flat.'

'Then where is she? Where did you take her?'

'I left her at my place. When I got back, she was gone. I don't know if they took her or if she got away.'

Millar doesn't respond straight away. I hear her voice, muffled; she's covering the phone and talking to someone else.

She comes back to me. 'I need to go. Listen to me, Cal. You need to get back here and hand yourself in, before the police catch up with you – or worse, before McArthur does. Running makes you look bad to us and him. They are going to try to tie up any loose ends that they think might hurt them in a trial. You already betrayed them once, they won't want you to tell your story to the police.'

'So you believe me now, about Elise?'

'How many times, Cal? It's not about what I believe. It's about what we can prove against them.' A pause. 'Get back here. And Cal, take care. They will be hunting for you.'

She hangs up. I'm left staring at the cow, who goes back to chewing the grass with disinterest.

29

Millar hasn't filled me with confidence, but my options are limited. I concede she's right. Hiding out here in the Highlands solves nothing. The problem is not going to disappear with time. The police are after me, which means they already know I have violated my parole. McArthur is after me and won't leave me alone. I know too much about Elise.

To top it all off, I am almost out of money and I can't think of any way to get more. Wild camping in the wilderness is about the only option left open to me, but it's not a viable long-term plan.

The single-track road takes me all the way to the southern end of Aviemore. I come out at the roundabout. One corner is occupied by a new travel hotel, the other by an Italian restaurant that I remember from our family holiday. Inside I can see the red and white checked tablecloths and the old pictures that cover the walls. I remember sitting at a table by the window with Dad and Mum and Marie. I was twelve years old. They served a kid's buffet and we kept going back, over and over again, for more pasta and cheese pizza until we were stuffed. Funny the little things you remember, like the old couple sitting at the table next to us, tutting and throwing looks at Mum and Dad for allowing their kids to make so much noise. Or the slice of pizza I dropped on the floor, cheese-side down. Or the unlimited ice-cream for dessert, from a machine. I topped mine with chocolate and marshmallows and smothered it in strawberry sauce. It seems like I am looking through the window to a different world now – someone else's life, someone else's past.

I follow the pavement back to the centre of the village and see families on their summer holidays and wonder where those kids will end up in the future. Will any of them end up on the run from the police and a criminal gang?

A shrill whistle from the train station makes me turn and look across the road. The main train from Edinburgh, stopping on its way to Inverness, is pulling away. Those that have just alighted are spilling out of the picturesque station, a fresh collection of hillwalkers and campers arriving to tackle the summits of the Cairngorms.

He sticks out like a sore thumb. He is the only one not carrying a rucksack or pulling a suitcase behind him. Black jeans, black t-shirt, camouflage-green jacket. I duck behind the wall that separates the front of the Cairngorm Hotel from the road. Dante turns and looks across the road in my direction. He doesn't see me. He carries on looking around and then decides to start walking into the village, scanning the people he passes. I am grateful for the influx of visitors that have destroyed the quaint charm of Aviemore and turned it into a crowded tourist destination. They give me cover.

Dante works his way along the street. I shadow him on the opposite side of the road, following twenty yards behind him, keeping him in sight.

How did he find me? Millar didn't know where I was. She mentioned CCTV. Are there enough road cameras to have tracked my route north? I stopped for petrol at the services in Perth; was I on camera paying in the station? I have kept my phone off most of the time, only switching it on occasionally, and I have called or messaged no one. They can't have traced the signal. I have paid cash for everything so there are no credit cards leaving an electronic trail to be followed.

Has someone betrayed me? Who could have guessed I would come here? My heart sinks. It might have been my sister or my mother. If they knew I had headed north, they could have pieced together where I was going. Marie would remember the family holiday. There wasn't anywhere else up this way that we had been before. My own family could have given away my location.

Dante stops at the Tourist Information centre, a small unit in the shopping arcade that runs along one side of the main street. He opens the door and goes inside. I sit on a low wall that runs behind a bus stop that provides me with cover and wait for him to emerge. I can't see inside the centre. I imagine him asking the assistant where someone might stay in Aviemore on a small budget. She smiles and obliges him with the obvious answer – pitching a tent at a campsite. *And where are the campsites around Aviemore that you would recommend staying at?* She takes out a map of the local area and points out the handful of locations, two to the south of the village, one to the north. *Much obliged.* Dante thanks her and pockets the map. *Mind if I take this?*

He exits and looks up and down the busy street. He looks straight ahead at the supermarket across the road, steps forward to the pedestrian crossing and waits for the traffic lights to stop the constant stream of cars going up and down the main street.

I crouch down further as the green man lights up and Dante crosses the road. He walks straight into the supermarket. Perhaps he's hungry after a long train journey. Perhaps he's looking for more information. It's the main grocery store in the village; everyone who stays in Aviemore visits the shop at some point.

Whatever his reason, it's my opportunity to get past him without being seen and get back to the campsite. If I wasn't sure about following Millar's instruction earlier to return to Glasgow and face the music, Dante's presence has made up my mind. Stay here and I'm a dead man. Head back and I've got a fifty-fifty chance of scraping through. Suppressing the urge to start sprinting through the crowds, drawing attention to myself, I walk at a brisk pace, passing the front of the supermarket and carrying on. After the roundabout at the top of the street, beyond the holiday crowds, I break into a jog along the clear pavement.

* * *

The tent is left behind. It lasted a week, but I have no plans to take a camping trip in the near future. I collect my few belongings, throw them into the Corsa and leave. I don't stop at reception to let the owner know I won't be back.

The needle on the petrol gauge is hovering around the bottom of its arc. The only petrol station is at the end of the main street. I will have to risk going through the village and filling up and hope I'm not spotted. I don't know where the next petrol station is to the south. It could be more than twenty-five or fifty miles away, and I don't want to end up stranded in the mountains.

I cast a wary eye around at the faces passing by as I drive down the main street, expecting to find Dante staring at me at any moment. There is no sign of him. Beyond the train station, I pull into the petrol station. No other cars are on the forecourt. I pull up to the pump furthest from the road, hidden from view, and fill the tank. At the desk inside I use the last of my cash to pay for the fuel, plus a bottled drink and a packaged sandwich for the drive.

I pull away, again looking up and down the street. No sign of him.

I am in the clear as I reach the roundabout that marks the southern boundary of Aviemore. Past that it's a straight drive down the A9 and then motorway from Perth all the way back to Glasgow.

A large fuel tanker is negotiating its way around the roundabout. I stop and wait for it to pass. I take a last look at the Italian restaurant. It's a shame I didn't get the chance to go there for a meal while I was here. I don't have many happy memories of family life before it all started to go wrong. This is one of them.

The door to the restaurant opens and Dante walks out. He's licking an ice cream cone. He stops with the cone halfway to his mouth. Our eyes meet. The ice cream drips down the side of the cone and over his large hand. Panic rises.

The road ahead is finally clear. A car behind me honks its horn. I look in the rear-view mirror at a red BMW, driven by an exasperated-looking man. I am frozen in inaction until Dante suddenly leaps forward, tossing his cone to one side, vaulting a low wall and diving across the road, heedless of any traffic. He grabs at the handle of the driver-side door. I come to my senses, shift into gear and floor the accelerator. The Corsa's engine screams in protest. I pull away and leave Dante in my wake, grasping at air. The driver in the red BMW blasts his horn again, this time at Dante, who stands in the middle of the road looking after my disappearing tail lights.

I've made it. He might call ahead and let McArthur and Murdo know I have been spotted, but for the moment I am safe.

At the turning onto the A9, I sit and watch a large trail of cars file past, stuck in a queue behind a slow-moving caravan on the single-carriageway road. I wait to join the back of the queue. In my rear-view mirror I see the red BMW approach. The angry man has caught up with me. The car gets closer and my gut tells me something is wrong. The car stops close to my rear bumper. Too close. It dunts into the back of me, threatening to push me out into the passing traffic. I look closer. The angry man who was in the driver's seat has been replaced by Dante. He pushes me forward again, into the path of the oncoming cars.

One car has left a slight gap. I slam the Corsa into gear, drop the clutch and spin out, slotting into the train of cars. Dante can't get out at the same time. He has to wait. The stream of cars continues behind me. I am round the bend and out of sight before the red BMW is able to pull out.

The A9 is a major road made up of stretches of single carriageway interspersed with dualled sections to allow faster-moving cars to overtake the slow-moving freight trucks. It's also one of the most dangerous roads in Scotland, with regular fatal accidents caused by impatient drivers attempting risky overtakes on blind bends. The campaign to have the entire length of the A9 dualled has been going on for years. I am grateful it has been delayed by bureaucratic indifference because the single carriageway offers me my only chance to stay ahead of Dante. In a straight race, his stolen BMW will eat my old Corsa up alive.

I try to remember where the first section of dual carriageway begins. I've got a few miles yet. I check the rear-view mirror. I can see ten cars back in the queue. No sign of the red BMW.

I think about pulling off the road at one of the occasional side roads, but if Dante sees me turn off, I'm a sitting duck. I just have to hope I can keep a few cars between us until we reach Perth and the busier traffic and multiple routes will offer more of a chance to evade him. It's about ninety miles to Perth, about an hour and a half's driving time. It's going to feel a lot longer.

30

When the train of cars hits the first stretch of dual carriageway there is a rush to pull out and get past the slow-moving caravan. I nip out, put my foot to the floor and push the Corsa to its limit, urging it to pick up the pace. Ideally, I will clear the caravan and get away, while Dante, too far back to clear the other cars, remains stuck, crawling at a snail's pace, for another spell of single carriageway. If that happens, I've got a good chance of making a clean getaway.

The engine complains as I insist on getting every ounce of horsepower from it. The chassis rattles around me, shuddering and jarring as I propel it forward against its will. I try to ignore it and keep my foot down on the accelerator. I risk a look behind. I can see a red car in the outside lane. It is behind three other cars. Dante is flashing his lights and blasting his horn to try to clear them out of the way. He knows what I am trying to do. If he doesn't clear the caravan this time, he knows I will be gone down the road.

The signpost flashes by. *Dual Carriageway Ends. 1 mile.* I am stuck behind a small Fiat whose driver is in no rush to clear the caravan. Incrementally, we are gaining.

Half a mile to go until the road narrows back to a single lane. I am alongside the rear end of the caravan. The red BMW is still stuck behind two other cars. I try not to be impatient. I try not to use my horn or my lights, but I do ride right on the bumper of the Fiat in front, urging it to go faster.

Quarter of a mile. My car is shaking. Each shuddering jolt shoots another dose of pain through the broken rib in my side. I can see the end of the dual carriageway. It's coming up on us fast. The Fiat finally makes it past the caravan and pulls in. I stay in the outside lane as the arrows painted on the road tell me to move in. I keep my foot down. With ten metres to spare, the Fiat driver sees what is about to happen and slows down to let me pull in in front of him. I am so elated I punch the steering wheel and shout at my old Corsa in delight.

Other cars that overtook the caravan are long gone, bigger engines sending them well on their way. I have got some clear road. I look behind me in time to see the red BMW swerve in behind the caravan. Dante didn't make it. I am home free.

Then my heart sinks.

A long straight opens up before me, dipping down into the valley and then climbing again on the other side. There is no traffic coming towards me in the opposite lane. In the rear-view mirror, the caravan comes round the bend. The red BMW follows. Dante sees his opportunity straight away and swoops out from behind the caravan into the oncoming lane. In a flash he's past the caravan and alongside the Fiat behind me. The driver of the Fiat looks bewildered as the BMW roars past, and then brakes as Dante pulls alongside me. As much as I stamp down on the accelerator and urge the Corsa forward, this race is no contest.

I look across at Dante. He's staring back at me. We're doing ninety miles an hour; my car is straining, he is cruising. He has one hand on the wheel. In the other, he raises a gun and points it in my direction. His passenger-side window opens. He won't do it, will he? He can't shoot me while we drive along. He's just threatening me. He thinks I will be scared into stopping and pulling over and then he can bundle me into his stolen car and deliver me to McArthur.

We have left the Fiat behind, the driver sensibly backing off and letting these two idiots drive like maniacs without him.

My only option is to keep going. I look from Dante to the road. I need someone to come the other way.

The window next to my head disintegrates into pieces before the noise of the gunshot registers. I throw one hand up to my face and duck down, while trying to keep the Corsa heading in a straight line on the road.

Dante is yelling something at me over the howling rush of wind between our cars. I get the gist. *Pull over. It's no use running. There is no escape.*

I am in shock. He actually shot at me. I have never been shot at before.

I believe he'll do it again. I believe he'll kill me if he has to.

The gun is still pointing at me. There's no glass between us now. In that split-second of desperation, reckless instinct takes over.

I yank the steering wheel to the right and the Corsa swerves wildly across the white line and into the side of the BMW. Dante is caught off guard. The gun drops and he throws both hands onto his steering wheel as our cars lock together. He swerves away and I steer back into my lane.

The Corsa won't take another hit like that. A new harsh screeching noise comes from the front tyre. I've damaged my car more than the BMW.

Dante is cursing at me and scrambling around for something. He's trying to pick the gun up, while driving at a hundred miles an hour.

The road starts to rise. On the uphill slope it starts to turn again, the long straight coming to an end.

The driver of the articulated lorry, from his higher viewpoint, sees the BMW on the wrong side of the road before the distracted Dante notices him. The furious blast of his loud horn fills the valley, accompanied by the squeal of brakes as he slams his foot down hard.

Dante sees him coming, but he only has time to throw the BMW to the right to avoid a head-on collision. He doesn't have time to check what lies on the far side of the road.

It happens in an instant. The flash of red hits the crash barrier and flips into the air. I lose sight of it as the lorry comes between us. There's the sound of screeching brakes everywhere, including my own. Tyre smoke fills the air. Over the din, the sound of a heavy impact, the shattering of metal and glass. I pull over onto a verge. My hands are shaking, I am gripping the wheel so tightly my knuckles are white. There's a queue of cars backed up behind the stationary lorry. Drivers are jumping out of their cars and rushing over to the side of the road.

The Fiat pulls up behind me. The driver gets out and comes to my car. He leans in the shattered window.

'You okay, mate? What was that idiot doing? Why didn't you just let him pass you?'

I try to open the door. It won't budge. It's dented from the impact with the BMW, bent out of shape and jammed shut. The Fiat driver goes around and opens the passenger door. I climb over the gear stick and he helps me out.

'I don't think he'll have survived that,' he says.

My head is pounding, the adrenalin still pumping. I stagger across the road and around the back of the lorry. The driver is on his phone. 'Police and ambulance please. There's been a traffic accident.'

I get to the barrier where the other drivers have gathered. Some have their phones out, filming and taking photos rather than calling anyone.

On the other side of the barrier is a twenty-foot drop. At the bottom of the drop there are pine trees and rocks. The red BMW is nestled on a slab of rock at the base of two tall trees, lying on its roof. The car is crushed flat. There is debris lying around it, broken shards of glass and metal and fibre glass. Smoke rises up from the wreckage.

There is no chance Dante has survived.

'They will be here in ten minutes.' The lorry driver stands at my shoulder. 'I told them not to bother sending the chopper. He's not going to need it. What the hell was he thinking? There's a dual carriageway another two miles up the road. How much of a rush was he in?'

Others continue to gawp over the side of the road. I start walking back towards my car. I get in the passenger side and climb over into the driver's seat before anyone notices.

The Fiat driver and the lorry driver start to shout at me.

'You can't just drive off! The police are on their way.'

I turn the key. The engine turns over but doesn't catch.

'Come on, you bastard,' I shout. 'Not now.'

It catches and sparks into life.

The lorry driver makes a desperate grab at me through the shattered window, and pulls back as he gets a shard of glass through his hand for his trouble.

There is a horrible screeching, grinding noise from the front of my car, but the old Corsa is made of stern stuff and it's still going.

I drive away from the scene of Dante's death.

No one follows me.

A mile up the road I hear sirens and a police car flies past, heading towards the accident site. Someone will have taken a note of my registration plate. Traffic cameras will follow my movement.

I don't care. I am getting back to Glasgow. There is no hiding from McArthur if he wants to find me. I know that now. And they will stop at nothing to get me.

My only hope is to face my problems head-on.

31

The Corsa miraculously makes it all the way back to Mount Florida and the parking space outside my flat. It makes a sad sound of defeat as I pull up. It won't start again after today.

Millar is waiting for me. She steps out of her car and joins me on the pavement.

'Is he dead?' I ask her as she pushes open the gate for me and follows me up the short path to my front door.

'On impact.'

I get inside and slump onto the sofa. Millar is on her phone. 'I've got him,' she says to whoever is on the other end of the call, and hangs up.

'What now?' I ask.

'Now you don't have many options. You either go on your own or you help us put McArthur away.' She sits down on the chair next to me. 'How's your face?'

'How does it look?'

'Just as well you weren't a looker before. Who did it?'

'Malky Thomson, on Murdo Smith's orders. You interrupted them just as it was getting interesting. I was about to start fighting back.'

'If you press charges we can add them to the case. We could use them to get Malky to flip and turn against his boss.'

I'm incredulous. How can she still not get it? 'He'll never betray McArthur. You must know that by now.'

'The threat of serious jail time can focus a mind.'

'He'll die before telling you anything. Prison won't scare him.'

Millar shrugs. 'I can make the car crash disappear so long as you co-operate with our investigation.'

'There were witnesses.'

'No one else was hurt; no one else damaged their car. There are no insurance claims to be investigated. The traffic police have their statements. A red BMW was driving erratically for over ten miles, harassing other drivers, taking risks to overtake on the wrong side of the road. The driver pushed his luck too far and paid the price. Turns out the car was stolen, so there's not much sympathy for the deceased. And Dante had no family that we know of. I don't think McArthur will push for a further police investigation.'

'What about the gun he shot at me with?'

'What gun?' Millar feigns ignorance. 'From what I hear, things got pretty badly smashed up in the end – not much left of anything.' So it's like that. 'All you have to do is testify to what you know, put what you've already told me on record.'

'I haven't told you anything you didn't already know.'

'I told you before, a case like this, it's not one big revelation. Save that for the movies. It's all the little pieces of evidence that build the case up. You are a part of that.'

'And Carmen Carmichael?' That gets Millar's attention. I haven't seen her since the night I snooped around the offices at Plein Soleil and learned that the club manager had also been talking to Millar. 'Why do you need me? She can tell you all you need to know.'

Millar regains her composure. 'Carmen has been feeding us information for a while. Long before you came along. Financial records about the club. Comings and goings. But she's not an insider, she's not part of the inner circle, the family. We also can't be sure if she is playing us straight or toying with us. She owes

McArthur, she might be too loyal to him. When I approached you, we didn't know you would be sent to work at her club. Our hope was you could get us closer to the centre, to the real power. We were getting there, but things moved faster than we expected. Even then, you help our case. You know about corroboration, right?'

I remember it from my trial a year ago. Unique to Scots Law, corroboration means any significant piece of evidence must have two independent sources to support it, before it can be admitted into evidence, like two independent witnesses. The prosecutor had plenty of corroborating witnesses to send me down after the car accident. All of Rose Black's friends saw what happened.

Millar continues, 'So, we have Carmen and we have you to corroborate her information. She's agreed to be a source at the trial, but wants to remain an anonymous witness. Hopefully the judge agrees.'

'I don't have that luxury?'

'You don't have anything to bargain with. Besides, I think you've blown your cover already.'

'I've hardly told you anything useful.'

'Don't be so sure about that. Maybe you haven't seen the latest headlines?'

She takes out her phone, taps the screen and waits for something to load. Then she hands it to me.

It's a BBC News webpage: "First Minister Questioned by Police in Fraud Trial". Underneath the headline, a subheading: "Two councillors in South Lanarkshire also quizzed in investigation into McArthur Business Empire".

Millar watches me read the screen and lets me take in the details. 'Your trip to East Kilbride, the meeting at the nightclub. Little pieces in the puzzle. Your statements tie in to other witnesses and paper trails. If one piece goes missing, we can't complete the jigsaw.'

I start to see the bigger picture. This goes way beyond the club and my small part in it. It reaches government and politics and corruption on a national scale. This could actually bring McArthur down.

It dawns on me. 'The night you turned up at Murdo Smith's house, the night I was taken there. You weren't there to rescue me. That was just coincidence.'

'You're important to me, but you're not that important. Call it luck.'

'It didn't feel lucky.'

'We ID'd the body in the flat that burned down. It belonged to Bilal Yousaf, Billy to everyone who knew him. Owner of the convenience store that burned down beneath him. The last landlord to be holding out in the block that had been bought up by various McArthur front businesses. We've got the paperwork to show it. We've got other members of the family testifying to the threats Billy received. And we've got a witness to Tony McArthur driving around with petrol cans in the back of his car on the day of the fire. Little pieces. It was enough to tip the balance for us and the Procurator Fiscal to move ahead. I wasn't at Murdo's house. I got to put the handcuffs on Francis McArthur himself.'

'I bet you enjoyed that.'

'Two years of work. I'm not going to lie, I thought it would be a sweet moment to see his face. We hit his offices and his home. Piles of paperwork, laptops, computers and phones seized. Everything we need to convict, we have. But he didn't give me the satisfaction. He looked at me with contempt, like he knew all along this was coming and that none of it would mean anything. He already has a way out of this, I can tell. Then you disappear and some of our jigsaw pieces disappear with you and it's all up in the air again. I didn't even get to pop the champagne.'

Millar stands up to leave. I pull myself up to follow her along the hallway.

'You stay here. I'm putting an officer in front of your house. McArthur isn't stupid enough to try anything now that the heat is on but just in case, this should dissuade him. I'll be in touch once I know more, we'll get you down to the station and you can make a statement.'

She reaches for the handle on the door to let herself out. I reach forward and put my hand on it first to stop her. She turns to look at me.

'There's one piece of the jigsaw you still haven't mentioned.'

'Cal, that's where corroboration becomes a pain in the ass. You're the only one who's said anything about Elise. Either she comes forward and presses charges, or—'

'Or you find her body in the River Clyde?'

Millar gives me another of her shrugs. 'We don't need her to make our case. McArthur goes down either way, with or without another charge.'

'I thought you would care more.'

'I've got enough on my plate.'

I could tell her about the baby, about Tony's indiscretion, about the plans for a forced abortion, but it's not going to sway Millar. Her case is made; she has her man. She thinks I was beaten up because they found out I was feeding the police information for their fraud case. I won't spoil it for her by telling her they only wanted to know where Elise was. I take my hand off the door handle and step out of the way.

Millar opens the door and stops.

My sister gets a fright as the door opens just as she is about to knock. Her immaculate eyeliner is smudged and her eyes are red. The glowing tan from her honeymoon has drained away. She looks from me to Millar and back to me again.

'I think you guys have some catching up to do,' says Millar, and she slides out of the door.

Marie watches her go, staring daggers at Millar's back as she leaves. When Millar gets to her car and gets in, Marie turns back to me.

'What the hell have you done, Cal?'

32

'You're talking to the police?'

'They wanted to talk to me.'

We have moved into my living room. The atmosphere is frosty. I felt more comfortable with Millar opposite me than I do with my sister leaning over me, hands clenched, face red, anger brimming near the surface.

'Dante's dead. A car crash this morning.' Marie is on the verge of tears again. I had no idea she was that close to her husband's henchmen. 'Tony said he was searching for you, trying to find you.'

'I had to get away.'

'You disappeared. Tony told me you vanished, left them all to be arrested while you took off over the garden wall.'

'That's not really the full story.' I tilt my face to the light and point at the yellow skin and cut marks on my face.

'What happened?'

'Malky did that, while Dante held me. On the orders of Murdo Smith and your new father-in-law.'

That gets a reaction, forces her to pause. 'I don't believe you. Why would they do that to you?'

'It might be better if you ask Tony.'

I haven't seen my sister since I found out her new husband had been having an affair with Elise, since I rescued Elise from the flat where McArthur was holding her, threatening to force her to abort her child. I don't want to tell her the truth. If I do, I know we will never be close again. Maybe it's already too late for us to ever be close again, but I can't bring myself to inflict that sort of pain on my little sister.

From my silence, Marie draws the wrong conclusion.

'Is it because you were talking to the police? Was it you who informed them about Francis and the business?'

She's half right.

'The police approached me after I got out of prison. They saw me at your wedding. They wanted me to take the job that McArthur offered me and use my family connection to get inside the business, give them information.'

'And you did it for them?'

'I didn't have a choice. I'm an offender out on parole. I took the job and told them nothing. I didn't have access to anything important. I told them about a couple of meetings at the nightclub, about the people that came. Enough to keep them off my back. That's all.'

A half-truth. Marie looks at me. It's like we are back living in the same house as teenagers. She's trying to guess if I am telling the truth or not. Like when I used to wind her up by hiding the TV remote or taking her phone or when I found out her Facebook password and posted on her account. She doesn't have Mum or Dad to call on now. She has to figure it out for herself. Just like back then, there is no trust between us.

'Why didn't you tell Tony the police were using you?'

'How could I? They would throw me back in prison. I figured if I played along a little bit, I could keep the police off my back and at the same time not betray Tony or Francis.' Now I'm lying to her. I told Millar everything that I saw and didn't care about the consequences for Tony or anyone else.

'But if you didn't tell the police anything, why did Malky beat you up?'

'Maybe they thought I was the one who had been informing on them.' I omit the truth – that they were looking for her husband's pregnant mistress.

'After everything Francis and Tony have done for you, how could you even think of betraying them?'

I look at her. I can see in her eyes that Tony has told her about the accident, about Rose Black, about how I managed to avoid doing time in prison after pleading guilty.

'Maybe you don't know your husband as well as you think you do.' It's as close to a confession about Tony's indiscretion as I am going to come to with Marie.

'I know his father kept you out of jail. You owe them both, and this is how you repay them?'

She throws her arms up in the air and then her resolve seems to collapse. She slumps down on the sofa next to me but not touching me. We're just not that close anymore, but she can still let her mask slip in front of me. All at once, she's my little sister again, talking to me like she's just got home after a bad date and needs to vent.

'It's been awful. The police have been in our house. They took Tony's computer, his phone; they emptied his office. Tony's not allowed to leave the country. He says it's all just a misunderstanding that will be cleared up eventually.'

'Is that all he has told you?'

She wipes her hands across her face, smudging her make-up further. 'He won't tell me anything else, but I've read the news. Is it really serious?'

'About as serious as it gets.'

She knows more than she is willing to admit to me. I can still read her. She knows McArthur has done some serious wrongdoing. What she can't figure out is how much Tony is involved. That's the reason she's here, not to check on my welfare.

'They're talking about arson, bribery, fraud.'

'Murder,' I add.

She should look more shocked than she does. She already knew it.

'So why was that police officer here?'

'Checking I was okay.'

She eyes me with suspicion. 'Where did you go?'

'Aviemore. You remember we went there on a family holiday?'

It dawns on her. She's not stupid. 'You drove back today?'

'This morning.'

'And Dante?'

'Crashed after chasing me down the A9 and trying to shoot me.'

'Why would he shoot at you?'

'You have to ask your father-in-law. I imagine he had orders to either bring me back alive so McArthur could deal with me, or if not, leave me dead in a ditch in some remote part of the Highlands.'

'I don't believe you. I won't. This is like some sort of nightmare.'

'I'm not asking you to believe me. You need to talk to Tony. But I did warn you, Marie. I told you not to get involved with the McArthurs. I told you not to marry him. If Tony told you about the accident, then he should also have told you the price that his kind gesture cost us. It cost Dad his dignity, his pride, his morality. It made him McArthur's puppet and in the end, it killed him.'

'You could have told me this before I got married to Tony.'

'Would it have made a difference? Would it have stopped you marrying him?'

'Does Mum know?'

'About the accident? She knows how Dad became worn down after it, about McArthur using him, about the money we had to pay him.'

Her anger is building again. In some ways it's reassuring to see she still has some fire left within her, that she's not beaten down and defeated yet. Maybe she will stand up to Tony after all.

Marie gets up. 'Tony wants to see you.'

'So that's why you're really here. You're his messenger now.'

'Will you come with me?'

Even if the prospect of facing Tony McArthur was one I was looking forward to, after the last week and the drive today, I'm in no fit state to go anywhere. All I want is to lie down in a comfy bed.

'Tell Tony if he wants to see me, he knows where to find me. He can come himself, instead of sending his wife to do his dirty work for him.'

She slaps me hard across the face. My cheek stings. She's hit me before, plenty of times, when we were kids, play fighting, wrestling on the sofa. We've had serious fights before, as we got older and hormones came into play and we tested each other's nerves and boundaries growing up in the small house together. This is different. This hurts more than all those other times put together. Behind this slap, there is real hatred. I can feel it in the stinging aftermath, I can see it in her face, I can taste it in the still air between us.

'Marie, I—'

Before I can apologise she turns and leaves, slamming the living room door behind her. The front door bangs shut a moment later. The whole flat shakes.

I walk through to the bedroom. The bed is unmade, the duvet crumpled where it was left a week ago when Elise slept in it.

I lie down and can still smell Elise on the pillow and the sheets. I close my eyes and fall asleep straight away, even though it's still early in the evening and the sunlight is blazing through the window.

I don't dream, I don't think of anyone. There is only black.

33

They come for me during the night. I don't hear them. I don't wake until strong hands pin me to the bed. There is no point in struggling. I lie still and offer no resistance as I am flipped onto my front. My hands are pulled behind my back and cable-tied together. Before I can see anything, a cloth bag is pulled over my head.

They pull me up onto my feet. One strong person has done all this and not made a sound. A second person joins them. They take an arm each and march me out of the room and down the hallway to the front door.

Outside a dog barks somewhere. Robbed of my sight, I listen. Hard breathing, heavy footsteps, a car engine running.

Hands push my head down and throw me into the back of the car. The people sit either side of me. Doors shut. The car pulls away; no squeal of tyres, no loud engine revs. They are calm and professional. They have done this sort of thing before.

No one has spoken a word.

I try to follow the route, feeling each turn and change of direction, sensing each stop for traffic lights and junctions. It's no use. They could be driving around in circles. After five minutes I give up, sit back and try to remain calm. Wherever they are taking me, there is nothing I can do to stop them.

After half an hour, the car stops and the engine is turned off. Doors open on either side of me. I am pulled out of the car and onto tarmac. Hands take hold of my arms again and march me across the hard ground. A car park of some kind? Or waste ground?

A heavy metal chain is pulled through a winch and a metal shutter rises. We go from exterior to interior, from fresh night air to damp and musty air. The tarmac under my feet changes to smooth concrete. Someone lets go of the metal chain and the shutter rumbles and clatters closed behind us. The noise echoes around. We are in a large, empty space. I am marched across the floor and turned around and pushed down onto a plastic chair. There is a strong light coming from somewhere that bleeds through the cloth covering my face.

Another set of footsteps walks across the floor, a strident, purposeful gait. They stop in front of me. The two who have brought me here now take up position behind me. The cloth sack is lifted from my head.

My eyes blink as they adjust to the bright light that shines straight into them. The figure in front of me is silhouetted, their face in shadow. When he speaks, I recognise him instantly. Turns out it is not just the son who wants to see me.

'A good man died today because of you,' says Francis McArthur. He steps forward and leans over me.

'I'm sorry about Dante, but it was his own fault, not mine.' I'm not that sorry. Dante was trying to shoot me when he crashed.

McArthur pulls another chair towards me and sits himself down. I take in my surroundings. We are inside a vast empty warehouse. The bright light is on a stand in front of me. The floor is bare grey concrete, the walls white and plain with steel pillars every few metres. The roof is slanted corrugated panels and from it hang air conditioning ducts and cable trays, snaking across the ceiling, stark and functional and industrial. The monotony of the bare white walls and grey concrete floor are only broken by a broom resting against the wall in the far corner, a pile of dust, dirt and bits of glass and metal shards gathered around it. Whoever last used this place gave it one final sweep before bailing out.

Francis smiles at me and leans back in his chair and crosses his legs. 'I underestimated you, Callum. You always were trouble, even when Anthony used to run around the streets with you. Even when you were both teenagers and started drinking and chasing girls together. Even after I kept you out of jail after the accident. I should have realised how much trouble you could still be, but I like to give people a second chance. I told you that at the wedding, remember? You've had your fair share of tragedy, losing your father, ending up in prison. For some reason, I thought there still might be a chance for you to make something of yourself, if you were given the right opportunity. When Anthony set his heart on marrying your sister, I thought you might take the institution of family seriously, that it might mean something to you.

'Murdo told me to be careful. He warned me against bringing you in. He told me to keep you at arm's length, that you would stay away and it would be better left like that. But family means something to me. It means *everything* to me. Not just blood relatives, but extended family and loyal friends. So I went against Murdo.' He stops and laughs to himself. 'You'd think I would know by now not to go against Murdo's better judgement, but here we are.

'You have thrown that lifeline back in my face. You've betrayed me. I can understand that. I know you blame me for what happened to your father, even after everything I did for you. I could have left you to rot in prison. Your father made his own choice; I don't accept any blame. He could still be alive now if he had just done the small favours I asked him to do for me and repaid his debt.' He shrugs, like he can't understand what is so unreasonable about coercing people to break the law for him. 'But how someone can betray his own family, his own friend, his own sister, his own mother? That I cannot understand and I cannot forgive.'

He hasn't said anything specific yet about what I am supposed to have done, so I call his bluff. 'I haven't betrayed anyone.'

McArthur puts on a sympathetic smile that says, *I pity how stupid you are, Cal Jackson.* That says, *You have no idea what a world of shit you are in.* He reaches into his pocket and takes out a smartphone. I feel my stomach lurch and sink. He holds it up to me, showing me the screen. 'You recognise this?' I don't answer. 'It looks like a pretty ordinary phone, a bit scratched, but it must be special in some way, because you keep it hidden behind a skirting board in your bedroom. Now why would you do that?'

'Sentimental value.'

'Sentimental value,' he repeats loudly and laughs, looking to the men behind me and encouraging them to share his joke. 'You are a funny guy, Callum, you always were. Cheeky, an attitude. I used to like that about you.' The false *bonhomie* drops, the laugh echoes away into the rafters. 'These days I find it quite tiresome.

'Patrick here is a bit of an expert with these things. He can get past the locking software with a click of his fingers. He tried to explain it to me once, but I'm getting on now, I don't pretend to understand modern technology.

'What a surprise to find only one number in the contacts on this special phone. Is it the number for an old flame? A past lover? Is that what you mean by "sentimental value"?

'And then I realise I recognise this number. Not exactly a mutual acquaintance, per se. Not someone I'm on the best terms with. In fact, Detective Simone Millar has become a bit of a problem for me of late. She's been making a nuisance of herself, poking her nose in where it's not welcome.

'Do you want to explain to me why you would have a police detective's number tucked away on a hidden phone? A police detective who has been harassing me and my people for the last couple of years? If it helps you, Callum, I already know the answer, but I want to hear you say it.'

I am not about to let him have this victory, but it is pointless to carry on any pretence. 'We both know I'm not your biggest problem. We both know I don't have much I can tell the police. I've only worked for you for a couple of months. I'm only a lowly bartender. If you're worried about Detective Millar, you need to look elsewhere to find out who really betrayed you.'

'Worried?' The laugh this time is more like a sneer of contempt. 'Do I look worried?' I have to be honest, he doesn't. 'This business with the police will blow over soon enough. Your Detective Millar is in way over her head. She'll learn that soon enough.' He shakes his head at me. 'After everything I did for you, Callum, this is how you repay me? Snitching on me to the police. What was it? Her good looks turn you astray? You like a powerful woman? You like to be ordered around?

'Let me guess. You work at the club, you've been snooping around where you shouldn't. You think you know a thing or two. You think you know Carmen Carmichael.' He sees my reaction before I can suppress it. 'You think Carmen is your friend. Carmen has been talking to Detective Millar as well.

'Surprise, Callum, Carmen is a smart girl. A lot smarter than you, it turns out. She has a sense of self-preservation that you lack. When Millar approached her a year ago, Carmen came to me and told me about it. We agreed this could work to my advantage. Rather than dismissing this crude attempt right out, we decided to treat it with the contempt it deserved. For the last year, Carmen has been drip-feeding the police false information, misdirection, titbits of scandal that go nowhere, things that can be disproved in court when the time comes. That has kept her sweet with the local police, which has allowed the club to operate without interference – and, more importantly, it has kept her in my good books too. If only you had made the same choice when Millar approached you.'

I can't hide my disappointment. Another small bit of hope vanishes. I thought Carmen was different. Turns out I don't have any allies within McArthur's family; not my own sister, not Carmen.

'Now you're thinking, *who else can I turn to? Who can I rely on?* The short answer is nobody, Callum. I am your only hope now. Did Millar tell you she could protect you? Did you believe her?'

I'm not sure if I'm supposed to answer. I don't say anything and McArthur carries on. I let him. He seems to like the sound of his own voice.

'Let me give you an example. The police officer left at your flat to guard your door tonight. Have you wondered what happened to them?'

Up until that point, I hadn't thought about them, but I can make a guess. I remember Millar's words to me in the museum, with the organ music swirling in the background: *We could try, but frankly, I wouldn't get your hopes up. There's a lot of corrupt coppers and McArthur has a lot of reach and resources.*

'You get it now, don't you? The penny has dropped. If the officer faces disciplinary action after it's discovered you disappeared on his watch, I will make sure he comes out of it alright. He'll deny seeing or hearing anything. As far as the police are concerned, you are still tucked up in bed and will be for the next few hours. No one is coming to rescue you.

'Another example. The pair of officers tasked with trailing my every move while I'm out on bail. Do you think they followed me here and have signalled the cavalry back at base to come and rescue you?'

I don't have to answer that question. Money talks, blackmail talks, threats talk. I'm starting to wonder if Millar is even immune from McArthur's reach. Why not? He seems to be able to buy off anyone he wants to.

'Your only hope now is to tell me what I want to know. Throw yourself on my mercy and you just might live a day longer.'

For the first time, McArthur's threat isn't veiled. It is as clear as the day that is dawning outside the warehouse. As things stand, I'm a dead man, and the only person who can stop that from happening is sitting in front of me. My life is in his hands again, just like it was on the night I hit Rose Black. For all Millar's promises and confidence in her case, I'm on my own here and now.

'I didn't tell them much about your business. I didn't have access to much. I told them you were looking to expand into East Kilbride. They already knew that. I told them—'

He cuts me off with a wave of his palm. 'I don't care about any of that. The business operations are watertight. I can afford lawyers that will tie the public prosecution up for years trying to untangle all the violations of procedure and underhand tactics that the police have employed. Nothing you can say about any of that is going to improve your situation here.'

I'm puzzled. 'Then what is it you want to know?'

'I want to know about the girl. Elise Moreau. Where is she?'

34

He waits for an answer. Why is Francis McArthur asking me about Elise? With charges of murder, arson, racketeering and fraud hanging over his head, he's asking me about a woman his son got pregnant. This isn't about business. That doesn't faze him; that situation is under control. What does matter to him is Tony and his infidelity. Does he care that much about family? Does the idea of family scandal, an extra-marital affair, a failed marriage, an illicit child mean more to him than the destruction of the business empire he has built over his entire lifetime? It doesn't fit with the man I know.

'That's why you brought me here? Because Tony can't control himself?'

'It affects your sister too. I would have thought you cared a little more about her?'

'She's a big girl, she can live with the consequences of what her husband gets up to.'

He uncrosses his legs and stands up. I look up into his face, squinting into the bright light shining over his shoulder.

'I don't have to justify anything to you, Callum. Your life is in my hands. What I want to know is where she is. Now tell me.'

'Your lapdog Murdo already tried to beat it out of me a week ago. I'll tell you the same thing I told him. I don't know where she is.'

'You were lying to him. She was in your flat the whole time.'

'A week ago, sure, she was. I told her to run if I didn't return home. Thanks to your goon squad taking me away and beating the shit out of me, she's gone. Now I am able to answer you with a clear conscience: I don't know where she is. And now I'm left to wonder, why do you care?'

In one motion, he steps forward and slaps me across the face. I feel the wound under my right eye open up and blood run down my cheek again. In all the time I've known him, in all the dealings I have had with him, I have never seen Francis McArthur use violence. Not once.

He wipes his hands on a handkerchief, regaining his calm, pretending like it's no big deal. 'My patience is wearing out, Callum. I'm going to ask you one more time. After that, Patrick will take over. He's a far more effective interrogator than I am.'

Patrick is one of the men standing behind me. I hope he and Dante were not close friends.

'You can keep asking until every bone in my body is broken. I can't tell you what I don't know.'

'Very well.' He steps aside and the light is blocked out by the enormous form of Patrick stepping in front of me. He's a man of few words. His only preamble is to crack his knuckles.

The blaring ringtone breaks the ominous mood. It echoes off the bare walls and floor and cuts through the silent night. Patrick looks unsure and glances at McArthur. On his signal, Patrick steps back, takes a phone from his pocket and answers it. The person on the other end of the call asks to speak to McArthur. Patrick hands the phone over to his boss. I have a reprieve as long as the phone call lasts.

McArthur listens and doesn't say anything. The call doesn't last long, but whatever is said to him, it brings about a sudden change of plan. He asks questions. 'You're sure that's where she is? And he's there too?' He hangs up and hands the phone back to Patrick. From his pocket he pulls out his old pocket watch attached to its chain, flips it open and looks at the time. It's a nervous tic. He knows what time it is. He's using the action to buy himself time while he thinks what to do. Then he decides. He snaps the watch shut and puts it back in his pocket. The chain glints in the light of the bright lamp.

'Leave him here. Gag him and tie him up tight. We'll come back for him if we need to. If not, he can have a long and painful death and be found years from now when only his bones remain.'

Patrick and the other man who manhandled me get to work. Patrick holds my ankles against the legs of the chair and cable ties are pulled tight. Hands pull my jaw down and a rough cloth is shoved into my mouth. The rough texture inside my dry mouth sends panic signals to my brain. I struggle to fight the reflex reaction. I try to resist, thrashing helplessly side to side until firm hands pin my body down and my wrists, already tied together, are secured to the back of the chair with another cable tie.

Their footsteps fade away. A plug is removed from a wall socket and the bright lamp goes out. The warehouse plunges into blackness. The chain rattles through its winch and the shutter rises, revealing a small rectangle of weak morning sunlight. Then the chain is released, the shutter rushes to the ground and slams closed, and I am left alone in the dark.

* * *

Whoever called McArthur, whatever they said, it was enough to make me irrelevant. They wanted information about Elise. The phone call gave him the information he needed. The phone call was about Elise. *He's there too?* My best guess is that "he" means Tony and wherever he is, Elise is there too. They've found her. Why isn't she a million miles away from here? What would make her stay here when she knows she is in danger?

Delphine Moreau in her living room, wasting away, alone, frail, staring at the pictures of her daughter on the sideboard. She is why Elise is still here. She can't leave her mother to rot and die alone. Not after all that her mother did for her, raising her on her own, fighting to give her a chance in life without any help. That is the only reason Elise would still be here. It's the only place she would risk going, even if she knew McArthur might be waiting for her.

The moment of revelation is tempered by my current situation. I'm trussed up like a turkey and no one is coming to my rescue. I need to get out of here and get to Elise. It might already be too late, but I have to try.

The cable ties around my wrists are tight enough to bite into and cut my skin, but the ones around my ankles were put on in a rush. They have some give, enough for me to be able to slide my ankles up and down the chair legs.

I use my whole body, wriggling backwards and forwards until the chair starts to rock along with me. I reach a tipping point and gravity takes over and the chair, with me attached, topples back. I wasn't prepared for the smack of concrete on the back of my head. It's enough to stun me for a moment. I try to slide my feet down past the base of the chair legs that are now pointing into the air. The rubber stoppers at the bottom of the chair legs are slightly wider. The cable ties resist and pull tighter, gripping and biting into my ankles and drawing blood. After further undignified pulling and muffled screams of pain suppressed by the cloth in my mouth, I get the cable ties over the end of the chair legs and my own legs are free.

I roll over onto my side, the chair stuck on my back like a shell. I use my tongue to push at the cloth in my mouth. My gag reflex kicks in again and I fight back the urge to vomit into my mouth. Choking on my own sick while scrambling around an empty warehouse tied to a chair is not how I want to go. Inch by inch, the gag falls out of my mouth until it's all gone. My mouth is dry. This is taking too long.

I roll over again, this time onto my front. With my legs free, I'm able to summon enough strength to get onto my feet. The chair prevents me from standing up straight, but I can shuffle around bent over at 90°.

The only way out of here is the metal shutter that needs to be operated by the winch. I need free hands to open it. I need to get the cable ties off my wrists.

There is nothing in the warehouse except the pile of swept-up rubbish in the corner. I hobble over to it, threatening to topple over with each step. I am thirsty and hungry and wish I had eaten a proper dinner before I went to bed last night. I am tired and dirty and running on empty, but I am still running. I have to keep going.

There is a piece of metal in amongst the dust and dirt. It's not sharp, but it does have an edge and that might be enough for the cable ties. I don't have any alternative. I get down on my knees and lie down on my side on top of the dirt pile. I shift my hands as far to the side as I can, trapped between my own back and the back of the chair. I feel around with my fingertips, stretching them as far as they will go. I shift my body. Dirt, specks of glass, wood, dust. Then I locate the piece of metal and I can hold the flat piece between two fingers and shimmy it into my palm and finally get a good grip of it. I roll back onto my front and up onto my knees.

I manoeuvre the metal strip between my hands and then push it against the cable tie. My hands are too weak, the metal too blunt. The cable tie barely moves. It's hopeless. All that effort for nothing. A loud drumming noise erupts above my head. Rain pouring onto the metal roof. Another storm is rolling in. They are regular now, interspersing the hot spells in between, releasing the humidity of the summer, winding the country slowly towards autumn.

I get back to my feet and waddle over in my crouched fashion to the metal shutter. Outside it is early morning. Maybe there is someone out there. Maybe this warehouse is part of an industrial estate with workers arriving for an early start. I throw myself against the metal shutter and it cracks like thunder, a metallic rolling crash. I do it again and again. I try to shout, my voice weak and dry and unable to cut through the sound of the clattering shutter and percussive rain.

'Is anyone out there? I'm locked in here.'

The last cry of the metal shutter rolls away and all that's left is the rain on the roof. It reminds me of lying in a caravan as a child on another family holiday, listening to the rain fall right above my head. I don't remember when. I wish I had paid more attention to my life back then. Happy memories are in short supply.

A last feeble crash of chair against shutter and then I'm down on my knees, sinking towards the concrete.

The metal shutter rattles again. That wasn't me. And again. Someone else is hitting it. Someone on the outside.

'In here!' I call out. I scramble back to my feet. I throw my shoulder against the shutter again. 'In here!'

An answering rattle. Then nothing. Have they left me here?

The shutter moves again. Someone is trying to open it. I hear metal hammering and then a thud as something falls. Then the shutter starts to lift up. Hands appear underneath it, then it is thrown up and Simone Millar stands under it, holding the shutter up above her head. At her feet lie a small sledgehammer and the remains of a padlock.

'You coming?' she says, 'I can't hold this forever.'

PART 5

BREATHLESS

35

We are somewhere to the north of the river, in amongst the old abandoned shipyards. A huge Titan Crane, now a tourist attraction lit up against the dawn, towers up amongst the rusting buildings and tells me we are close to the town of Clydebank, to the northwest of Glasgow.

Millar guns the engine and runs red lights on the quiet roads that are just beginning to stir with the coming of dawn. The low sun glares through the windscreen from gaps between buildings, flickering and flashing and not helping my sore head. Millar flips her sunglasses out and puts them on, then bears down harder on the accelerator.

I tell her to head to Stepps, to the home of Delphine Moreau. I tell her about the phone call Francis received in the warehouse just as he was about to torture me. I tell her that's where we will find Francis McArthur and Tony and Elise. I just hope we are not too late.

'Why is he so desperate to find this girl?'

I haven't figured that out yet.

While she focuses on driving, she explains.

'I got a GPS ping from the phone I gave you.' I remember Francis holding it up in front of me and gloating. 'I figured there wouldn't be a good reason for you to be visiting an industrial estate in the old shipyards. You won't be surprised to find out who owns most of the warehouses around there.'

'They broke into my flat and took me. The officer that you left at my door let them do it.'

She shows no surprise. 'What can I say? McArthur has a big balance book and a long payroll. Police Scotland can't match his pay offers.'

'What about the officers that are meant to be following his every move?'

'They're my team; they're clean.'

I'm not convinced. 'So where are they?'

'They're clean, but we all make mistakes.' The brakes slam on and we slither around a bin lorry reversing onto the road. Millar downshifts and punches the accelerator again. 'It was planned. Malky was at McArthur's house. They came out together and got into separate black SUVs. There were five of them, the whole fleet. We tried to follow the right ones. We guessed right with Malky. We guessed wrong with Francis. He gave us the slip.'

We hit the expressway and Millar starts weaving in and out of the early morning traffic. Angry horns trail behind us.

'You don't have a siren in this thing?'

'Afraid not.' She blasts her own car horn as an unsuspecting commuter is too slow to get out of the way. She is enjoying this way too much. After months wading through paper trails and business law, this is real action.

She makes the sharp left at the end of the expressway, then guns the car along the slip road that rises up and drops onto the M8 motorway. Morning rush hour traffic has already started to build. Millar uses the hard shoulder and blasts past the waiting queues. I hold onto the grab handle above the door with one hand and brace myself against the dashboard with the other.

'Why Elise? Why Stepps?'

'It's where we grew up, where her mum still lives. Delphine Moreau. She was my old French teacher at school. She suffers from Alzheimer's now. Elise was taking care of her. Her mother is the only reason she would still be anywhere near Glasgow.'

'But what is Elise to McArthur? Why would he risk breaking cover to abduct you, knowing we're watching his every step?'

'I don't know the full story, but I know she's pregnant and that Tony is the father.'

That's enough for Millar to take her eyes off the road for a split second and look at me. 'How does your sister feel about that?'

'She doesn't know.'

'You didn't tell her yesterday?'

'I don't have the heart to kick her when she's down.'

'She has the right to know.'

'Feel free to tell her yourself.'

Millar wrenches the car to the left, crosses three lanes of traffic and dives off the motorway and onto the slip road. She powers through a red light onto Cumbernauld Road and passes Hogganfield Loch on our right. We are back where I grew up, racing Marie round the loch on our bikes, feeding the swans, getting an ice cream from the café. A lifetime ago.

'That explains why Tony is desperate to find Elise, why he would risk it all. But not Francis – he would be happy if she disappeared,' says Millar.

'Maybe that is what he wants to happen. Make her disappear permanently. Let's hope we're not too late.'

Millar yanks the steering wheel hard to the right and skirts round a stationary double-decker bus. My head smacks against the passenger side window. She floors it across the four-way intersection. 'Point taken, Cal. I should have listened to you sooner about Elise.'

It is as close as I am going to get to an apology, or Millar admitting she was wrong. 'Better late than never.'

'Let's hope so.'

The road rises and crosses over a railway line. Millar grabs the handbrake and turns a hard left onto Whitehill Avenue. The road is narrow, made more so by the parked cars that line both sides. The church passes in a blur out my window and there's a *clunk* as the wing mirror connects with a parked car and disappears behind us.

'Which house?'

'Right at the end.'

Millar hits the brakes and slows. Up ahead, a black SUV is parked on the apex of the corner, jutting out into the road, abandoned there in a hurry. After the breathless speed of the journey, Millar slows to a crawl and approaches with caution. She drives past the house and the SUV and turns the corner. Parked on the kerb is Tony's Porsche Panamera.

'Didn't you have people tailing Tony?'

Millar shakes her head. 'Not continuously. Budget doesn't cover it. We had people checking in on him when we could.'

'What do we do now?'

'There's two choices: sit and wait to see who comes out, or go in and interrupt whatever is going on in there.'

She gets to the bottom of the road, U-turns at the wide junction and pulls over on the opposite side of the street. Commuters leaving houses walk to their cars and glance at the abandoned SUV and the white Porsche, but no one stops to ask any questions. Delphine's house is quiet; there is no sign of movement from where we sit.

'Shouldn't you call for back-up?'

'I'll call in to my team and tell them I've picked up Francis again.'

I wait while she talks into the police radio. 'We should go in.'

'I agree.'

'You don't have a gun?'

'Of course I don't have a gun. This isn't America.'

'McArthur's people carry guns.'

'We'll add it to the charge sheet. Come on.'

Millar gets out of the car and goes to the boot. She opens it, pulls out a stab vest and pulls it over her head, sticking the Velcro sides around her.

'You don't have a spare?' I ask.

'No. Here, you can have this.' She hands me a small spray can.

'What's this?'

'Pepper spray.'

'You're giving me pepper spray?'

'Welcome to Police Scotland.' Millar picks up an extendable truncheon and hangs it from her belt, next to police-issue handcuffs. 'This is what we have to work with.'

'You don't even have a Taser?'

Millar shrugs and starts to walk across the road. I follow, thinking about the gun I found at the flat on Walton Street and the bullet that shattered my car window.

Whatever is about to happen, we are woefully underprepared for it.

* * *

The tall hedge gives us cover as we approach the house. We enter the garden by a side gate. There is a path that leads to a back door, which must lead into the kitchen where Delphine almost made me a cup of coffee when I visited her.

Millar reaches the wall of the house and presses against it. She gestures for me to join her and I tuck in next to her. She signals with her fingers for me to keep a look out while she goes forward and ducks around the corner of the house to the bay window that juts out at the front. A car goes past on the road. I feel ridiculous, like we are playing some childhood game of hide-and-seek while the world goes on around us, refusing to acknowledge the unfolding life-or-death drama. I once played hide-and-seek around these streets, and cops and robbers. Birdsong chirps from the rooftops above me. It is a normal summer's day in the north of Glasgow. The heat is starting to build again and promises another sweltering few hours until evening. It is warmer than the sun-filled days of childhood ever were.

No sound escapes from inside the house. I hear Millar's footsteps on the gravel and she reappears, bringing herself up from a crouch as she returns.

'No one in the living room,' she half-whispers to me.

'We should wait until your colleagues arrive.'

'For weeks you've been going on about finding this woman. Now you want to wait?' Incredulity drips from her hushed sarcasm. She's right. If Elise is in there with Francis and Tony then she is in danger, and I haven't come this far to leave it too late when it really counts.

Millar nudges me in the side and points to the back door. There's a small set of three stairs that rise up to it. 'Come on,' she urges, and pushes me towards it.

The door is solid wood painted garish yellow with no window. The handle is an old-style iron knob. I turn it in my hand and can feel the chunky mechanism click and turn. A bolt scrapes back. It's unlocked.

I check with Millar, who beckons me on with a determined nod of her head. I push the door open. The bottom of it scrapes along the linoleum floor of the kitchen. There is no one in the room. I walk through and Millar follows, closing the door softly behind us.

The kitchen is still a mess of dirty plates and cutlery and open food packets and tins that have been left forgotten on the worktops. The smell of curdled milk comes from an open plastic carton that has been left out of the fridge. The sink is full of murky water soaking unwashed dishes. The dining table in the middle of the room is covered in junk mail, newspapers, books and scribbled Post-it notes. If Elise has been staying with Delphine, she hasn't got round to cleaning the kitchen up.

Millar takes her extendable baton from her belt and flicks it open. The metal shaft in her hand looks about as threatening as a magician's magic wand. I can't see McArthur feeling scared by it. It occurs to me to find a weapon for myself, something more practical than the small canister of pepper spray I am holding. I look around and see a kitchen knife holder with five empty slits in the top of it. Either they are all lying in the dirty sink water or Elise had the sharp objects removed for her mother's safety. I will have to make do with the spray.

We make our way across the kitchen, careful to avoid obstacles that litter the way – discarded footwear and clothes, a bucket and mop, a dining room chair that has been pulled out and abandoned in the doorway that leads to the narrow hallway. Millar takes the lead and I follow her along the hall.

Above our heads an old floorboard creaks. Someone is upstairs. We move further into the hallway. I can hear voices. Millar tenses; she can hear them too. They are muffled behind closed doors. I can't make out what is being said, but the tone is unmistakeable. Whoever is up there is arguing.

The staircase runs alongside the hallway. As we move forward, Millar turns and looks up to the landing at the top of the stairs. No one is there. We reach the foot of the staircase, which sits next to the door to the living room. Millar gestures to me, pointing at her eyes and then the living room.

I nod understanding and step past her and go into the living room, confirming what Millar saw through the window. The room is empty. I turn to back out of the room and the picture of Elise as a teenage girl on the sideboard catches my eye. She was a striking teenager. There is a dark, exotic quality to her that she has grown into in the intervening years.

I am about to leave the room when I stop and my breath catches in my throat. Millar notices me pause and sees the look of realisation on my face. She glances up the stairs and, still seeing no one, risks leaving her position to come in to the living room beside me.

'What is it?' she hisses.

It all makes sense now. I point to the photo of Elise on the sideboard. Not the one of her in her school days but the one tucked behind it, the one of her as a newborn baby.

'Elise?' asks Millar. 'What about it?'

Millar only sees the dark hair and the snub nose and the flush skin. I am looking beyond the baby girl to the arms that are holding her. I should have seen it the first time I looked at the picture. I should have made the connection. I thought at the time that the arms and hands in the photo belonged to a man, maybe Elise's unknown father. Now, I know they belong to him.

I pick the photograph up in its frame and point at the detail in the corner that has caught my attention. The thing I missed the first time round. Millar doesn't see it at first.

'What?' she urges.

I point again, jabbing at it and getting her to focus on the tiny glint of metal that has been caught in the flashbulb of the camera. It is a tiny mark, a few millimetres of a chain that creeps out of the man's pocket and disappears behind the cradled infant's head. It's small, but it's there, and it's unmistakeable. I flip the photo over and unfasten the clips holding the frame in place. I take the photograph out. The card border of the frame is hiding a fraction more detail that is now exposed. It is a watch chain, one of those old antique chains used to attach pocket watches to waistcoats. No one wears them anymore. No one wore them thirty years ago. Only one person I have ever known wears one; only one person connected to Elise and Tony wears one.

Millar finally sees what I am pointing out to her. She only knows one person who wears an antique watch chain too.

The man holding the newborn girl in the photograph, cradling Elise moments after she was born, is Francis McArthur.

36

Millar recovers first, though I can tell she gets it too – the enormity of it, the horror of it, the fallout that will follow when the truth comes out. I am frozen, struggling to unwrap the full implications of what this means for the people involved. Millar takes the photograph from my hand and places it back on the sideboard.

'Come on,' she orders me. 'We need to stop them.'

I understand her meaning. Stop them before they kill each other. That is what will happen.

Just as Millar pushes me into action, a scream pierces the air. A woman's scream, a mix of anger and despair. It comes from upstairs.

Maybe we are too late already.

* * *

Millar's training and experience kick into action as a reflex. Someone is in trouble; it is her duty to run to their aid. She rounds the bannister and sprints up the stairs three at a time, her baton still in her hand, poised to be used if needed. A second scream breaks me out of my inertia and I run after her.

The upstairs landing has four doors leading off it. Straight ahead is a bathroom. To the right is a door to a bedroom that must sit above the kitchen at the back of the house. The voices are clearer now. Millar follows the sound. It is coming from one of the rooms at the front. The door to one lies open. There is no sign of anyone inside, just an unmade bed and drawn curtains, through which the morning sun is penetrating the gloom.

That leaves door number four.

I recognise Tony's raised voice. He is telling someone to calm down, to stop, to take a moment to think about what they are doing.

The woman screams again. A wild and uncontrolled wail. It belongs to Delphine Moreau.

Millar halts outside the door. She knows rushing into an unknown and tense situation can have unintended consequences. She puts her foot to the bottom of the door and nudges it open a fraction. The screaming gets louder as the noise escapes from the room. Millar kicks the door wide and steps back. I enter first, trying not to barge in, trying to contain my fear and adrenalin. I stop two paces into the room. Millar follows me and stands beside me. The four people in the room turn and stare at us.

Delphine Moreau stops mid-scream. She is on the floor at the bay window. Her hair is deranged, straggly and tangled and unkempt. She's wearing a nightie that hangs from her emaciated frame. She is being held in the arms of her daughter.

Elise is on her knees, her arms wrapped around her mother, clinging to her, protecting her and trying to soothe her. Her dark hair is tied back, a few loose strands framing her face. Her look is defiant and menacing. Her dark eyes smoulder with hatred that is directed across the room at the man standing in the opposite corner, tucked behind the door Millar and I have just come through.

Francis McArthur holds the handgun in front of him, pointing it towards the window at Elise and Delphine. When he sees us, the gun sways towards us and then back again. He can't decide who he should keep in his sights. I have never seen him look so emotional before. His eyes are red and wide, his face streaked with tears. He looks distraught and out of control. He is still wearing the same coat and suit he wore at the warehouse, but the smart confidence he exuded then has left him. He looks like a broken man.

The fourth person stands in the middle of the room, between Francis and the mother and daughter. Tony McArthur has his hands raised towards his father, palms up in a gesture of supplication and restraint. He is shielding Elise and Delphine from his own father, pleading with him to stop and put the gun down.

As Millar and I stumble into the scene, it's not clear who knows the truth.

'What the hell are you doing here?' yells Francis, breaking the momentary stalemate. He is shouting at Detective Millar. 'This has nothing to do with you; this is family business.'

Millar raises her hands. The extendable baton looks particularly useless as McArthur's gun turns towards her. She tries to placate him. 'I'm here to stop you doing something you will regret. Forget about everything else. Forget about me and the investigation. You don't want to hurt anyone here. Your family means everything to you, so let's put the gun away and talk.'

For a second I think he might actually listen to her, but it is a short-lived hope as McArthur's face turns to a sneer and the gun swivels back in the direction of Tony, Elise and Delphine.

'You have no idea what you've walked into,' he says. 'This can't be allowed to go on.' He talks to his son. 'I'm trying to do what's best for you, what's best for the family. I've only ever tried to do that, to look out for your interests.'

'I have a good idea of what's going on.' I can hear my voice carry across the room and can't believe I have spoken. I should just keep my mouth shut and walk away, leave them to destroy each other, but I care about Elise; maybe I empathise with her plight at the hands of this bully, the same man who tore my family apart.

The gun swings back and now it is facing me. I had never looked down the barrel of a gun until a couple of days ago. Now they are pointing at me on a regular basis.

'You understand?' Francis shouts at me. 'You? After everything I did for you? I kept you out of prison. I gave you a way back into some sort of life. I should have let you rot after the accident. Only Tony insisted I help you.'

'I wish you had let me rot. Maybe then my father would still be alive. Maybe then I would have some sort of family, something that I could protect. You took my family from me – first my parents, now my sister.' I turn to Tony. 'Does Marie know about any of this, Tony? Have you told her anything?'

Tony shakes his head. 'I didn't mean for this to happen. It's just something we've always done. We're drawn to each other. It was harmless until—'

'Until you got her pregnant,' I interrupt him. I realise he still doesn't know the full horror of it all. He hasn't even thought about why Elise and he might be drawn to each other so powerfully that they couldn't stay apart, even when he was engaged to another woman. I don't want to be the one to explain it to him.

I turn back to Francis. 'Tell him why you are so set against this child being born. Tell him why you warned him to stay away from Elise when you found out about their affair. Tell him why you kidnapped Elise and were going to force her to have an abortion.'

The gunshot reverberates around the room. For an instant I think he has shot me, but I don't feel any pain after the immediate shock. The gun points at the ceiling and a shower of dust and plaster falls to the floor. It is a warning shot. A shot to stop me before I reveal too much.

'Enough,' Francis shouts.

I have come too far for it to be enough. 'Ask him, Tony. Ask him what this is really about.'

Tony looks unsure for the first time. 'What does he mean, Dad? What's he talking about?' He thinks it has been about his marriage, about protecting the McArthur name from scandal and gossip. He thinks it is because his father disapproves of an illicit child. He doesn't realise there is something more.

Does Elise know? She is looking from one McArthur to the other and then to me. Her eyes meet mine. My heart goes out to her for what she is about to hear. Her mother knew at one time. Not about her daughter's affair, but the truth about her father. If the horrible disease hadn't robbed her of her mind, she could have warned her. She had chosen not to tell Elise about her father. Delphine had done the right thing. She wasn't to know it would end up like this. Now she can't tell her the truth because it is lost in the haze of her forgotten memories. Delphine looks around, her face a mask of uncomprehending terror.

'Tell me,' demands Tony.

Francis is caught by the truth. He is looking for a way out. He has always seen a path out of trouble before. He has been able to predict and plan and mitigate. For the first time, Francis McArthur feels his life spiralling out of control. He is getting to experience what the rest of us have to live with every day.

'Tell them,' I urge him, hoping I am not pushing him over the edge into violence, 'or I will.'

'You can't. You wouldn't dare. It will crush her.' Francis waves the gun at Elise. He's right, but she needs to know. They both do.

'I was wrong, Millar,' I say, hoping to defuse the tension a little. 'I thought it was Tony who took Elise and was urging her to get rid of the baby in order to protect his new marriage. But Tony was willing to live with his mistake to some degree, to take a bit of responsibility. It was only Francis who knew the full story and why he needed Elise and the baby to disappear. I should have seen it sooner, when I first looked at that photograph downstairs – the photograph of Elise when she was born.'

'What photograph? What are you talking about?' Francis tries to cut me off.

The photograph that Delphine sits and stares at blankly on her sideboard every day. The one picture that exists of Elise and her father before he abandoned her.

'I should have recognised the watch chain the first time I saw it, but I wasn't looking to make any connection.' Silence fills the room. 'The photograph of you holding your newborn daughter.'

I expect an explosion as the grenade detonates, but there is only silence. No one says anything. Tony turns and looks at his father and then at Elise and back again. Elise stares at Tony. Tony didn't know. Elise only looks down. I realise she already knew. Did she guess or had she worked it out for herself? Had she spotted the glint of the watch chain in the corner of the photograph while she cared for her ailing mother? When did she find out? After she had slept with Tony for the last time? After she was pregnant? Before?

Delphine speaks first, her voice fragile and broken. 'What's going on, Elise? What is it?'

Elise soothes her mother. 'Sssh, it's okay, Mum.' She leans forward and kisses the top of her head as she cradles her in her lap, wiping Delphine's hair from her face, the daughter caring for her mother.

Tony looks at Elise. His lover, his half-sister. 'I didn't know,' he tries, but words can't suffice in this situation. He turns to Francis. 'Why didn't you tell me?'

'How could I? I didn't know you had been together until it was too late. Now you understand, though, why the baby must be terminated?' The gun is pointing at Tony. Francis looks broken and panicked. 'I can't allow it to be born.'

'You son of a bitch!' Tony's anger finally spills over and he lunges at his father. Another gunshot explodes. I don't know if Francis means for the gun to go off, if it's instinct or self-preservation, or if he has lost control of his mind and his actions. Tony goes down before he can reach his father, crumpling to the floor. He screams in pain and shock; pain from the bullet that has shattered his right kneecap, shock that his own father would do this to him.

Delphine screams. Elise jumps up, but Francis swivels the gun to point at her and she freezes in front of the window. Millar scurries over to Tony, props him up against the wall and puts pressure on his wound, trying to stem the blood that is pumping onto the carpet. I don't move.

'For the last time,' Francis snarls at Elise, 'either you get rid of the baby or I will do it myself.' The gun drops to point at Elise's stomach.

Elise puts her hands across her midriff, the mother's instinct to protect already strong. 'You couldn't do that. I'm your daughter. This is your grandchild. What sort of a monster are you? You left us. You left my mother with nothing. Can you imagine what it is like to grow up seeing "unknown" typed next to "father" on my birth certificate? You could have helped us, you could have been a part of our lives.'

'Not without losing everything I had built up. My family, my wife, my business. They meant everything to me. Your mother was a stupid mistake. One time. I wasn't going to let that ruin everything. I wanted her to get rid of you. She refused. She called me when you were born. She promised she would leave me alone, she would tell no one and ask for nothing. I should have known my mistake would return to haunt me one day.'

'Is that what I am to you? A mistake?'

'There's no point in lying about it. I didn't want you. I wanted you to be gone. Then I find out my son has made the exact same mistake. I can't let that happen to him. I can't let him have the same guilt eating away at him for the rest of his life.'

Francis has lost all control. Thirty years of stifled pressure has been released. Every time he saw Delphine Moreau at his son's school, every time he saw his illegitimate daughter around the village, he would have been reminded of what he had done. He would have been reminded of how easily he could lose everything that meant so much to him.

In the distance, police sirens approach, responding to either Millar's call for back-up or the gunshots heard in the quiet street. The ever-vigilant neighbour next door must have noticed something by now.

'How could you?' cries the mother's voice. Delphine Moreau gets to her feet and stands in front of her daughter. There is a new look on her face. One of determination and fight, the same emotions that helped her raise a daughter on her own, without any help from Francis McArthur. She watched his empire grow, his wealth grow, his status grow, and all the time she knew his secret. Yet she never demanded anything from him and never betrayed him, even though she had the power to destroy him. And this is how he repays them. From somewhere in the depths of her confused mind, a moment of clarity surfaces, a memory strong enough to fight against the chaos and erasure. 'How could you do this to us after all this time? I left you alone. I told you I would want nothing from you. You chose to leave us and I let you go. You should have stayed away from us.'

'How could I? When I found out, I should have made sure she was never born,' Francis shouts back at her.

Delphine steps towards him. He sees her as a harmless, broken old woman. She is small and frail and thin. She is not a threat to him.

'Leave us alone!' Delphine screams, as I imagine she did thirty-four years ago when Francis first walked away from them.

I see the blade too late. My mind flashes back to the empty knife holder in the kitchen. As Delphine staggers forward, her arm folds out from behind her. Francis moves to push her out of the way. He doesn't see the blade in her hand either, not until it is swinging down and piercing his chest. Delphine summons strength from somewhere within her soul and the knife plunges deep into him, right up to the hilt.

Francis doesn't cry out. He looks down at the handle. There is no dramatic spray of blood; instead, a gradual circle of red creeps across his shirt. He staggers backwards. Delphine stands unmoving, her face blank. Her vengeance complete, her mind retreats back into the shadowy world of half-memories and forgotten lives where she lives now.

McArthur drops the gun and brings his hand up to the knife. It must have entered his heart, on the left side of his chest. There is nothing anyone can do to help him. He doesn't have the strength to pull it out. He fumbles and sways and blood dribbles from his mouth. His life ebbs away in front of us. He seems to smile, thinking about the way it has ended for him. He has survived at the top of a corrupt empire for so long, using threats, force and violence, even murder, to control his world and his business, and in the end it is a woman he abandoned thirty years ago who has returned to destroy him.

He staggers forward, making one final effort. Tony is near to him, but it is not to his stricken son that he stretches out his hand. It is towards the daughter he never knew, towards Elise. Is it one final attempt at an apology for his past sins? If it is, it's too late. He topples forward and lands on the floor with a deadening thud.

Downstairs the front door crashes open and footsteps charge up the stairs.

Murdo Smith bursts into the room, chased by two police detectives. He sees his boss face-down on the floor, the pool of blood gathering underneath his inert body. He cries out, 'No!' and lurches down to hold Francis McArthur's lifeless form.

37

Delphine Moreau is back in her usual chair in the living room. Elise sits on the sofa next to her. A slew of official vehicles is outside. Various officers, coroners, forensic investigators and detectives come in and go out, up and down the stairs.

An ambulance has already taken Tony McArthur away. He might walk with a limp for the rest of his life, but he will survive.

Through the window, Murdo Smith is helped into the back of a police car. He had found out where Francis and Tony had gone and he knew the implications, he knew Francis McArthur's secret. The police officers had been watching his house when he suddenly left, driving across the north of the city at a furious pace. When Millar put the call out for back-up, the officers put two-and-two together. Whatever Murdo's bond to Francis McArthur – friendship, devotion, love – the sight of the dead body broke something. He sat sobbing, cradling McArthur's head, until Millar and the other officers were able to pry him away.

There is a heavy clunk outside and a trolley is wheeled along the front path. Through the living room doorway I can see the bottom of the stairs. A coroner's assistant appears. He is holding one end of a sealed black body bag. His colleague follows, holding the other end. They manoeuvre out the front door and put the body on the waiting trolley. Francis McArthur is taken away and a few moments later the coroner's van leaves.

No one in the living room has spoken yet. Elise holds her mother's hand on her lap. She looks at the photograph, the one of her as a baby being held by her father.

I have to ask. 'When did you know?' She stirs from whatever place she had retreated to and looks at me. 'When did you know that Francis was your father? That you and Tony were…?' I can't bring myself to say it.

Elise looks at me with disgust. 'After, of course. After I found out I was pregnant. You don't think I deliberately…' She can't bring herself to spell it out either. 'I would never have known if it wasn't for Mum's dementia. She would have taken the secret to her grave if she had been in her right mind. When I told her I was pregnant, it triggered something in her memory. She said it straight out, like it was a fact that I already knew, that she had told me before. *I hope he treats you better than that bastard Francis McArthur did us.*

'I was horrified, but it was too late to change anything. I knew I would keep the baby. I told Tony about it – the baby, that is, not about his father and my mother. He wasn't happy, but he eventually came round to the idea. Said we would figure something out in time, just please not to tell Marie or anyone else.'

'Then why did you turn up at the wedding?'

'Tony had started to ignore me. Francis had found out and told Tony to ditch me – you know the real reason now. He started to threaten me and the baby. I wanted to make sure they got the message. I could ruin his new marriage if Tony didn't keep his word.

'I didn't tell Tony the rest, but I wanted to let Francis know what he had done, the consequence of his actions all those years ago, what it had led to. I wanted to wipe the smug grin off his face. All his talk of putting family first and family meaning the world to him… not me, not his daughter or the woman he abandoned.'

'So you turned up at the club?'

'It was foolish. I should have stayed away. I knew what Francis could be like. Tony had warned me often enough, told me things about how he did business, but I wanted to punish him, to show him what had become of his sin. To avenge my mother, rotting away without anyone to care for her while he lived the good life. I didn't know it would end like this. I didn't want this.'

'Don't blame yourself for what he did,' I warn her. 'This was all his fault. He got what was coming to him.'

Millar is in the hallway. She is talking to an older man in police uniform with lots of stripes on his shoulders, I assume some sort of Police Commissioner or Head of Police Scotland. The killing of a prominent individual, one already embroiled and charged in a major police investigation, has brought out the top brass.

'What now?' I ask Elise, before we are separated and taken away for statements and questioning.

'It depends what they will do to Mum.'

'I mean about the baby.'

'Nothing has changed,' she says, which seems to me to be ignoring the actuality of our surroundings. She sees my disbelieving look. 'I'm having this baby whether the McArthurs like it or not, whether Tony will act like a father or not.'

'Your mother will be okay. Diminished capacity. They can't put her in prison in her condition.'

Millar enters and interrupts us. It helps that she saw exactly what happened. It helps that she saw me tied up in a warehouse. She is on our side.

'Elise, will you accompany your mother to the station with these officers?'

Two plain clothes officers are behind her in the hallway, a man and a woman. I recognise the man; he is the officer I have seen with Millar before.

Elise kneels in front of Delphine, explaining that they have to go with the police and answer some questions. Delphine smiles at her and takes her face in her palm. 'Of course, dear. You're such a good girl, always looking after me.' I can't tell if she even remembers what has just happened, or if her memory of her act of ultimate revenge has already gone, a ghost of a memory evaporating among the misfiring neurons inside her brain.

Millar watches them leave then turns to me. 'You're with me.'

* * *

Outside, the commotion has faded away. The police have driven away Tony's Porsche and the abandoned SUV. The last of the blue lights departs, leaving behind one car and two officers to stand guard in front of the police tape that surrounds the house on the corner.

Millar takes me to her car, which is still parked where we left it earlier.

'What now?' I ask her over the top of the car, the same question I asked Elise moments before.

'Now you have some questions to answer.'

We both slide into the car and shut the doors. Millar guns the engine and pulls away.

'This is going to take some explaining to my parole officer.' I'm making light of it, but the prospect of a return to prison is a very real possibility.

'I'll put in a good word for you. You were only there because I put you there. And I can vouch that you didn't actually commit a crime, that you were trying to prevent one.'

As we pass the house next door, I see the neighbour I'd spoken to before. She's talking to one of the police officers left to stand guard.

We turn back onto Cumbernauld Road and head back towards the city. I wonder if I'll ever have a reason to return to Stepps again.

'What about your case?'

'It's not great, the main suspect being dead and all, but we've still got other avenues to pursue. McArthur's dealings spread quite a web of corruption and we still have all his files and paperwork to go through.'

'It would have been nice to put him behind bars though, after all your work.'

Millar sighs. 'Yes, it really would have been.'

I admire her pragmatism. Inside, I imagine she is seething with anger. Maybe it's better this way. McArthur seemed pretty sure he would beat the corruption and fraud charges in court. Millar would not have been able to contain her anger if he had got away scot-free in the end.

Delphine Moreau has just made sure he can't get away with it this time.

PART 6

WITHOUT SUN

38

Festive season in Glasgow. The heatwave of the summer is a distant memory; a mild and wet autumn has been replaced by a freeze that has lasted since mid-November. The city is covered in a picture-postcard blanket of white frost that is four inches thick in places. Ice-covered pavements make walking anywhere treacherous. The main roads are passable thanks to the continuous work of the council's grit lorries. The trees have shed their leaves and branches now resemble white, crooked fingers. Icicles hang from gutters and plumes of steam rise from boiler flues.

The houses along Roman Road are burning through enough electricity to power a small country. Each mansion is festooned with twinkling fairy lights from head to foot, wrapped around doorways, along fences and bordering windows. Some twinkle and sparkle; some are colourful, others ice white. Glittering reindeers sit on the front lawns, backed by huge inflatable snowmen. Signs cry out for Santa to stop here and multi-coloured candy canes line driveways. The tall trees that border the gardens are bedecked in their own shimmering, winking décor. It all feels forced, like everyone is in a competition and no one wants to be left out.

No. 24 has joined in the parade. A string of colourful bulbs runs along the top of the low wall that runs around the property.

The tree in the driveway is covered in a net of white fairy lights and from the alcove over the front door hang electric icicles. Garlands wind their way up the pillars on either side of the porch.

As I park my car, I can see Christmas trees in the windows of the kitchen and the lounge. I am sure Marie has paid an interior designer to come in and do all this for her. There's no way she did it herself.

The BMW sits in the same space as before. The Porsche is absent. I deliberately park my small Toyota where it used to be. The Corsa never did recover from its high-speed chase. I got fifty quid for scrapping it. The Toyota Aygo is all I can afford on finance. It takes up twenty percent of my monthly wage and is tiny, but it always starts first time.

As I get out of the car, Marie opens the front door to meet me.

We haven't seen each other since summer. There have been text messages, but not much more. I wasn't sure if she wanted to see me. I wasn't sure what I should tell her. It was easier to avoid each other. We've had plenty of practice at that over the last few years anyway.

Then she called last week. The day before, Tony had had his arraignment hearing in court. After the death of Francis McArthur, and with Tony's injury, the trial was delayed. Tony pled not guilty to all charges against him. The case won't be heard until well into the New Year. This might have been the trigger that made Marie call me. She invited me over to her house. Just me. No Tony, no Mum, no Michelin-star chef in the kitchen.

'Hey,' I greet her, walking up to the door.

'Hey,' she replies and leans in for a forced embrace and a brush kiss on the cheek. She steps back and looks me up and down. 'You look better.'

'Thanks.' I have filled out since the summer, putting on some of the weight I lost in prison. 'You look well.' She does. Why should I be surprised? Marie was never one to let herself stay down for long, always rising to the next challenge.

'Come on through.'

She leads me into the living room we sat in when I was last here. A bundle of brown fur jumps up to greet me as I walk in.

'This is Harley. A springer spaniel. He's only three months old, still a puppy and still in need of training, although we've managed to get him to go outside for the toilet and sleep through the night now.'

I pat Harley on the head as he leaps about like he's tripping on a particularly powerful substance. He licks my hands and nuzzles in between my legs, almost tripping me up. Marie rescues me by pulling him away and disappears to bundle him into another room.

'Never had you as a dog person,' I say when she returns. We sit on opposing sofas. The room hasn't changed, save for the blankets draped over the sofas to protect them from the over-enthusiastic dog.

'I never was. Still not really. It was Tony's idea. He didn't want me to be alone in the house.'

'How is he?'

'Doing well.' Marie forces a smile. 'Walking with a crutch now. Still has a lot of rehab to get through, but they're confident he'll walk again without a limp.'

'And the court case?'

She shrugs. 'He doesn't tell me much about it. He seems confident though. I think the lawyers are talking and they'll offer a deal before it gets to trial. They'll break up the business, but he hopes they will let him keep a part of it – he thinks the construction and demolition business will be his, but he will be forced to sell the land and property, and the clubs. We will be able to keep the house, just need to cut back on some things.'

Millar has told me the same thing. The appetite for a long, drawn-out, complicated fraud trial evaporated with the death of Francis McArthur. He was the one they were really after. Now the authorities are going to settle for breaking up the McArthur empire.

Tony was relatively low down in the business. Francis shielded him from the worst of it.

Murdo Smith and Malky Thomson have a harder task ahead of them to find a plea bargain that will keep them out of prison. They were McArthur's right-hand men; they were responsible for implementing his blackmail and extortion schemes.

The arson and murder of Bilal Yousaf has been pinned on Dante, acting on Francis's orders. All are conveniently deceased. The Yousaf family will never get their day in court.

The body in the swimming pool has been declared "Death by Misadventure (Drowning)" by the coroner. No charges are pending. Without the headline of bringing down Francis McArthur, the appetite of Police Scotland to continue a lengthy and expensive investigation has waned.

There is an awkward silence between us. Marie stares at me. I look around the room. The decorated tree stands in the window. There is no other sign of decoration in the room. It's all just for show, like so much of the lifestyle of the rich around here.

'Seen much of Mum?' I ask.

'She comes round every week. She wants to see more of you.'

'I know, I should make more of an effort. Just busy, you know?' Marie chooses not to pursue an argument even though she knows I am lying. Working at the club takes up four evenings a week. The rest of the time I have to myself. There is no excuse for not seeing Mum more, other than my own reluctance to do it. She calls and messages; I respond without enthusiasm.

'I was just going to phone in a take-away for dinner, if that's alright. Nothing fancy, I'm afraid.'

'Sounds perfect.'

'Chinese okay?'

'Great, whatever.'

Marie gets up and leaves the room and I can hear her talking on the telephone, calling in an order to be delivered to the house.

She comes back and brings two bottles of lager with her. She has forgotten I have given up alcohol since my release from prison. I don't remind her as she puts a bottle on the table in front of me and takes her seat.

The small talk is leading up to something, and I can guess what she wants to ask me.

'And how are you after everything that happened?'

'I'm not going to lie, Marie, I'm doing pretty good. Steady income, settled, and I no longer have Francis and Murdo breathing down my neck.'

She gives me a look of shock. It's hard to tell if it's genuine or not. 'I know he had his faults, but there's no need to be cruel.'

'They had no problem being cruel to others.'

'He's dead, Cal. Leave him in peace.'

I don't know how much Marie really knows about her father-in-law and what went on. She can't be that naïve.

'I wanted to ask you,' she starts, building up to the real reason I've been invited, 'about that day. What actually happened? What really happened to Tony?'

'Don't you think you're better off asking him?'

'I've tried. He shuts me out.'

I know why Tony doesn't want to talk about it with his wife. This is the reason she has invited me over to the house after months with only sporadic communication.

'Where is Tony?' I ask.

'Away for a couple of nights at a health spa. Rolling in some business meetings too. New investors, expansion.' She waves her hand in the air; either she doesn't care, doesn't understand or a mixture of both. 'You're not answering my question.'

'What has he told you?'

'That Francis went crazy. Pulled a gun on Elise and her mother. Turns out Francis was the girl's father. Tony tried to stop him and Francis shot him. Then the woman stabbed Francis.'

'That's what happened.'

'You were looking for Elise? That's why you were there?'

'She disappeared after being thrown out of the club. I wanted to find out what happened to her.'

Marie knows there's something more, but she knows I'm not going to tell her anything else. It is left unsaid, hanging between us.

Elise's pregnancy, the child fathered by Tony, remains a secret to Marie. Tony isn't going to tell her, but Marie has a right to know. On the other hand, what business is it of mine to interfere in their marriage? Maybe if we were close I would tell her the truth, but we're not, and there is no point in pretending that we are. We lead separate lives now and move in separate worlds. This life, and everything that comes with it, is what Marie chose.

'Mum and Sheila are spending a lot of time together. Sheila says Mum has been a great comfort to her since she lost Francis.'

Mum would know how Sheila feels, losing her husband. Francis's death makes it easier for Mum to accept her new in-laws. The man who took her husband from her has himself gone. Did Anita Jackson share a small, private smile when she heard what had happened? I doubt it – she's not that sort of person – but the shadow cast by Francis has lifted and Mum has a new family she can be part of.

We manage to spend an hour together and maintain a civil flow of conversation. Marie asks about work and the club. The food arrives and we eat in front of the television, the inane background noise filling in the pauses. I help tidy away the leftover food and cutlery and then make my excuses to leave.

It is a relief to make it to the door. This is how it will be between my sister and me from now on. There will always be this unspoken secret between us.

I put my coat on, bracing myself to move from the warm house into the cold winter evening. 'Tell Mum I was asking for her. Maybe see you both over Christmas.' My hand is on the door handle when Marie places her hand on top of mine and stops me from going.

'Tony and Elise. Were they close? Is that why he was there? Did he know they were related?'

She tries to read the response in my face and I can see behind her eyes what she really wants to know. She feels it, her gut tells her it's the truth, but she won't admit it to herself. She knows Tony and Elise were together as lovers. She knows Tony has betrayed her.

And I can see what will happen if she finds out the real truth. Her marriage will be over; her happiness, such as it is, destroyed. Tony will never tell her about the child and the truth behind their relationship, and I know I can't either.

Once, she would have been able to read the truth from my reaction, but the years of distance between us have broken that connection. We are strangers to one another now.

She puts her hand on my chest. 'I'm pregnant, Cal,' she announces.

She waits for my congratulations. That seals it. I can't tell her about Elise, and I hope she never finds out, for the sake of her unborn, innocent child.

'That's great.' I lean in and give her a light kiss on the cheek.

Her hand leaves mine and I can escape.

'I'll let you know how it goes. You're going to be an uncle.'

I open the door and step out into the cold, my breath forming a cloud around me. 'That's great,' I say again, trying to muster more of a smile.

She is still standing at the door as I drive away, lit by the overhead light, like a halo in the darkness, alone among the false stars. I retrace my way along Roman Road and back to the city, leaving the mansions and the money behind. I'm in no hurry to return any time soon.

39

I pass Hogganfield Loch. The childhood memories come to the surface, refusing to be replaced by more recent events. It would be quicker to get to the nursing home by leaving the motorway at the following junction, but I like to come this way. At the intersection, instead of going straight on to Stepps, I turn right and head down Avenue End Road.

The care home sits under the motorway. The hum of cars passing is constant. It is a specialist home for those living with dementia.

The visitor car park is quiet. It's a weekday, when relatives have jobs to do before visiting in the evenings.

Gillian is behind reception. She sees me approach the door and presses the security release to let me in. The glass door slides open.

'Mr Jackson, how are you today?'

'Good, Gillian. How are you?'

'Same as always.'

'How did Chloe's show go?' Gillian's eldest is appearing in her musical theatre group's Christmas pantomime.

Gillian is pleased I have remembered. 'She was fantastic. There were a few mishaps, but she remembered all her lines and her dance steps. She is convinced she wants to be an actress now. Star of stage and screen.'

'I'm sure she'll do it, too.'

In the four months I've been visiting the home, I have got to know the team of receptionists at the front desk. Snippets of polite conversation are unavoidable while I sign the visitor log and fill out the paperwork attached to each visit.

Under "Resident Visiting" I write "Delphine Moreau".

They no longer question why I come to visit Delphine, despite not being related to her. I fill in the usual sentence in the box under "Reason for Visit", which all those unrelated to the residents of the home must complete. "Family abroad wish to be kept updated on her situation, Mrs Moreau has no relations in the country and no one else to visit her."

'How has she been this week?'

'Absolutely fine. No incidents. She's properly settled in now.'

The first weeks were difficult. Delphine had enough of her mind left to know she was being moved out of the home she had lived in for most of her adult life, the home she had raised Elise in.

She doesn't seem to have any memory of what happened in the bedroom that day in July. She never mentions Francis McArthur, she never has nightmares about stabbing the father of her daughter to death, there is no mention of gunshots. It has been erased from her memory, either by her own will or by the disease that continues to eat away at her mind.

'Any mail for her?' I ask this every time I visit. The answer is always negative, but as Gillian is on the verge of delivering her customary "no", she remembers something.

'Oh yes, there is in fact. Came yesterday.' Gillian turns away from behind her desk to a cupboard and rummages through a tray of letters. 'It stood out as we don't get much air mail from France here. Her family getting in touch with her at last, I guess?' She hands over the thin envelope to me.

'I expect so. Thanks.' I can tell she wants me to open it in front of her, but is too professional to say it. I pocket the letter, hiding my emotions about the unexpected delivery. 'Okay to go through?'

'Sure, let me get the door for you.'

I walk across the reception room to another glass door and Gillian pushes another release button to slide it open for me.

* * *

Delphine sits in her chair, the same chair that used to sit in her living room at No. 64 Whitehill Avenue. Residents are allowed to bring some of their own furniture and belongings into the home. It helps to settle them.

She looks healthier. She is no longer like a skeleton covered in skin. A regimen of timetabled meals has filled out her face and brought colour back into her pale, grey skin. Her hair is clean and brushed.

The chair faces out of the window, onto the area of garden to the rear of the building. It's landscaped with an artificial grass lawn, bare trees and empty flower beds. The bulbs have been planted and colour will return in the spring. There is a greenhouse and allotment to one side, where residents can plant fruit and vegetables, and a gravel path that runs around and across the garden. Even though it is a cool December day, a nurse supports an elderly man wrapped up in a winter coat on her arm – his other hand holds a shaking walking stick – and guides him around the path.

If you can ignore the looming grey concrete pillars that prop up the motorway overpass behind the back wall and the constant traffic pollution, it's a picturesque scene.

There is no other chair in the room, so I sit on the edge of the bed as usual. 'Morning, Madame Moreau.'

I never know what sort of response I will get. Today, she reacts; other days she doesn't even notice I am here. 'Hello there, young man,' she smiles. I know she says "young man" because she can't remember who I am.

'How are you today?'

'Very well, very well. I was just watching old Maurice out there in this frosty weather. He'll catch a chill. It will go straight to his chest.' Her French lilt is still there, the voice stronger and clearer than it was in the summer. The move into the care home has been good for her.

I introduce myself as I do every visit. 'It's me, Cal Jackson. You used to teach me French at school.' She nods. Behind the eyes, I can sense the panic. She doesn't remember me at all. 'I am friends with Elise, your daughter.'

At Elise's name, her focus returns. She cannot forget her daughter, at least not yet. In time, the disease will take Elise from her too.

'You know Elise? Will she come and visit me soon?'

I don't have the heart to tell her how unlikely it is that she will see Elise again. Most likely, Delphine won't remember this conversation in a couple of hours' time anyway, so there is no point in upsetting her. 'I'm sure she is desperate to see you.'

'I do miss her terribly.'

I pick up the envelope Gillian handed to me at reception. 'I haven't heard from her for a few months, but she sent you this.'

It is too late. When I turn back, Delphine is looking out of the window once more. Her attention has gone, her mind drifting into unknowable space and time. I don't know if she has delved into the distant past or if she sees only blankness and emptiness in these moments. Sometimes she will return to the present and pick up the conversation as though nothing has happened; other times I leave and she forgets she ever spoke to me.

I look at the envelope, addressed to Madame Delphine Moreau, care of Craigview Care Home. The franking mark says Reims. My French geography isn't great, but I know it's a city in the north, not too far from Paris. Next to the franking mark is another stamp that says postage has been paid. The rest of the envelope is blank. No return address.

I should leave it for Delphine – it's addressed to her – but I know who it is from already, and I think Elise will know it is me who receives this mail and opens it. It is intended for me as much as it is for Delphine.

I carefully rip open the corner and slide my finger along the top of the envelope. Delphine doesn't stir in her chair. I pull open the sides. There is a single piece of card inside. I pull it out. It is a photograph, printed out on glossy paper.

It is a picture of a baby girl. She is no more than a month or two old, with a mop of jet-black hair, chubby cheeks and legs sticking out of a sleepsuit. Her eyes are hazelnut brown and wide, her face drawn into a laughing smile as she reaches forward towards the camera. I turn the photograph over. On the back, handwritten in a flowing cursive script, is a name and date.

Delphine Moreau, cinquième Novembre.

I double-check the envelope, but there is nothing more. No accompanying letter, no contact details for Elise. Nothing more is needed. Elise has said all that needs to be passed on for the moment. If she was in trouble, if there was more to say, she would have written more. She is letting us know they are okay, her and her daughter.

A smile creeps across my face, unbidden and unexpected.

For a moment longer I sit on the bed and look at the picture of the newborn Delphine. Madame Moreau doesn't stir so I take my leave. Today she does not need the company or someone to talk to. Perhaps next time she will.

I get up from the bed, walk around the chair and place the photograph on the window sill in front of her, then step away. I will leave her to discover the photograph in her own time, when her mind allows her to see it.

As I reach the door, I hear her move. I look back. She stands at the window, holding the photograph in her hand. Her face is beaming with a joy I have not seen from her before.

She holds the picture up to show me and points at it. 'Elise,' she says, 'my Elise. Isn't she the most beautiful little thing?'

'She is, Madame Moreau, she is.'

I smile at her and close the door slowly behind me as I leave her to the memories of the daughter she still treasures.

40

The Thursday before Christmas, and the start of another work week at the nightclub. It is still called Plein Soleil at the moment, but Carmen plans to change it in the New Year, if she can settle on a new name. I suggest continuing the French theme with "Sans Soleil". Without sun. It feels like an appropriate name for a nightclub as well as marking the change in management. My suggestion wasn't met with much enthusiasm.

The club is busy tonight. A band from Edinburgh called Full Fat are playing a live gig downstairs and they seem to have brought a loyal following with them. The concert crowd is boosted by the traditional "Christmas night out" office revellers. It promises to be a good night.

Carmen and I haven't spoken about Francis McArthur. It remains unacknowledged between us. She knows what I did. I know what she did. Sort of. Did she play both sides off against each other? Was she really working for McArthur all along, feeding Millar just enough information to keep the police off her back? She's smart enough to have played that game. It's hard not to feel Carmen Carmichael is always the smartest person in any room she walks into.

Not only does she still run the club, but she now owns it as well. How that came about is a mystery. McArthur's empire has still to be formally torn apart by the authorities, but somehow Carmen has already procured her slice of it. Did she have the money to buy it? Was it left to her by Francis McArthur in his will, or did Murdo or Tony bequeath it to her out of the kindness of their hearts?

However she managed it, I am not complaining. She agreed to keep on a novice ex-con approaching his mid-thirties with no prior experience of bar work, who requires an exemption from the police to retain his position while he remains on parole. I have met her family now – her partner Charlotte and their kid, Lewis.

There are still six months to go before I am entirely free from the justice system. Millar kept her word and vouched for my involvement in McArthur's death. She made it sound like I was the good guy, trying to rescue a bad situation and unable to do so. I guess that part wasn't made up.

Georgia and Lauryn still work in the club. Marc has moved on after dropping out of university and deciding to travel the world. Andy didn't show up one week and never returned, although Lauryn says she stills sees him around the university campus. The girls have finally managed to teach me the basics of cocktail mixing, although I still feel a wave of relief when a customer approaches and asks for a lager and a glass of wine rather than one of the many concoctions on the menu. It's hard to say if I am considered a friend. There is an age gap and a wariness about my past that will always create distance, but they accept me. There is even a hint of rapport between us now.

Carmen has other plans for the club. The décor is to be redone, the lighting redesigned, the upper office space to be divided to create a chill-out room. She wants to attract a wider clientele with the rebrand, not just the older, upper-market crowd.

There are new faces. Behind the bar, Carmen has hired Jenny to run things as the Head Bartender. It's nice to have someone my own age to talk to. Malky Thomson is no longer in charge of security. The door is manned by three brothers originally from the

Outer Hebrides, the Johnsons, who each look like they have spent their lives working out in a gym and tearing mammals apart with their bare hands for fun, before feeding on the raw meat. They guarantee there will be no trouble inside the club.

We make a pretty happy team.

Carmen approaches me at the bar. She slaps a newspaper down in front of me. 'Your doing?' she asks with a raised eyebrow, before walking off again to tend to business.

I unfold the *Record* and read the headline, splashed across the full front page, and the sub header that follows:

FIRST MINISTER RESIGNS
Links to murdered businessman expose corruption at the heart of Scottish Government

The story has been bubbling along ever since McArthur was charged and his connections to various politicians exposed. It progressed from councillors and aides to party donations for favours and finally to cabinet ministers, and now to the head of the government at Holyrood. Andrea Fulton quit early on in the unfolding scandal and disappeared from public view. The deal to renovate East Kilbride town centre collapsed. The burned-out building on Woodlands Road remains behind safety fencing and scaffolding, in limbo until a new developer is appointed to salvage or destroy what the fire didn't get.

Despite what Millar thought would happen, she is still attached to the case, working alongside forensic accountants and business lawyers to unpick everything. She keeps in touch, and whenever I do see her, I get the sense she is done with Francis McArthur and the trail of paperwork he has left behind. She knows no one will go to jail for any of it in the end, least of all the first minister of the country. She is ready for a new challenge, someone else to get her teeth into.

I have followed the story at a distance. The article gives little detail beyond the dramatic headline. It is all couched in innuendo and hints – a journalist who has the story but not enough proof to print all they know for fear of libel. Most of it, Millar has already told me.

It turns out the first minister attended a number of functions and fundraisers on behalf of McArthur businesses and didn't declare any income from them to the parliament's Register of Interests. That in itself is enough to garner censure. On top of that, the first minister's government has interceded on behalf of McArthur businesses on several occasions and always, without fail, decided in favour of Francis McArthur. On three occasions the government called in planning permissions rejected by local councils and overturned the decisions in favour of McArthur construction. The public has grown too cynical with politicians not to be able to read the glaring space between the lines.

It should interest me more, but all of it feels secondary to what I remember about the summer heatwave. Francis McArthur is gone and his empire with him. Murdo Smith sits in his mansion in Bearsden and waits for his day in court, the power he once wielded swept away. Soon enough their place will be taken by the next opportunist. The cycle will begin again, only next time it will have nothing to do with me, and I am happy about that.

In the last few months I have found some sort of contentment with work at the club, the beginnings of friendship with colleagues and my visits to Delphine Moreau. The flat in Mount Florida feels more like a home. I have caught myself thinking about Jenny and wondering if there could be something more there. We get on together, work well together and make each other laugh. It's a start, although relationships have never been my strong point.

Thinking about Jenny has taken my mind off the other woman who haunts my dreams. Millar has stuck to her word. She refuses to tell me anything about Rose Black for my own good. She is right, of course. Only now, with the clarity of the last few months, do I realise how unhealthy my fascination with her was. Some sort of aggressor-victim mentality that will take years of therapy to unravel. It is better forgotten about. Everything that happened with Elise has cured me of my Rose Black infatuation.

The band kicks off their gig downstairs. The floor shakes as a bass drum kicks in and a guitar joins in. The crowd reacts with a collective cheer.

* * *

Two hours later the concert ends and there is a rush at the bar as the crowd spills up the stairs and looks for refreshment. Jenny and I are rushed off our feet and Carmen comes behind the bar to help, while Lauryn and Georgia deal with table service and glass collection. Two of the Johnson brothers disappear downstairs to help the band de-rig.

I don't see Millar enter the club. The front doors have been closed for an hour, so she is not here as a punter, and if she had a ticket for the gig, she has missed it.

The first I notice of her is when I turn round from the till and expect to find the next customer pushed up against the bar. Instead, I see Millar's face and straight away I know something is wrong. Her eyes are wide, her mouth a serious frown. She leans over the bar. 'I need to talk to you,' she yells above the noise of the background music and chatter.

'Wait over there until I can get away.'

Carmen sees her and looks at us with suspicion. Millar sees her look. 'It's nothing to do with McArthur or the club,' she reassures Carmen, before fighting her way back out of the scrum at the bar and finding an empty stool in the corner.

It takes ten minutes for the rush to die down. In that time, my mind careers around the various scenarios that would lead

Detective Millar to turn up at the club after midnight in the week before Christmas. It has to be something to do with Marie or Tony. Is it about Marie's unborn baby? Or has something happened with the case against Murdo and Malky? Are they getting off scot-free and Millar is here to warn me they might be coming for me?

None of these scenarios fill me with joy, but I can feel it is not any of them. Something about the way Millar keeps looking over at me tells me it's something more, something that she knows is going to break me and the small world I have slowly built for myself in the last few months.

'We can cope here for five minutes. Go and see what she wants,' says Carmen, who notices how distracted I am. 'Could you also tell her that having a police detective show up on duty isn't great for business?'

Jenny glances at me as I pass behind her and go around the end of the bar. She knows a bit about my past, but not everything. She hasn't met Millar before, but she must sense trouble in the same way I can.

'What is it?' I still have to raise my voice to be heard over the din as I stand next to Millar.

'Is there somewhere quieter we can talk?'

Carmen is watching from the other end of the bar. I jerk my thumb in the direction of the stairs up to the office, asking her permission. She nods.

Through the double doors, at the bottom of the stairs, the noise is reduced to a dull throb.

'What is it?' I ask again, trying to hide the creeping anxiety. Millar's eyes look moist, like she's on the verge of tears. It is not like her to show emotion, happy or sad. She is always in control and contained.

'It's Rose Black,' she says. 'She's dead.'

My world collapses in on itself. I sway back and hit the wall. I feel faint and sick. What has Millar just said? I can't have heard her right. I hear her say 'I'm sorry,' and she reaches out her hand, trying to support me as I slide to the floor.

Just when I thought that part of my life could be left behind – McArthur, Tony, my dad and the accident that started it all a decade ago – just when I thought I could move on and make something of what was left of my life, the shadow of Rose Black returns.

I want to ask how, and why, and find out all the details, but my mind won't be still. I am on the floor and Millar is beside me, trying to soothe me, saying something about finding the bastards that did this.

I can't take it in. I see the windscreen of Tony's car smashing, I hear the tyres shriek and the screams.

I will never escape my sins.

CAL JACKSON WILL RETURN

ABOUT THE AUTHOR

Iain Kelly was born in Glasgow and now lives in East Kilbride, Scotland. He works as an editor in the television industry and is married with two children. *Full Sun* is his sixth novel.

For more information visit his website: www.iainkellywriting.com

Follow on Social Media:

Facebook: iainkellywriting
Instagram + Threads: @iain_kelly_writing
X / Twitter: @IainK_Writing
LinkedIn: iain-kelly-writing

ALSO AVAILABLE

ALL WE CANNOT LEAVE BEHIND

Edinburgh, 1920. Three children are missing, abducted from the poorhouses of the city.

When a body is found near the town of Liberton, Dr Thomas Stevenson, still suffering from the trauma of the First World War, finds himself drawn into the police investigation. But suspicion falls on the woman with the mysterious past who lives with Thomas. Could she be guilty of the brutal murder?

With time running out and lives at stake, Thomas must prove her innocence, but to do that he has to find the real killer and unlock the truth about her secret past.

A past that casts a long, dark shadow.

Praise for All We Cannot Leave Behind:

- 'An incredibly atmospheric piece of writing. [The] description of Edinburgh and every location throughout the novel feels authentic and his characters fit perfectly into each setting. This is a wonderful piece of fiction and a highly recommended read...'

- 'The writing is beautiful and I was left feeling quite emotional as the story unfolded. The characterisation is excellent, I was invested from the start, and I really felt compassion for Dr Thomas and Louise. This is a beautiful work of fiction, which I highly recommend.'

- 'An emotive read and had my heart aching. [Kelly] draws the reader into a powerful, dark, all-encompassing narrative. Kelly writes with a brutal honesty that is all at once gritty and gentle, hard-hitting and empathetic.'

- 'An absolutely gripping read. Great characterisation and a well-researched historical thriller.'

ALSO AVAILABLE

THE BARRA BOY

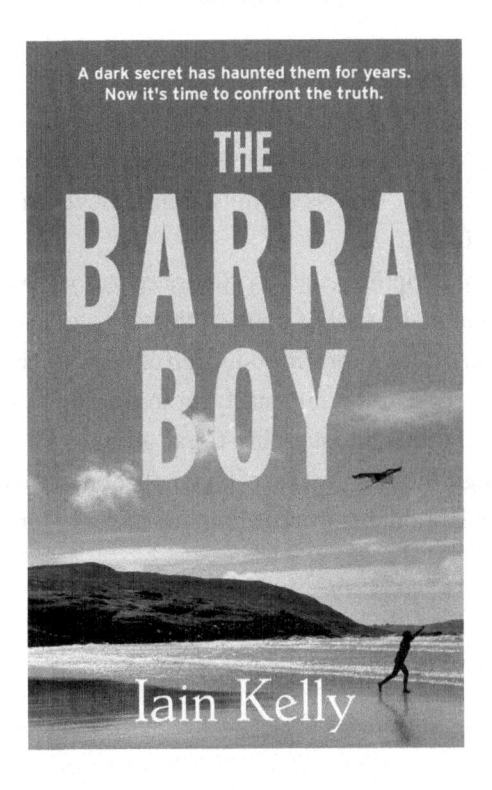

1982. Thirteen-year-old Ewan Fraser is sent to the remote island of Barra, off Scotland's west coast, to stay with his aunt and uncle.

Resigned to a monotonous summer of boredom, he is befriended by local girl Laura Robertson; together they explore the golden beaches and rocky coves of the idyllic island.

But a dark secret that connects Laura to the mysterious outcast

Mhairi Matheson and her son, Billy, is hidden beneath the tranquil surface...

A secret that threatens to tear the small community apart. Forty years later, Ewan returns to confront the truth about the formative summer of his adolescence, and finally learn the truth about Laura and the boy from Barra.

Praise for 'The Barra Boy':

– '[A] superbly written, character driven story that ranks as one of my favourite reads of the year. The author has a wonderful feel for locations... This is an outstanding novel from an author with a great future.'

– 'rich in description, superbly controlled pace of reveal... we have lots and lots of praise for this book – highly enjoyable setting, utterly pleasurable to imagine, early introduction of suspense that lasted right through to the conclusion, and satisfying answers to the mysteries that you encounter during the storyline. Great, great work.'

– 'a thoughtful combination of literary fiction and coming-of-age novel, and will undoubtedly remain in my memory for a long while.'

ALSO AVAILABLE

A JUSTIFIED STATE

Book One of The State Trilogy

The future.
The socially reformist Central Alliance Party rules unopposed.
Poverty and homelessness have been eradicated, but overpopulation, an energy crisis and an ongoing war jeopardise the stability of the country. When a local politician is assassinated, Detective Danny Samson finds himself at the centre of an investigation that threatens not only his life, but the entire future of The State.

Praise for 'A Justified State':

– 'the action is pacey and exciting, the characters fleshed out, nuanced and believable, the mystery…is genuinely intriguing and alarming.'

– 'the writing brought to mind Phillip Marlow, *Do Androids Dream of Electric Sheep?* the world of George Smiley, and Robert Harris' *Fatherland.*'

– 'This is a superbly well written fast paced, suspenseful mystery. A page turner as the action…makes you gasp.'

ALSO AVAILABLE

STATE OF DENIAL

Book Two of The State Trilogy

Election time in The State, the citizens prepare to vote.

A journalist from the Capital City heads north to report on growing resistance to the powerful ruling Party.

An ex-police detective returns to the city he once fled.

Together they become entangled in a burgeoning opposition movement.

Soon they learn the Party will do whatever it takes to remain in power, and one life is all it takes to spark a revolution.

Praise for 'State of Denial':
– 'Well paced and full of drama. A great sequel.'
– 'Well written, the plot flows effortlessly… A gripping sci-fi that is a little bit horrifying and a lot entertaining.'
– 'Get lost in the pages…through passages that may have you holding your breath.'

ALSO AVAILABLE

STATE OF WAR

Book Three of The State Trilogy

The State is at war at home and abroad. While the global First Strike War continues, a civil war threatens to bring down the ruling Central Alliance Party.

Daniel Samson – Citizen, Traitor, Survivor. Gabriella Marino – Soldier, Assassin, Fighter.

Caught between The State Forces and the rebels, hunted by both sides, they must choose between their own survival and protecting the city and the citizens trapped within the war zone. Are they willing to sacrifice their own chance of happiness to save a city from destruction?

The thrilling conclusion to The State Trilogy sees Danny and Gabriella join forces against their enemies in a fight that will determine the fate of The State, and the lives of all those who live there.

Praise for 'State of War':

– 'A lot of writers could learn how to create a believable future by studying Kelly's novels.'

– 'More action, more emotional stakes and this time the wrong move will not only end their lives but take a city with them.'